Jane Lane

The Severed Crown

SIMON AND SCHUSTER   NEW YORK

SBN 671-21567-1
Library of Congress Catalog Card Number: 73-1127
Manufactured in the United States of America
Printed by Mahony & Roese, Inc., New York, N.Y.
Bound by The Plimpton Press, Norwood, Mass.

1   2   3   4   5   6   7   8   9   10

For my dear son, Stewart

Contents

I am like a captain who has defended a place well, and his superiors not being able to succour him, he has leave to surrender it. But though they cannot relieve me in time, yet will I hold out, until I have made this fort my tombstone.

King Charles I during the Treaty of Newport

Summons

I

*Correspondence of Jean de Montreuil
with Cardinal Mazarin*

Oxford. January 2nd, 1646.

Since my replacing the former French Resident, M. Sabran, I have been at pains to scrutinize the state of each of the parties who won the civil war in England, that by keeping the balance of dissension among them equal, your Eminence may prevent them from meddling in our war with Spain.

Briefly, Eminence, it has become clear to me that the Parliament (or rather the shrunken remnant who still sit at Westminster) are for deposing King Charles and setting up a puppet monarch in his room, which would be a very ill example to our own malcontents. For the Army, they begin to boast that the kingdom is theirs by conquest, and I suspect would form some sort of military republic. This could prove extremely dangerous to France. Only the Scots still swear they are ready to preserve the King's just rights, so long as he subscribes to their Solemn League and Covenant. If an alliance between him and them could be brought about by me, he will be in great debt to France, whereas throughout his reign he has inclined more to the Spanish interest.

I must add that while the Parliament and the Army are increasingly jealous of each other, both are determined to get rid of the Scots, whom they called in to their aid when the King was like to prove victorious.

I have, therefore, held close correspondence with the Scotch Commissioners in London. Your Eminence instructed me that it would be prudent to avoid the subject of religion. I have found, however, that this is the one topic impossible to shun. The fine shades of difference between so many heretics would be laughable, were not the situation so serious. Yet I have come to the conclusion that beneath their pious mask, the real anxiety of the Scots is for the price of what they term their Brotherly Assistance, claiming that no less than £500,000 was promised them by Parliament if they came to its aid. They are, in fact, mere mercenaries like the Swiss; theirs is a war of the purse.

Having reached a stage in my talks with their Commissioners which necessitated a personal interview with the King, I travelled here to Oxford which is still his headquarters, though he has no longer any army capable of taking the field. I was at once made aware that if the victors in this civil war are at loggerheads, no less are the losers. I was escorted to the Presence Chamber by Colonel Ashburnham, Treasurer, who in the space of five yards whispered to me as many names among his fellow Councillors who, said he, were by no means to be trusted.

The opinion I formed of the King of Great Britain in this first private audience was that while he has an excellent understanding, he is not confident enough of it, which, I suspect, oftentimes makes him change his own view for a worse, being overborne more by the importunities than the arguments of others. Further than this, it is plain to me that he lacks all those talents necessary to win a game by political finesse. He knows nothing of the ambiguous phrase, the making men believe he means one thing while in fact he intends something different, the inflammation of allies against one another. His scrupulosity where his personal honour is concerned, while it does him credit, will prove a disadvantage in negotiations with those who, from my acquaintance with them, are well equipped with the talents I have mentioned above. Though he is fully aware of the rift between the several parties who vanquished him in the field, he suffers from the romantical illusion that all these his enemies are as anxious as he is himself to obtain an equitable peace treaty.

'Throughout this past winter,' said he, 'I have been sending message after message to the Parliament, conjuring them to promote a peace, as indeed I have done since the beginning of armed rebellion. I have gone so far as to offer to disband my forces and dismantle my garrisons, so long as those who adhered to me had liberty to live in their own houses without molestation. Yet all such overtures have been flung back in my face with insolence.'

I marvelled in myself that he should be so artless. Like any other conqueror, the Parliament is resolved to enjoy the full fruits of victory, and is busy arranging a grand confiscation of the estates and revenues of his adherents. Only when they have obtained his consent to such spoliation will they consider his overtures. Aloud I said I was sure that his best hope lay in an alliance with the Scots.

'It is my own opinion,' he replied, 'for they are my fellow-countrymen, upon whom I have lavished a thousand favours, and very sure I am they wish me well.'

I repressed my dismay at such unrealistic sentiment; and since at the outset he had begged me to use freedom in what I had to say, I spoke as one statesman to another thus:

'I am assured by the Scotch Commissioners in London that the only concession they will ask of Your Majesty is that you impose their presbyterian church system upon your kingdoms of England and Ireland. My humble advice, therefore, is that you make use of the Scots by subscribing to their Covenant, and then trust to a freely elected parliament to abrogate it as soon as you have regained your throne through Scotch aid.'

I was astounded by his reaction. It was as though I had uttered some blasphemy! He said with vigour:

'My conscience will not permit me to violate my Coronation Oath, wherein I swore to maintain the Church of England, and I would rather lose my crown than my soul.'

But then, controlling his passion, he told me he was confident that the Scots could be persuaded to come to an honourable agreement with him, which he was the more anxious to obtain because of his fears for the safety of the Marquis of Montrose, the most devoted of his Scotch adherents, who has been a fugitive in his native land since his defeat at Philiphaugh.

'Moreover,' said the King, 'I am aware that before very long Oxford will be closely invested, and I am resolved to avoid capture by the rebel armies, since as a prisoner I could not negotiate freely. You would put me greatly in your debt if you could persuade the Scottish Commissioners to promise freedom to my conscience, honour to my person, and protection to my friends, if I should place myself in their midst.'

To this I readily agreed. For I take great care to remember

your Eminence's observation that Scotland is a power often useful to us in opposition to the might of England. I have already dropped some hints to their Commissioners that the monies they received underhand from the late Cardinal Richelieu to aid them in their rebellion against this King in the days of his prosperity, might be continued by your Eminence in the present situation.

*　　*　　*

Southwell in Nottinghamshire. April 6th, 1646.

Your Eminence will excuse, I trust, my long silence, but I would not trouble you with writings until I had something definite to report. Receiving very little satisfaction from the Scotch Commissioners in London, I resolved to try whether I could induce those in command of their armies to be more tractable, and therefore came to this place seven miles from Newark, which town the Scots are besieging.

I will not weary your Eminence with a description of their forces who, while very numerous, have no military air about them, and who spend the most of their time either plundering the countryside or wrangling about fine points of theology. There is such a host of Geneva gowns in their ranks as makes me feel I am come into the Church Militant. I had the curiosity to hear one of their sermons, which ran for the space of two hour-glasses, and was to the tune that they took up arms only to convert the English, whom they appear to regard as perfect heathens.

Their general, the Earl of Leven (created so by His Majesty in 1641), is a little old mercenary, so ignorant that he cannot spell his own name, and as tortuous in speech as he is crooked in body. I showed him my letters of credit, wherein I am empowered to engage the honour of France as security that the Scots perform all they promise, and that the King of Great Britain shall make good whatever is undertaken by him. General Leven expressed unbounded joy when I dropped a hint that His Majesty might consider confiding his person to them. I had, I confess, a passing suspicion that it was a joy resembling that of the spider when she sees a succulent fly approach her web, but I am sure I wronged him.

6

In my conferences with him and his principal officers, I spoke home, showing them that they ought to feel but little interest in establishing their church government in England and ruling over the consciences of their neighbours, compared with the more pressing necessity of preserving their lives, their property and their liberty, all which they would lose whenever they abandoned their King. For I made it plain I was fully aware that the Parliament is now only anxious to be rid of them, they having served its turn. But in a burst of candour they told me, it was the Army rather than the Parliament who were their unfriends, for the most of those in the Army were of what they termed the 'Gathered Churches'.

It seems that these two sets of heretics, the presbyterians and the independents, hate one another as heartily as both do our Holy Catholic Faith. I was fain to hide a smile when they repeated with high indignation a speech made by Lieutenant-General Cromwell (who is the ruling spirit in the Army), wherein he asserted that the Scots had done nothing since coming into England except live upon the country, and pressed hard for their being sent home without the fee for their Brotherly Assistance.

'Why, then,' said I, 'there is the more reason for you to come to terms with His Majesty, whose authority will lend weight to all your just demands.'

They explained most earnestly that while nothing would gratify them more than the presence of their beloved Sovereign in their midst, they dared not invite him because this would violate the article in the Solemn League and Covenant wherein they and the Parliament swore never to suffer themselves to be divided. For the same reason they could not receive any of his adherents particularly obnoxious to their ally. I concealed my contempt for such equivocation, and continued to press them to a conclusion. While they still insisted I must excuse them from a written engagement with the King, at length they yielded so far as to permit me to write down their offers to him in their presence, pledging their word that such engagement would be as binding on them as if it bore their names. And this, your Eminence, is what I wrote:

'I do promise in the name of His Most Christian Majesty and the Queen Regent, my master and mistress, that if the King of Great

Britain shall put himself into the Scotch army he shall be there received as their natural Sovereign, and that he shall be with them in all freedom of his conscience and honour. That all his servants as shall come with him shall have protection. That the Scots shall really and effectively join with him for his preservation, and protect all his party to the uttermost of their power. That they shall employ their armies to assist His Majesty in the procuring of a happy and well-grounded peace, for the good of His Majesty and his kingdoms, and in recovering his just rights.'

2

Diary of Colonel Jack Ashburnham

April 15th, 1646. Ascending Magdalen tower, I espied through a perspective-glass the rebel dogs within cannon-shot on north and east of us. Boarstall House closely besieged and Woodstock threatened with assault. H.M. at his dressing this morning expressed to me his painful concern that he has received no further word from M. de Montreuil for near upon a fortnight.

April 16th. H.M. late at the daily council of war, a most unusual circumstance. I supposed it due to his having received a letter from the Queen, who must still be meddling in his affairs though she is, praise God, away from us in France. But when H.M. entered the council chamber, his countenance was much clouded, and it transpired that the letter which had delayed him was not from his wife but from M. de Montreuil.

Since the Frenchman's last dispatch, those sneaking factious turnabouts, the Scots, have deprived him of all means of communication with us, and he has spent the past fortnight searching out ways to convey a warning to His Majesty. For they had the impudence to tell him that having debated further, they required H.M. to impose their plaguy Covenant on England and Ireland before they would receive him. Moreover, they were now willing

8

to receive with H.M. only Prince Rupert, his brother Maurice, and myself, and even we must be surrendered if Parliament demanded it.

'This,' says the King, 'is all the account now made of the solemn promises formerly given to M. de Montreuil, and the best offers he was able to obtain after a long wrangle, for what they proposed at first was still more rude.'

'In short,' said I, 'they are abominable relapsed rogues, who have tacked about most villainously, and thank God Your Majesty has seen their true colours in time.'

Then must Rupert thrust in his oar as usual, saying what should be done. With H.M.'s permission, he has accepted of a parliamentary pass to go beyond seas with his brother and a large train of servants. He could smuggle H.M. along with him, says he, for the only hope lay in French arms, which according to the Queen are promised lavishly by Mazarin, so long as H.M.'s person is secure. Others in the chamber took up the same cry, tempting my poor master with the delight of being reunited with his wife and such of his children who are overseas.

The which, I observed, set up a sore conflict in him, he being too apt to fall into a shall-I, shall-I-not humour. But at length he told us that if he left England voluntarily, it would be given out that he had abdicated, and this he would by no means risk. So nothing decided.

April 22nd. After supper, I was summoned to H.M.'s cabinet, where I found Rupert, the Duke of Richmond, and Sir Thomas Glenham, Governor of Oxford. The door being secured, H.M. pledged us all to secrecy, and then informed us that he had taken a resolution of placing his person in the hands of the Scots, notwithstanding their weathercock behaviour.

'For I am advised by Sir Thomas here,' says he, 'that within the next few days Oxford will be closely besieged, and I am resolved to try by personal negotiation with the Scots to come to an agreement with them which shall safeguard all my adherents.'

Ere any of the rest of us could express an opinion, we must needs hear Rupert voice his. Despite his mutiny (to give it its true name) last year, he still presumes to rule the roost, and takes it for granted that he knows best in all matters.

'To reach Newark from Oxford in November last,' says he, most brazenly referring to that escapade when he was absolutely forbidden to intrude himself into H.M.'s presence at Newark, 'I was obliged to cut my way with a hundred and twenty horse in a series of hot skirmishes. If Your Majesty is determined to go to the Scots, you must permit me to accompany you, and I'll warrant to beat any troops who bar your passage.'

'Dear Rupert,' says his uncle, 'your great height would betray you, my purpose being to go to Newark very secretly.'

I, who have served the King since I was a page in the out-rooms of Whitehall, knew well the reason was, H.M. has never trusted Rupert since that ruffler's base surrender of Bristol and rude carriage afterwards.

When the others retired, H.M. beckoned me to stay behind, and says:

'Jack, you shall come with me, if you please.'

'Sir,' said I, 'I was taught by my father to stick by the crown, though it hung upon a bush, and so I will readily venture among these blue-cap swads of Scotland.' I had nearly added somewhat anent their cursed Covenant compiled by the Devil, but though H.M. excuses my blunt tongue, he can never away with swearing.

On his inquiring of me if I could obtain a pass which would enable us to travel in freedom, I answered there was nothing simpler. For, says I, there are a vast number of the honest party making their way to London to compound for their estates with the caterpillar Parliament, protected by such passes, and I know I can borrow a safe-conduct.

'To London,' he repeated, in a tone which was strangely thoughtful, but he did not enlarge on what lay in his mind. Then he says, we must have a third in our party, one who knows the by-ways as you and I do not.

'Dr Michael Hudson is the very man,' I told him. 'Your Majesty may remember how he forsook his parsonage at the beginning of this hellish rebellion, and since has been scout-master in several of your armies. Plain and blunt, Sir, but brave as a lion and cunning as a fox when it comes to secret travel.'

H.M. liked well my suggestion, and bade me, without loss of time, set about the borrowing of a pass.

April 27th. At half past two of the clock this morning, I was admitted by H.M. as appointed by the privy door into his bed-chamber, bringing with me a suit and cloak of sad-coloured cloth such as befits a serving-man, for my dear royal master is to pass as my groom upon our journey.

'You must turn barber, Jack,' says he, 'cut my hair close and shave off my beard.'

This took me aback, for though he detests any ostentation in appearance, he loves to be trim, and I know nothing of barbering. He smiled a little wryly when he saw the result of my scissors-work, but says it would pass muster for a groom. And from the moment we leave Christ Church, says he, you must remember to address me as 'Harry', and to use such behaviour towards me as fits with that of a master to his servant.

With that he picks up a cloak-bag containing our necessaries, insisting that he carry it to help with his disguise. Ere we left the apartment, I noticed his glance linger on a chessboard, where the pieces were set out in the midst of a game. I remembered how it was his custom to play at chess each evening with the Duke of York, the only one of his children not either overseas or a prisoner of the snivelling crop-pates.

'Poor James,' sighed he, fingering one of the chessmen.

At the foot of the backstair we found Dr Hudson awaiting us with horses, having at H.M.'s command selected an inferior beast for 'Harry'. So we set forth upon this perilous venture. At the East Gate we called the password, and it was answered by Sir Thomas Glenham in person, who saluted us by our assumed names, Durrington and Veale, and in a loud voice bade 'Harry' have a care of his masters.

Hudson led the way, having most painfully traced out a route to Newark which would shun the high roads and the rebel garrisons. But we had not progressed far when H.M. calls softly to him, and says he, I have taken a resolution, which I would not till now disclose, to go instead to London.

We both exclaimed in horror, for it was as if an unarmed man should throw himself into a den of lions. But H.M. said he had heard much talk of the widespread disaffection of the citizens to Parliament, they groaning under such heavy taxes and their trade gone down the wind. Thus had he taken a romantical notion to go privily into London, conceiving that his presence there would put such heart into the cits that they would compel Parliament to negotiate with him an honourable peace. I had misliked the idea of going to the Scots, whom I suspect, for all their fulsome promises, of boatmanlike rowing one way while they look another; but to venture instead into the City, the birthplace of this damnable rebellion, seemed to me plain suicide. However, nothing Hudson or I could say would wean H.M. from this fantastical scheme, and so with hearts like lead we took the London road.

We were come some dozen miles from Uxbridge, when who should join himself to our company but a redcoat cornet, whom we must speak fair, though at the sight of his uniform I could scarce keep my hand from my hilt.

3

Unfinished Autobiography of Cornet George Joyce

[*Editorial Note.* The scriptural passages quoted by Cornet Joyce being so numerous as to weary the reader, many of them are in this edition omitted.]

. . . I must here recount my first meeting with the Man of Blood, Charles Stuart, though the Lord was pleased to conceal him in a disguise, lest perchance my righteous wrath would have impelled me to act out the device I chose for my colours, wherein a bloody sword is thrust through a crown. Whereas the Lord designed him for a more public destruction, and predestined me, His poor servant, to be the instrument of it. For he was the one most vile,

12

spoken of by Daniel, who should be destroyed neither in rage nor in battle.

It happened upon April 27th, in the year 1646, that I was sent by my captain to bear the news to Parliament of our storming of Woodstock. I rode at a sober pace, for my saddle-bags were weighted with the spoils we had taken from the Midianites, which being purified in the waters of separation, belong to the men of war. These I purposed to sell in the common market at Uxbridge, my pay being in arrears. I was composing in my mind a sermon I would preach in camp from a tract newly put forth against the dipping of infants, entitled *Baby Baptism mere Babyism*. For whosoever has received the gift of preaching may freely preach, of what calling or condition he be, and this I had retorted upon my captain when he bade me forbear, telling him further that if I might not preach I would not fight. And likewise did I accuse him to my colonel for singing a lewd song, hoping to be promoted in his room.

It pleased the Lord that as I was passing a by-way in the neighbourhood of Uxbridge, three horsemen emerged from it on to the high road, whom I challenged, requiring of them to inform me who they were, whither they were bound, and to see their passes. For the land was thronged with Malignants who crept about in jesuitical disguises, still seeking to hurt the Saints, though their party had been made as stubble to our swords.

One of them, with a great show of frankness, told me he was a Cavalier, Colonel Durrington, upon his way to London to compound for his estates, his companion being Mr Veale, a member of the Commons' House, absent from Westminster of late by reason of an ague. I narrowly inspected their passes, which were indeed made out in those names, with the addition of a body-servant. Whereat I exulted to them upon our storming of Woodstock, whose garrison, being crypto-papists, could receive no quarter, and on the spoil of gold and silver we took, according to the command of the Lord not to leave Egypt empty-handed. On this they would have parted from me, saying they intended to bait at Uxbridge, having ridden far and the ways being foul.

'Your souls,' said I, 'are destined for the fouler way to Hell.

13

And since I too would bait at Uxbridge, I will instruct you upon the wrath to come and upon the lake of fire burning with brimstone into which you will be cast, whose names are not written in the Book of Life.'

This I said to them not excepting the man Veale, for he confessed he was of the presbyterians, who hold the damnable doctrine of free will and believe that Jehovah may be placated by penance and good works. Whereas it is plain from Scripture that the race of man is accursed, all save those whom the Lord chose to be of His Elect from Eternity, and who are commissioned to cut off the ungodly with another sword from that of the spirit. You presbyterians, said I to Veale, are as the rebellious sons of Levi whom the earth swallowed and they went down alive into Hell.

'I marvel, sir,' says he, 'at your knowledge of Holy Writ, though it appears to be confined to the Old Testament.'

I showed him my *Soldier's Pocket Bible*, kept ever in my knapsack, containing those passages which give the qualifications of a fit soldier to fight the Lord's battles, and told him I dug daily in this sacred mine, chewing and squeezing each verse till I had sucked some virtue from it. It was with the word of God in our mouths and a two-edged sword in our hands, that we, the Hosts of Israel, had scattered His enemies. Such discourse made the miles pass with a sweet savour for me until we came to Uxbridge. As we sat down to meat, the Malignant, Durrington, inquired of me of what regiment I was, how long I had been in the Army, and whether impressed or a volunteer.

'I am,' said I, condescending to his idle curiosity, 'cornet in the Lord General Fairfax's regiment of Life Guards. And since you would know how I came to the colours, I will indulge you, that you may perceive the marvellous way of the Lord with those few souls whom He pleased to spare when, at the Fall, the race of man was sentenced to eternal damnation.'

And since the reader cannot hear repeated without relish the history of one of the Elect, I will oblige him by setting down here again what I regaled him with at the beginning.

I was born of honest and sufficient parents in the City of London and particularly in Three Needles Street, and received my profane learning at our ward school, whence I was put in my indentures to a master tailor. Though my skill was such that as soon as I was out of my apprenticeship my master engaged me as his journeyman, the Lord had prepared for me a sharper weapon than my needle, and a more glorious work than the cutting out of coats.

Being yet unconverted, I imagined in my folly that a visit to my mother's kinsfolk in the town of Huntingdon, which I made in the year 1642, was but an ordinary occasion, and it vexed me to discover the town full of talk anent a civil war. I gave a rough answer to the recruiting-sergeant who was urging all the young men of Huntingdon to enlist in a troop of horse just then raised by one who bore the name of *Cromwell*.

Ah, ah! how strange are the ways of the Lord. That name of His most valiant captain, another Joshua, excited no emotion in my bosom. I knew it indeed, for my maternal kinsfolk were natives of Huntingdon, and besides that our great Oliver's father was the principal brewer in that town, the Cromwells and their kin by marriage owned all the estates within the county, ay, and in Cambridgeshire and Rutland besides, great rich gentlemen, their revenues far exceeding those who sit in the House of Lords, that pimp of tyrants.

Though my hardness of heart caused me to turn a deaf ear to the recruiting-sergeant, it pleased me in an idle hour to go view a muster at the backside of the town; and there for the first time I saw Captain Cromwell (as he then was), and as I listened to his voice which, though sharp and untunable, was full of fervour and command, directing the raw recruits, it was the Lord Himself who spoke to me that I should join myself to their number. What drew me to Cromwell at the first was the declaration he made at this muster. Says he:

'I will not deceive or cozen you by the perplexed and involved expressions in my commission to fight for King and Parliament. If the King chanced to be in the body of the enemy I was to charge, I would as soon fire my pistol upon him as any private person. Therefore if your consciences will not permit you to do the like, I advise you to enlist yourselves in a troop not under my command.'

This made me deem him a man for my turn, upon whom I

15

might depend to go thoroughpaced with any work he undertook. That he knew how to cozen is quite true, but always it was in the Lord's service and to perform His will. And though he was so rich a gentleman, there was no vanity in him, he being very ordinarily apparelled, his linen plain and by no means clean, and his suit made by an ill country tailor.

I had scarce enlisted when I received my reward. It was nine minutes past noon upon Saturday, August 15th of that year, when being in my chamber I was visited with a sudden inward conviction that I was of the Elect. Nor was the Lord content to bestow on me conversion, but straightway I began to have visions, being transported from earth to heaven, where I conversed with Christ, who opened to me the Book of Life and permitted me to read the names therein, likewise of those He had sent to the Devil wholesale, as papists, episcopalians, presbyterians, et cetera. Then did I begin to preach and grew renowned in the Army, who were accustomed to receive my exhortations with such lamentable groans, such plentiful tears and smitings of the breast as testified to the extraordinary presence of the Holy Ghost within me. But these my fellow travellers at Uxbridge, being of the Damned, heard me in a sullen silence and without any marks of a just conviction of sin.

Being somewhat wearied by my eloquence, I fell silent as the cloth was withdrawn, and the Malignant, Durrington, calling to his servant Harry to fetch wine, asked me what news I heard of public matters. Condescending to his carnality, I told him there was a rumour buzzed about our camp at Woodstock that the King had left Oxford secretly, going no man knew whither.

'It may be,' remarked the presbyterian, Veale, 'that since we in the Parliament have been petitioning His Majesty to return to us ever since the outbreak of war, that we may negotiate personally with him, he is now resolved to do this, so he be assured of security and respect for his person.'

I would be gone to sell my lawful plunder in the market-place and disdained to share their sottish guzzlings. Yet ere I left I told the unregenerate Veale it was plain he had been absent from Westminster.

'For the latest advice we have from thence,' said I, 'is that the

16

godly among the Commons have voted an ordinance whereby any man within the cities of London and Westminster who presumes to harbour or assist the King will be proceeded against as a traitor.'

4

Correspondence of Jean de Montreuil with Cardinal Mazarin

Southwell. May 3rd, 1646.

I informed your Eminence in my last how these perfidious rogues among whom I am, did their best, soon after my coming to their camp, to deprive me of all communication with the King of Great Britain, and of how it was not till a fortnight after my arrival that I contrived to get a cipher message through to him, warning him of their giddiness. With what result I knew not until yesterday, when I received a visitor disguised as a travelling chapman, who disclosed himself to me as one Dr Michael Hudson, and who brought me extraordinary tidings.

It seems that Oxford being threatened with close besiegement, the King removed from thence in a very secret manner upon the 27th of last month, having for companions only this Dr Hudson and Colonel Ashburnham. It did not over-much surprise me to hear that he had a whim to make for London, there to cast himself upon the affections of the citizens, for I had before observed this romantic flaw in him. However, being yet some distance from the capital, it chanced that an enemy trooper rode a stage in their company, who remarked in conversation that Parliament has proclaimed any man assisting him a traitor. Therefore did he and his companions turn north, and on April 30th put up at an obscure inn at Downham Market in the county of Norfolk, whence Dr Hudson came by devious ways to me.

While I have been baffled by the Scots' prevarications and disgusted by their equivocal talk (such of it as I can comprehend, for these barbarous creatures have no French, and their English is a kind of patois), I have persevered in my negotiations with them in accordance with your Eminence's instructions to foment continued strife within these realms. Though your Eminence must pardon me if I say that I would sooner converse with beasts, which these upon two legs resemble, only that they have more cunning.

Last evening I summoned the principal officers to wait on me again, Dr Hudson being present on the strict understanding that he should not disclose to them precisely where the King is lodged at present. Their first question was, had His Majesty gone to London? for there was a strong rumour that so he had. I at once perceived that the idea of this put them in an agony, for if he should make a treaty with Parliament, farewell to all their hopes of obtaining the price of their Brotherly Assistance.

'Why,' says Hudson, 'as to that, I can tell you only that His Majesty inclines to it, having learned from M. l'Ambassadeur here that you will not honour your former large promises to him.'

They were voluble in their explanations and excuses. After harping at length on their ridiculous Covenant, they blurted out that they were in mortal dread lest the Army turned to rend them if they invited the King into their midst, while on the other hand they feared for the safety of his sacred person if he ventured into London.

'Ah,' sighs General Leven, 'if only His Majesty would come to us without invitation, we would do more for him than can be expressed.' (Thus I translate him, for I am not able to reproduce his outlandish dialect.)

Upon this I nailed them down hard. If they sincerely wished His Majesty well, why did they not ally themselves with the Marquis of Montrose, who has yet some scattered troops in Scotland, for the protection of the King? At which they expressed great horror, saying that the Marquis being excommunicated by their Kirk, it was not to be thought of. But so far as they were concerned, he was free to transport himself overseas. This one point gained (for I know King Charles's painful anxiety for Montrose), I dangled a bait before them. Suppose, said I, His Majesty is yet undecided whether to go to London or entrust his person to you, what new offers are you prepared to make him? In such a fret were they lest the King pursued his whim of making for London, that they proposed an engagement far beyond my hopes. It is true they still refused to put it in writing, for fear such a document offend their former allies, but they permitted Dr Hudson to set down the following in their presence, swearing as formerly that it would be binding upon them:

'That they would condescend to all the demands which His Majesty and M. de Montreuil had agreed to make them before M. de Montreuil came from Oxford. That they would secure His Majesty in his person and honour. That they would not press His Majesty to do anything contrary to his conscience. That Mr Ashburnham and I should be protected. That if the Parliament refused, upon a message from His Majesty, to restore him to his just rights, they would declare for him, with all their army. That a body of their horse should be sent out to protect His Majesty on his way to their camp.'

Leven being still a-fidget lest this precious paper might be seized upon during Dr Hudson's journey to the King, Hudson rolled it up very small and encased it in melted lead the size of a little bullet. Says he:

'The good Lord gave me an iron stomach to begin with, and by now it has become a perfect arsenal. I cannot count the number of secret writings I have been obliged to swallow through my years as scout-master. I remember once I was caught by the rebel Earl of Stamford, who having stripped me naked and found no messages hidden about my person, forced me to drink two powerful emetics, his lordship so far honouring me as to hold a bowl with his own hands to receive the result. But he was disappointed!'

*   *   *

Southwell. May 12th, 1646.

There was never a letter I wrote in my life which mortified me more than this I now pen to your Eminence. In my years at the Paris Bar I have encountered many villains, yet they were perfect angels compared with these treacherous Scots.

At six in the morning of May 5th, I was roused by my servant with the news that His Majesty had just arrived at my lodging, and hasted down to greet him. I recognized him only by his slight stature and slow, deliberate speech, for his beard was shaved off, his hair most ill cropped, and his person befouled with mire. He told me he had ridden all night from Stamford, and for the past two days had scarce been out of saddle.

I was in the midst of ordering my servants to prepare a bath and food for His Majesty, when there came a great clatter of horsemen in the street, and in walks the Earl of Lothian, one of the principal Scotch commanders. He expressed the utmost astonishment at finding His Majesty in their camp, and I could scarce believe my ears when I heard the rogue say:

'It does not become me to inquire into the causes which persuaded Your Majesty to come into our midst, but to endeavour that Your Majesty's being here may be improved to the best advantage for promoting the work of uniformity in religion.'

'What becomes your lordship,' said I, 'is to withdraw, that His Majesty may refresh himself after a journey he took at your invitation, and upon which he ought to have been protected by your promised troop of horse.'

'It waits outside,' says Lothian brazenly, 'to escort His Majesty to our headquarters at Kelham House, where we shall do our poor best to entertain him. But first we must have Your Majesty's signature to this,' and he whips out a copy of the Solemn League and Covenant.

I observed the King flush with anger, but he answered nothing.

'Next,' continued Lothian, 'we require Your Majesty to order Lord Bellasis to surrender to us the town of Newark.'

'To this,' replied the King in a level tone, 'I willingly condescend, so the terms offered him are honourable, for I earnestly desire to avoid any more bloodshed.'

'And finally,' says this insect who wears an earl's coronet, 'you must command James Grahame' (thus did he refer to the Marquis of Montrose) 'to lay down arms.'

'I bid you remember, my lord,' says the King, 'that he who made you an earl, made James Grahame a marquis.'

This so majestical rebuke recovered for me the use of my

20

tongue, which I spared not against Lothian, hotly upbraiding him for his perfidy, and demanding to know what had become of his and his colleagues' solemn promises to receive His Majesty into their camp with honour and respect to his person and freedom to his conscience. Promises made, I added, not only to their Sovereign Lord, but to me as representing His Most Christian Majesty, whose honour I had pledged for their fulfilment.

'Why,' sneers this gutter-earl, 'if Monsieur chose to write down promises, that is his affair; we ourselves set nothing in writing, and Monsieur must have misunderstood us, not having full command of our language. However, we approve of His Majesty coming *uninvited* into our camp to settle a just peace, the first condition of which is his signature to the Covenant we have made with the Lord God.'

'I thought it was with the English Parliament, your paymasters,' said I bitterly; but His Majesty made me such a look as told me he much misliked that mode of speaking.

Nothing I could say would move Lothian to stay while His Majesty washed away the stains of his journey, but off they must go at full speed to Kelham House. Later in the day, when I judged the King would have had leisure to refresh himself, I rode thither, where at my first coming I was met by a person who told me he was captain of a guard of honour appointed by the Scots for the protection of His Majesty. It was with much ado that I prevailed on him to admit me to the King's chamber, where I at once observed new bars set at all the windows. He smiled sadly, and says to me:

'They assure me that these, like my guard of honour, are for my protection, but to speak plain, I am a prisoner.'

I began to say to him how aghast I was that I should have been the unwitting instrument of enticing him into this trap, from which the bait is now withdrawn. But he begged me not to concern myself over a matter in which he knew me entirely innocent. His immediate anxiety, said he, was for the Marquis of Montrose, the Scots having broken all their other promises. Since my professed coming from France was to obtain recruits for French service, he asked me whether I could not send a commission to Montrose, who thus would come under the protection of His Most Christian Majesty. This I promised to contrive without delay.

I next demanded a conference with the principal officers to try if I could not bring them to some sense of shame. I told them roundly that they had lured their King into their camp with pledges every one of which they had broken. To which Lothian had the impudence to reply:

'We have honoured our pledges by providing a guard of honour to protect His Majesty's person, and I assure you we shall serve him on the knee as becomes our Sovereign. In the matter of the Covenant, we intend to use gentle persuasion, not force, to reform His Majesty's conscience.'

I find that, having got the King into their clutches, they are in tearing haste to be gone, their destination being the town of Newcastle, where I suppose they will sit down and dun for their money, and whence they can retreat into their own country if need arises. Upon a rumour that the King was making towards their camp, Parliament sent them a very sharp message, which Lothian showed me: 'That the House of Commons deems it unreasonable that the Scots, being but a hired army in their pay, should assume the authority to dispose of the King otherwise than by their orders, resolving further that His Majesty shall be conducted to the castle of Warwick.'

This verbal rebuke, says Lothian, will certainly be followed up by deed, and it is our duty to remove His Majesty to a distance where he will be safe from capture by the Parliament's soldiers. So tomorrow they break camp, and begin a rapid march towards the Border with their royal hostage.

Your Eminence may be pleased to excuse me in that this letter is writ in a style very unbecoming to be addressed to a Prince of the Church, and penned by one who has the honour to be the Ambassador of His Most Christian Majesty. But in truth, Eminence, my profound humiliation at the way I have been hoodwinked, and my choler at the outrageous perfidy of the Scots, have altogether discomposed me. I cannot enough admire the equanimity with which the King of Great Britain supports their rude treatment, he having a courteous demeanour to those who have broken their sworn word to him.

5

Exchange of Letters between King Charles and his wife

Anderson House, Newcastle. May 27th, 1646.

My dear heart, Montreuil being recalled to France (and I fear in some disgrace) will carry both this letter and Jack Ashburnham with him, Jack being threatened sore by the Scots, only for his fidelity to me. I owe him £9,200, which I earnestly recommend you would assist him in for his repayment, Parliament having seized upon all my revenues.

I am much beholden to the Portugal Agent for conveying your letter of May 3rd to me, which gave me such contentment as you may better judge than I describe; the which, that you may better do, know that I was full three weeks without hearing from or of you, but in scurvy public prints which made you retired into a convent. Which though I did not believe, it vexed me sore that I could not prove them liars. I conjure you, dear heart, by your constant love to me, that if I should miscarry (whether by being taken by the rebel soldiers or otherwise), to continue the same active endeavours for Prince Charles as you have done for me, and not to whine for me in a convent, but like your father's daughter, vigorously assist Prince Charles to regain his own.

The Scots afford me the trappings of a king, yet a captive one. Here, as at Newark, there are bars at all my windows; I may not ride abroad without what they please to term my guard of honour; and they have taken from me that good trusty man, Dr Hudson, the other companion on my journey to their camp. Being desirous that such of my old servants at Oxford who would be willing to share my captivity, might have leave to come, I made a list which I purposed sending to Secretary Nicholas; but my jailers drew their pen through the names of all but seven. And what irks me most, they deny me any of my chaplains. Instead of whom, they obtrude their ministers upon me, and while I respect these for what piety and worth may be in them, yet their judgments are in opposition to mine. Some remedies are worse than the disease, and some comforters more miserable than misery itself.

Their behaviour resembles that of besiegers, who issue a summons and will have no parley. I never knew what it was to be barbarously baited before, and these five or six days last have much surpassed in rude pressure upon my conscience all the rest since I came into the Scottish camp. For nothing will serve but my signing the Covenant, declaring without reserve for presbyterian government and receiving their Directory in my family in place of the Book of Common Prayer, with a like command for England and Ireland. But I answer them ever the same: That what they require is against my conscience, which may be persuaded, but cannot be forced by anything they can speak or do. And assure yourself of this certain truth, that no danger of death or misery (which I think much worse) shall make me do aught unworthy of your love, in which I triumph still, you having confirmed it by a deed of time and sealed by constancy.

Though such as would deprive me of my kingly power, would no less enforce me to live without liturgy and sacraments, I shall never think myself less than myself while I am able to preserve the integrity of my conscience, the only jewel (save your love) left me which is worth keeping. Comfort me, as often as you can, with your letters; and do you not think that to know particulars of your health, or how you spend your time, are pleasing subjects to me, though you have no other business to write of?

Montreuil being ready to leave, I can say no more but that I am eternally thine.

*   *   *

From my bed at the Louvre. June 14th, 1646.
Dear heart, M. Bellièvre, President of the French Law Courts, being sent by the Cardinal to replace Montreuil, does me the favour of carrying this letter to you. He assures me he will neglect neither

prayers nor threats to make you save yourself on any terms; for which he has my blessing.

You wrote me in your last that I should be my father's daughter. My father confounded all his enemies and won the throne of France by embracing the Catholic Faith. What you have to do to gain a like reward is much simpler. Except for a few forms and ceremonies, there is no difference between episcopacy and presbyterianism, for are they not all Protestants? (I would have written heretics, but that you would be sure to take offence.) Is not London worth the Covenant? You were always of old so ready to make concessions, so yielding to advice. Now you stick upon a mere trifle.

I am making every day such efforts for you. Mazarin has assured me that there will be peace between France and Spain by Christmas, and then he will be in a position to spare you some troops, but he must have the support of the Scots. And he will not have the support of the Scots unless you sign their Covenant, which is just a bit of paper presented to you at pistol point; *et voilà*, when the pistol is withdrawn, you tear the paper up. If you will not sign, it appears to me that your throne has become nothing to you, nor my company.

Forgive me, if you please, my faults of spelling, but I am obliged to write letters myself, having dismissed my secretary to save his wages. My clothes are so ragged that I am ashamed to walk abroad. Every sou of my French pension I spend on bribes, humiliating myself by appeals to my most bitter enemies.

You desire to know particulars of my health. I have a seizure of paralysis in the legs and all over the body. It seems to me as though my bowels and stomach weighed more than a hundred pounds, and as though I were so tightly squeezed in the region of the heart that I am suffocating; and at times I am like a person poisoned. I can scarcely stir and am doubled up. The same weight is upon my back; one of my arms has no feeling, and my legs and knees are colder than ice. This is perhaps the last letter you will ever receive from me. Let it not trouble you, I beg. Adieu, dear heart.

*   *   *

Anderson House, Newcastle. July 12th, 1646.

My sweet heart, since your letter conveyed to me by M. Bellièvre I have been upon the rack, each day expecting to hear news of your death. Now comes Will Davenant, who tells me you are very well in your physical being, and my sighs and tears are exchanged for *Te Deums*. Only I must confess that the letter he brought me from you has stifled some of my joy, for therein you accuse me of wicked obstinacy and lack of love for you and our children, repeating withal your old threat of retiring into a convent.

I must tell you that you will break my heart if you undertake any more to force my consent to part with the Church of England. If you do, I shall not be able to support my daily miseries. I am assailed on all sides, my cousin Hamilton, M. Bellièvre, and now Will Davenant (who though he be capable of penning a graceful lyric, understands not anything of divinity), urging me that to abandon the Church is the only way to save my throne. I find myself condemned by all my best friends of such a high destructive and unheard of kind of wilfulness, that I am thought to stand single in my opinion, and to be ignorant of my main foundation, to wit, conscience.

I have already written to you several times upon the reasons which forbid me to sign the Covenant, my grief being the only thing I desired to conceal from you, with which I am as full now as I can be without bursting. You write that I was too yielding in the past, and now stick upon a trifle. I must confess to my shame and sorrow that heretofore I have for public respects (yet I believe that if your personal safety had not been at stake I might have hazarded the rest) yielded unto things that were no less against my conscience than this, in particular my sacrificing the Earl of Strafford. For which I have been so deservedly punished that a relapse now would be insufferable.

As long ago as the abortive Treaty of Uxbridge, I told the Parliament's Commissioners that they had all my shop could afford, and that I would sooner die in a ditch than abandon the Church, injure my successors, or forsake my friends. The difference between episcopacy and presbyterianism is no bare matter of form and ceremonies, but so real that if I should give way and sign the

26

Covenant, there would be no Church of England, and by no human probability ever to be recovered. Pray make the case your own. With what patience would you give ear to him who would persuade you, for worldly respects, to leave the communion of the Church of Rome for any other? Indeed, sweet heart, this is my case.

For the rest, you cannot but be confident that there is no danger which I will not hazard, or pains that I will not undergo, to enjoy the happiness of your company, so they may not make me less worthy of you. I can write no more, my heart is too full, and my mind much fatigued by my theological disputation with Dr Henderson, an eminent Scottish divine. There was never man so alone as I. All the comfort I have is in your love and a clear conscience. I know the first will not fail me, nor (by the grace of God) the other. I am eternally and absolutely thine.

6

Letter from Dr Alexander Henderson to the Moderator of the General Assembly of the Kirk of Scotland

Newcastle. July 16th, 1646.

Reverend Sir, I have now these two months past endeavoured the conversion of His Majesty, exchanging divers papers with him in the form of a theological disputation, but all to no purpose. Being now very infirm in my body and sick at heart, I start my journey to Edinburgh tomorrow (the Lord willing), and shall take care that all these papers be laid before the Assembly. Lest my infirmity prevent me from giving you a verbal account of my mission, I write this for your eyes only.

His Majesty most willingly consented to the disputation, promising to bring an open mind to any arguments I might advance, so they be rational. (I am sorry to say it, Reverend Sir, but some of our ministers who were with him before my coming, had more zeal than discretion, His Majesty complaining to me that their driving was too much like Jehu's.) He pressed me hard at the beginning that he might have some Anglican divine to assist him; said he, 'I know very well what a great disadvantage it is for me to maintain an argument of divinity with so able and learned a man as yourself, it being your, not my, profession.' But according as I was instructed, I excused the granting of this request.

And as it transpired, His Majesty had no need of such reinforoment. I must confess that had his armies been as strong as his reason is, he had been every way unconquerable, since the Lord forbid I should have the disingenuity to deny the great advantage he had over me in all these writings. And this when the help of his chaplains could not be suspected, they being far from him.

I called upon all my powers of persuasion in conjuring His Majesty to join with us in continuing the blessed work of reformation, pleading his oft-expressed desire for the peace of his realms. To which he answered, 'It is strange there can be no method of peace but by making war upon my soul. If the straitness of my conscience will not give me leave to swallow down this camel of a Covenant, you have no more cause to quarrel with me than this, that my throat is not sufficient wide.' Upon my warning him of the loss of his throne if he let slip so glorious an opportunity, I found I had gone the wrong way with him; the least hint of a threat makes him cold. When I begged him to consider that there is no shame for anŷ man to change for the better, he answered me home, 'As I shall not be ashamed to change for the better, so I must see it is the better before I change. For example, I deem you for the present the best preacher in Newcastle, yet I believe it possible a better preacher may come in your place. Till then I retain my opinion.'

Wae's me, he has a sharp wit and abundance of learning. He was pleased to say I carried a library in my brain; the which is rather to be said of him, for in all these debates he had no books to assist him, save only the Bible which it is his habit to read daily. I for my part have come near to blindness by the consulting of so many ancient authors. Imagine my mortification when I, through

28

fatigue, having made a slip in quoting from Jerome, His Majesty most courteously corrected me in his next paper.

I besought him earnestly to consider, if the ghost of his royal father, of happy memory, could now speak, whether he would not advise His Majesty to perfect the work of reformation begun in England by King Henry VIII. To which he replied with some tartness that he had the happiness to know his royal father better than I, and desired me not to be too confident in the knowledge of how his ghost would speak. On my offering to show that our Saviour did not appoint archbishops, and that there were none in primitive times, he challenged me, not without a smile, did He appoint moderators of a Kirk Assembly?

Upon occasion, to show how sincere was his intent to hearken to the tenets of our Kirk, he consented to attend service at Nicholas's in the mercat-square. I much regret that the minister was so rude as to insult over His Majesty, calling on the congregation to recite with him Psalm 52, the opening words of which, said he, he intended taking for the text of his sermon, 'Why boasteth thou thyself, thou tyrant?' But straightway did His Majesty arise from his seat, and calls instead for Psalm 56, 'Be merciful unto me, O God, for man goeth about to devour me.' Then did the whole congregation join with him, betraying much emotion. For I must warn you, Reverend Sir, that there is a most dangerous discontent among the common folk here against our countrymen, ay, and the same lack of affection towards us is spread throughout England.

I believe the chief cause is, there is a rumour bruited that our Commissioners in London would yield up the person of our native-born Sovereign to the English Parliament if they may have in exchange the fee for our Brotherly Assistance. I abhor to think of it, and I am sure we would never be so base as to render up our prince's person which in our Covenant we swore to protect, and who came to us for succour on our invitation.

I spoke home on the subject to my Lord Argyll, new come from London. But he is dark as ever in his speech, and the only reply he would make me was, that if His Majesty will not embrace the only truly reformed religion, we could not in conscience take a pharaoh back with us to Scotland.

7

Correspondence of President Bellièvre with Cardinal Mazarin

Newcastle. August 9th, 1646.

I have made haste to observe your Eminence's command that I inspect the fine collection of pictures assembled by this King at Whitehall, and have sent your Eminence details thereof by my secretary. Speaking with the chief men in Parliament, I find they are indeed considering the sale of these treasures, being extreme straitened in their purses, notwithstanding the huge taxes with which they mulct the nation. I shall take care to drive a hard bargain with them.

I find that your Eminence's displeasure with M. de Montreuil has too much bottom. His indiscreet reproaches on the Scots have made Parliament suspect how far France was engaged in the negotiations concerning the King of Great Britain going to the Scotch camp. Your Eminence may rest assured that I shall take the utmost care not to compromise the neutrality France professes; and I am happy to inform your Eminence that I find myself *persona grata* with all three parties who won the late war. I have impressed upon them that the Prince of Wales came not into France from Jersey upon invitation, and is not officially received by His Most Christian Majesty. But since he is come, they should suffer less inconvenience by his residence there than if he were in any other part of Europe. Lest my dealings with them reach the ears of this King, I have my excuse ready: that France, and all his true friends, are convinced that nothing can be done for him unless he will part with the Church of England.

Yesterday there left here some Commissioners from Parliament, who had come hither with new propositions to the King, though they transpired to be the same as were offered him formerly, with the added threat that if he would not yield, he would be deposed, and his youngest son, the six-year-old Duke of Gloucester, set up in his room. This threat, he confided to me, caused him keen anguish, since it would lead to that perpetual strife between rival Regents, which devastated Scotland during his father's minority.

I was present at the conferences, and could not but admire the acumen displayed by Parliament in securing their own interests. They presented a vast and detailed proscription list of all who in any capacity whatsoever have served their King, carefully docketed with the proportion of plunder to be extracted from each victim, from two-thirds of their property for 'high delinquents' to one-third for the more fortunate. To which was added the names of those to be exempt from pardon, thoughtfully contrived to catch the biggest fish whose whole possessions can thus be thrown into the pool.

The King, rejecting both this and the imposition of the Covenant upon England and Ireland, offered counter proposals, which they would not so much as consider, saying they had no power to treat. At which he said, with an outburst of anger rare in him, that in that case a trumpeter would have served as well.

My brother writes me from London that the House of Commons has just passed a resolution, 'That this kingdom has no further need of our brethren the Scots in this kingdom' (hitherto it has always been 'our dear brethren'), and has offered them £100,000 to be off. To which they replied reproachfully 'that they came into England out of affection and not in a mercenary way', with much pious talk about religion, somewhat marred by their adding a demand for their £500,000 to the last farthing. They are as anxious to go home as the Parliament is to take farewell of them, for there is considerable discontent in Scotland, which it may require Leven's army to quell, and they have become so hated in these northern counties of England, where they live at free quarter, that they fear uprisings against them.

I was about to seal this letter, when I received a new dispatch from my brother. As a gentle hint that they are prepared to give value for money, the Scots have inserted into a paper on the subject this very pregnant question, 'What was to be done regarding the person of the King?' In other words, they have decided to regard him as a marketable commodity, and are prepared to sell him for cash down.

* * *

Newcastle. September 30th, 1646.

My brother writes me, that the bargain of which I advised your Eminence in my dispatch of August 9th, is at length concluded. In return for handing over the person of the King, the Scots are to have the fee for their Brotherly Assistance, though they have been obliged to allow a heavy discount.

They have always stated and offered to show that they owe in England £200,000, and this it is agreed that they shall have before they quit the kingdom. They are promised a further £50,000 in three months' time, a similar sum in six months, and £100,000 within the space of two years. My brother tells me there are unseemly wrangles over the nature of the securities to be given to the Scots for these future payments, they demanding hostages. But on the whole they are pleased, as well they may be, for they have driven a hard bargain with niggards who at first tried to foist them off with a bare fifth.

All that remains to complete the deal is for Parliament to find the initial £200,000, and this is proving unexpectedly difficult. They had no doubt that the City of London would oblige, it being their friend, yet it has made the condition that the Army be disbanded forthwith. There is nothing the Parliament would like better, but it would be impolitic to offend the Army (whose pay is many months in arrears) until Parliament has the King safely in its hands as a hostage. My brother writes me that Parliament is at odds with itself anent the disposal of the King's person, many being much averse to his being brought to London, for there is little doubt that the citizens would clamour for his restoration, so great is the tide of feeling changed in his favour among them.

I rejoice to inform your Eminence that I have bought from Parliament, for a sum but a fraction of its value, the Rubens *Nativity*, of which I wrote your Eminence, and which hangs in the King's Council Chamber at Whitehall.

* * *

Newcastle. January 2nd, 1647.

This evening there arrived here the Scotch Chancellor, Loudoun, bringing with him a letter to the effect that the Parliament's Commissioners are on their way to receive the King's person. His Majesty was playing at chess with me at the time; he betrayed not the slightest emotion, but continued the game and won it. As he was putting up the pieces into their box, Loudoun, with a somewhat reddened countenance, spoke thus:

'There is nothing would have gladdened us more than to have taken Your Majesty home with us as the covenanted king of a covenanted people. Yet I assure you, Sir, we have stipulated with the English Parliament that you be received by them with all honour and safety.'

Upon which the King spoke as it were to himself, saying:

'I am bought and sold. I am ashamed that my price is so much higher than my Saviour's.'

My brother writes to me that on Christmas Day (a festival the presbyterians do not observe), thirty-six carts laden with gold left London for this town, strongly guarded by soldiers who complained to see such largesse given to the Scots while their own pay is in arrears. And further, that when the Scotch Commissioners came to take farewell of their former allies, they received a public rebuff. For it being moved in the House of Commons that they be thanked for their civilities and good offices since their invasion on the side of the Parliament, it was carried by twenty-four votes that they be thanked for the former only.

And so all those noble characters they were wont to give the Scots upon every occasion concluded now in this, that they had proved civil. Never were people more complimented at their arrival, more obliged while they were wanted, and more contemned at their departure.

*   *   *

Newcastle. February 12th, 1647.

I am now to give your Eminence an account of the final scene in this extraordinary exchange of a king for cash.

Yesterday the Scotch drums beat for their return march over

the Border, and their Commissioners came to take leave of His Majesty. Crocodile tears they shed in abundance, lamenting that he and they must now part. To which he replied coldly:

'In truth I would rather go with those who bought me than remain with my fellow-countrymen who sold me.'

But for all that, I doubt not he will trust them upon a future occasion, for I never encountered a more irresolute and sentimental man. He watched with me from the window as the carts laden with gold rumbled over the cobbles on their journey north, the people of this place being so hot against the Scots that only the English garrison marching in prevented a riot. There was a pasquinade being sold, which I take leave to quote to your Eminence as typical of the feeling of the vulgar here:

> The Scots must have two hundred thousand pound
> To sell their King and quit our English ground;
> And Judas-like I hope 'twill be their lots
> To hang themselves – so farewell, lousy Scots.

The King is much cheered by many cumulative evidences that he has the heart of the common people on his side, but sets too great store by it. For the voice of the people has ceased to be decisive in these realms. Likewise has he strong hopes, which I predict will prove vain, of treating personally with his Lords and Commons, now they have him. I suspect that on the contrary they will hide him away in some remote dwelling in the character of a hostage, while they lay the devil they raised in the shape of this great New Model Army. I know not which most to despise, the obstinacy of the King, the greed of the Scots, or the imbecility of the Parliament, who actually speak as though they can disband the Army without paying its arrears.

I will observe to make some court to the chief officers of the Army, that your Eminence may lay the foundations of a treaty with them, should they become the *de facto* power, and thus ensure their friendship, or at least their neutrality, in our quarrel with Spain.

Blockade

I

Secret Memoirs of Thomas Herbert

For my own satisfaction, I think good to write down my experiences since the time when I was constrained to set foot upon the public stage.

I had never in my life the least inclination to be about the Court, it being filled, so I understood, with frothy and vain persons, and noted for popish and superstitious practices. Moreover I was ever catched easily by fevers and fluxes, and so delicate a constitution required a sequestered mode of life. Before the flame of war broke out in the top of the chimney, I removed to my country seat, though there was smoke enough there, yet I contrived to live tranquilly. Towards the end of the year 1646, I began to fear that I had the running gout, and was come to London to undergo a course of physic with an eminent doctor. I had scarce commenced it, when I received a command to wait upon my noble kinsman, the Earl of Pembroke, who told me, it was the pleasure of the Parliament that I form one of the new Household appointed to attend upon the King.

I excused myself on account of my frail health, but his lordship answered me with some roughness:

'If you spent your days with hawk and hound, and your nights with wine and wenches, your friends would not be plagued by this everlasting talk about your lungs and your guts.'

I must here confess that his lordship was himself too much addicted to such pleasures, especially to wine, which made him exceedingly choleric. He was without learning, having been but three or four months at Oxford when he was taken thence, in the latter end of Queen Elizabeth's reign, to follow the Court. When his present Majesty ascended the throne, my lord bought the office of Lord Chamberlain, but espoused the cause of the Parliament at the beginning of the troubles, by reason of a hot grudge he bore King Charles for refusing to intervene when the House of Lords committed him to the Tower for striking a fellow Peer in the chamber.

'Since you love to live retired,' he said to me now, 'your new office should prove congenial. It is the Parliament's design to lodge His Majesty in one of his own houses which is a perfect backwater, that of Holmby in Northamptonshire. You are to be a Groom of the Chamber, which is a civil alias for gentleman warder.'

Nothing I could say would have me excused; and so having made my will and set my affairs in order (for I was sure my health would break down under this trial), I took coach with the rest of those appointed, early in the year 1647. Had it not been for my travelling medicine-chest I was like to have died, the cold being intense, the roads abominable, and at the inns where we lodged I durst not go to bed, for I was sure the linen was not aired. Arrived at Newcastle, my lord and the other Commissioners, the Earl of Denbigh, the Lord Montagu, and Major-General Brown, presented themselves to the King at Anderson House, carrying with them myself and the gentleman appointed my fellow Groom, Mr James Harrington.

I was in some curiosity to view the King at close quarters, though much prejudiced against him. The character I had heard of His Majesty was, that he was temperate, grave and chaste, a most excellent judge of paintings and carvings, but an encroacher upon the spiritual and civil liberties of his subjects, and unsatisfied till he should reduce his realms to perfect slavery. It was bruited further by those who were his most severe critics that his firm adherence to prelacy was not from conscience, but from a mistaken principle that kingly government in the State could not stand without episcopal government in the Church. And it was the common cry of the town that his papist Queen had entire dominion over him, he being a most uxorious husband.

His Majesty was seated in a chair of estate, and while the Commissioners kissed his hand, I had leisure to observe him. His stature was less than the middle size, but his shape neat and so exactly proportioned as to resemble a miniature painted by a master hand. His features seemed more inclined to melancholy than mirth, but neither crabbed nor peevish; his dress rich but not gaudy. Above all, he had such a majestic grandeur, as it were hung about him, that it struck a kind of awe in me, and I was sure must command respect from the rudest.

Though he received the Commissioners with formality, he showed a cheerfulness surprising in a situation which must needs be mortifying to him, rallying my Lord Pembroke upon performing a winterly journey at his advanced age. But when Mr Harrington and I were presented, by the austere knit of his brow he seemed not to like us, and inquired whether those old servants of his, but seven in number, who had been permitted by the Scots to attend him, might not be continued in their posts.

The Commissioners told him, 'for the present', and my lord whispered me aside that His Majesty had ever intensely disliked the close company of strangers. But to his earnest request that his chaplains be restored to him, the Commissioners replied that it was not to be thought of, the presbyterian religion being now established by an ordinance of Parliament. To which His Majesty retorted with heat, that they had crucified the Church of England by an ordinance.

A few days being passed at Newcastle to refresh ourselves, I made the acquaintance of my fellow attendants. Mr Harrington was of a very genteel Lincolnshire family, much travelled and having the command of several languages, so like to prove a pleasant companion. He was ardent for the republican form of government, and told me at our first meeting that he was engaged on making notes for a book he intended to write, remodelling our Constitution on the lines of the Greek democracies, to be entitled, *The Commonwealth of Oceana.*

For the rest, the Steward and Treasurer was Mr Francis Cresset, long in the service of my Lord Pembroke. Mr Henry Firebrace, a low-born youth but a neat scribe (whereby he obtained the post of secretary to my Lord Denbigh) was Page of the Backstair. No less than six of the new Household had served in the Parliament's armies, and I was thankful that they did not mess with the Grooms, for my stomach was ever swift to take offence and their table manners were those of the camp. In addition there were some menial servants, and two eminent presbyterian divines, Mr Sprigge and Mr Foxley.

During our stay at Newcastle, neither Mr Harrington nor I was admitted by the King to attend upon him, he insisting still to have in his chamber two of his own gentlemen who had come to him from Oxford, ancient Mr Patrick Maule and Mr James Maxwell. The latter gentleman was married to the widow of one Ryder, Surveyor of the Stables to King James, and had in his family Ryder's daughter, Mrs Jane Whorwood, a meddlesome and mannish female with the voice of a sergeant-major and a face so pitted with the smallpox that she was a perfect eyesore. Though she had a husband and family in Oxfordshire, she must needs intrude herself into the King's new Household in the capacity of laundress, for which I deemed her most unsuited.

Our journey to Holmby occupied two weeks, and the reason for this sluggish mode of travel very much offended the Commissioners. For though they had most strictly forbidden any official welcome to the King in the towns and villages through which we passed, the vulgar sort gathered in multitudes everywhere to impede us, crying God-bless-yous and wrestling with our escort to kiss His Majesty's hand. Ay, and at Leeds, a town always strong for the Parliament, folk lined the road for full two miles, so that our passing became a kind of royal progress.

Outside Nottingham, the Lord General Fairfax greeted His Majesty, dismounting to kneel at his stirrup and kiss hands, and afterwards riding at the King's side bareheaded. I heard His Majesty remark at parting, he had ever held the opinion that Sir Thomas Fairfax was an honourable gentleman, speaking much in his praise. Which made me marvel, seeing that Sir Thomas was in command of the Army which had vanquished him in the field.

The mansion called Holdenby, corrupted to Holmby, is the largest country house in England, designed in the Italianate manner for Sir Christopher Hatton, Chamberlain to Queen Elizabeth, and purchased for his present Majesty by his mother when he was Prince of Wales. It is situated three and six-eighths of a mile from Northampton, in a district very well-affected to the

Parliament, and is within a day's posting of London. At the time of which I write, it had a garrison of sixty men, commanded by Colonel Richard Greaves and Major Matthew Thomlinson, both of the Old Model Army, as were their soldiers, part of whose duties consisted in protecting His Majesty whensoever he was permitted to ride abroad. For letters, he must write none save in the presence of the Commissioners, nor was he allowed to receive any unopened by them.

Within a few days of our arrival, Mr Maule and Mr Maxwell received their dismissal, in consequence of a resolution passed at Westminster, 'that His Majesty's Household be composed only of such as had not been in arms or assisted in this late unnatural war against the Parliament, or adhered to the enemy'. So were Mr Harrington and I obliged to force our presence upon the King, which, while he concealed not his dislike of it, yet he endured it with patience. And albeit he was ever most strict in our observing the proper formalities, he excused our awkwardness with a grave smile, and took pains to instruct us in courtly etiquette.

At our first coming to Holmby, His Majesty inquired several times of the Commissioners whether there was word of new negotiations being offered him by the Parliament, since he assumed that this was the reason why he had been taken from the custody of the Scots. But my Lord Pembroke, being one night in his cups, informed the King with very little seemliness that His Majesty's rejection of the propositions offered him in August last, had obliged the Parliament to resolve they would give neither His Majesty nor themselves the pains to treat any further with him.

For a while I was confident that our most secluded manner of life was as congenial to His Majesty as it was to me. I was quickly made aware that he was by nature devoted to an exact routine. In his diet he was very sparing and temperate; he made but one meal a day, at which he drank a little glass of sack or claret, which glass he used also in the morning for his breakfast with a morsel of bread. His supper was ordinarily an egg and a draught of small-beer. Which spartan diet, he told me, had always been his by choice, of necessity while he captained his armies in the field, and now agreeable to his restricted exercise. To supply the want of hunting, which was forbidden him, he walked regularly in the gardens or around the galleries if it rained, with so fast a step I found it hard to keep up with him. On occasion, he was permitted to ride over to Althorp, the seat of my Lord Stanhope, for a game of bowls.

A circumstance which saddened me was His Majesty's steadfast refusal of the ministrations of Mr Sprigge and Mr Foxley. He shut himself up in his bedchamber on the Sabbath to read Morning Prayer in solitude, and he was ordinarily half-way through dinner before these godly divines had finished saying grace, he having recited his own in the old superstitious manner. This grieved me so much that I took the boldness to cry up these ministers to him, telling him that Mr Sprigge preached to admiration; to which he replied that there should be less preaching and more praying. For the first, said he, breeds faction, but the second, devotion. And said further:

'I hold it better to seem undevout, and to hear no man's prayers, than to be forced to comply with those petitions to which my heart cannot consent, nor my tongue say Amen, without contradicting my understanding, or belying my soul. I had rather be condemned to solitude than to hypocrisy, by seeming to pray what I cannot approve.'

These words I wrote down, and began the custom of recording in my journal others the King spoke which left a strong impression upon me. His Majesty, growing more easy in my company, laid aside his stiff coldness which he wore among strangers, and permitted me to see something of his true character concealed behind this mask. I found myself not exceeding sick at Holmby, only I could not sleep and was fain to send for an apothecary to procure some rest; upon my mentioning this to the King, he told me very kindly that I should take more exercise, and invited me to a turn with him in the gardens. I demurred, telling him I took care never to be wet-shoed in the morning dew, and said further I feared that he himself, being so delicately bred, and passing all his life to beyond his fortieth year in the soft comforts of a Court, might contract a chill. He gave me his smile which had a peculiar charm, as it were lighting up his grave features, and says he:

'I think you forget, Mr Herbert, that until lately I have been a soldier on active service.'

After supper that evening, he showed me a rough diary of some campaign he had conducted during the war, which mightily astonished me, for I had imagined that, though he had been his own general, he would not have tasted the true hardships of a military life. With his permission I copied down some entries which gave a picture of his painful marches. 'No dinner this day' was often recorded, as was likewise, 'Lay in my coach in the field all night'. Frequently he would be in saddle from dawn till late evening; and if he could procure a bed at the end of it, the fact was noted as a rare luxury.

'I am apt,' observed the King, 'for all physical hardship, and delight in every sort of exercise of mind and body. At Newcastle my wits were kept keen, both in resisting the daily baiting of the Scots to make me sign the Covenant, and in my written disputation with Dr Henderson. But here I am left as it were to stagnate, and this, I confess, irks me.'

I murmured something, I know not what, being much moved; for so great was his outward calm that I had not imagined he suffered. And then, as though fearing he seemed to pity himself, he added:

'As God has given me afflictions to exercise my patience, so has He given me patience to bear my afflictions. What armies and tumults could not obtain, neither shall these tedious restraints. Though my enemies shall destroy me, yet they shall never have cause to despise me.'

I was much startled to hear him speak the word 'destroy', as if our godly Parliament, or indeed any man who had the right to call himself a Christian and good subject, would lift up a hand against the person of the Lord's Anointed. I feared His Majesty was by nature melancholic, for he continued to speak as though expecting some violent death.

2

Unfinished Autobiography of Cornet George Joyce

When Parliament had bought Charles Stuart from the Scots, the unregenerate who formed a majority in the Commons' House were for disbanding the army of the Lord of Hosts. Ay, they durst propose disbandment when Egypt was but a day's march in the rear, and we had yet so many heathen tribes to conquer and their cities to lay waste, ere we could possess the Land of Promise. For we were the mighty men of valour chosen by the Lord to root out, not only in England, but in popish France and Spain, the Philistines and Hittites and all those who bore the mark of the Beast upon their foreheads.

And they would disband us without payment of arrears, which were eighteen months behind for the foot, and forty-three weeks for the horse and dragoons, the grand total being half as much again as was paid to the Scots to be rid of them. Instead of our just pay, we received debentures secured upon the public faith, and these we were fain to sell by the bundle to our officers for one and sixpence in the pound, who invested them in the forfeited estates of Malignants. A corporal in my troop was condemned to ride the wooden horse only for having holes in his shoes. How could it be thought that a poor soldier was able to give four shillings for new ammunition-shoes, who never received so much in the last year, and who, the war against Charles Stuart being ended, could have no more lawful plunder?

This Parliament that would cart the Ark and give laws to the Saints, who licked their fingers and shared out the fat of the land among themselves, got passed in March, 1647, an ordinance disbanding us, not at one blow, for there must be some spared to wreak the Lord's vengeance upon popish Ireland. For which force men were invited to volunteer, all their commanders being of the Old Model, lickspigots of the Parliament, and those who declined were to be disbanded forthwith, without their arrears of pay.

Now though I myself was of the Old Model, I had been favoured from the beginning with a vision, wherein it was revealed to me that we must march on until the Lord Himself bid us disband. And now this mole-eyed Parliament would transport us to a waste and popish country, where they might starve or relieve us at their pleasure, and if we would not go, we were to be turned adrift without our pay. And so we, both of the Old and the New Model, sent forth a petition, praying for our arrears, for pensions for our widows and orphans, and freedom from impressment in time to come.

To which we received a currish answer, denouncing our petition as mutinous, fulminating against the impudence, as they termed it, of soldiers in the employ of the Parliament presuming to question an ordinance passed by both Houses, and threatening to indict any man who promoted such petitions as a public enemy.

Aha! They had reckoned without our most precious Saint, Lieutenant-General Cromwell. He with his godly son-in-law, Commissary Ireton, played the knave with the knave (which is lawful), and swore from his seat in the House that he would rather be burnt alive with his whole family than permit the Army to resist disbandment. But within the Army he set up a parliament of our own, with a Council of Officers and another of all ranks below that of captain, two from each regiment being elected, at first termed Adjudicators, but soon becoming known as Agitators, since their business was to agitate such questions as the interests of the Army required. And at the first meeting of this lower Council, it was resolved that henceforth the term 'common soldier' be changed to that of 'private'; for we were not a band of janizaries hired to fight the Parliament's battles, but the Hosts of the Lord, and it was we, and not the Parliament, whom God had blessed in the field.

I being elected an Agitator in the Lord General Fairfax's regiment, our great Cromwell sent for me, and told me he would have me put into the privates' minds what he wished there. Further bidding me search out and report to him the designs of the levellers, who much increased in our ranks, to the decay of discipline. To be a spy, said he, was a very honourable office, reminding me of the godly spies in Scripture, as for example . . . [Here

Mr Joyce occupies two full pages with citations from the Old Testament, which are omitted. Ed.]

These levellers would have it that the Army was in as much need of reform as the kingdom, pressing that all landlords and masters be abolished, the owning of property prohibited, and no obedience given to King, magistrate or superior officer. Some among them said to me that soon the appointed days would be spent, and then should the he-goat cease from troubling the sanctuary. I was like to come to blows with them when I discovered they would have our great Cromwell intended by the prophet Daniel as this he-goat, which destroyed the ram only that he might become as great.

I rejoiced to find that my captain was a leveller, and hasted to accuse him to Cromwell. For my former accusation against him, of singing a lewd song, had not procured his dismissal, he saying he knew not the words of it, but sang it only for the tune. I had long been aware that he was not of the Elect, for when challenged he could not recite the dimensions of the Temple, nor the number of the companies that came to David at Ziklag, nor name the thirty-one kings slain by Moses and Joshua.

Our swords being at present in sheath, all our time was passed in drawing up in our two Councils censures of parliamentary ordinances, likewise remonstrances and petitions; which caused some ribald wag among the Cavaliers to say, that Parliament was hoist with its own petard, since these were the same methods Parliament had used against Charles Stuart before the war. Our privates took to wearing paper cockades in their hats, setting forth their grievances, and the watchword of the hour became *Purge*. The Parliament must be purged of those who had become as wicked tyrants as Charles Stuart; and here were we, twenty thousand Saints, to see that it was so.

Now our great Cromwell, being warned that Parliament was resolved to impeach him, because they suspected he was the ruling spirit behind our resistance to disbandment, spoke with holy cunning in the House, swearing once again that the Army was willing to do as Parliament decreed. And the Lord having blinded their eyes, they positively ordered disbandment, beginning in the

46

month of May, 1647, with the Lord General's regiment, then quartered at Chelmsford. The Commissioners who came to read the order to disband were answered from the ranks with jeers and angry hums. And my captain made a drum-head sermon, shouting forth that we would not worship their new idol, the presbyterian Parliament, and that we, who had loosed the chains in which this nation was altogether bound by the oppressor, were those who henceforth must give the law. Upon which our privates seized the colours, mine among them, and marched away to join with the main body at Newmarket, looting on the road, for they were in a righteous fury.

But the Lord spoke to me to turn aside and report to our new Joshua what had befallen. For though we were right to resist disbandment without our arrears, here was like to be a mutiny stirred up by my captain, and I was still hopeful of getting his place.

I rode hard for London. When I came to Cromwell's house in Drury Lane, I was informed he was shut up in close conference with Commissary Ireton, but upon a message that I carried urgent tidings, I was admitted to his presence. I told him first what had fallen out at Chelmsford, laying the whole blame upon my captain, and excusing our privates on account of their just grievances. Then, the Spirit moving strongly in me, I spoke as I was inspired thus:

'Sir, it grows to be a sad wonder that the most zealous promoters of the cause are now more spitefully inclined towards their own faithful armies, by whom the Lord perfected their victories, than against Pharaoh himself. They denounce our petitions as scandalous, and care only for enriching themselves, and that the camels of the Malignants shall be their booty and the multitude of their cattle a spoil. Whereas when the Hosts of Israel fought in the wilderness, the spoil belonged only to the men of war.'

'Alack,' he groaned, 'they have just now passed an ordinance whereby all estates of Malignants concealed and uncompounded for, shall be forfeit, one half to the Parliament and the other half to the discoverer. There are clerks and solicitors who make a trade of hunting out such discoveries; while my poor precious Saints remain without their just pay.'

At this I was the more incensed, and cried:

47

'As if it were not enough that these Parliament-men during the war should through their committees in every garrison and portion of the Army presume to dictate when to sally and when to fight. But now while they feed their coffers from the King's revenue and the estates of Malignants, we the Hosts of the Lord must starve. There are some of our privates who cry, Why do we suffer these fellows to vapour thus? Let us clout them out of their seats.'

Commissary Ireton made me a sharp look, as though he thought I had presumed too high; but our new Joshua let fall a sudden ocean of tears, being quite unable to speak for several minutes. The unregenerate would have it that he was of a morbid nature, ay, and I have heard a physician affirm that in his youth he was what they term *melancholicus*, and suffered such phantasies that on occasion he had threatened to lay violent hands upon himself. But those who speak so know nothing of the movings of the Spirit. Anon, smiting himself upon the breast, he moaned:

'As we find out new sins every year to provoke the Lord, so the Lord finds out new punishments to afflict us. Alas, that the poor godly people should be persecuted by Saul.'

I was somewhat at a stand to know whom he meant by Saul; but when he spoke of the poor godly people he meant always his soldiers. So taking courage, I said to him that it was but a few months since thirty-six carts laden with gold were sent to the unregenerate Scots, while we, the Lord's instruments in breaking the rod of the oppressor, were forced to pinch our bellies, being denied the wages we had earned with our blood. He looked upon me with a thoughtful air, and then says he:

'The Scots had something to give in exchange for this gold.'

'Pray set a guard upon your tongue, sir,' cried Commissary Ireton, with a warning glance at me. But Cromwell paid him no heed, beginning to pace the apartment and as it were musing aloud:

'When I opened my bible this morning, the first words upon which my eyes lighted were these in 2nd Samuel: "And the men of Israel answered the men of Judah and said, We have ten parts of the kingdom and we have also more right in the King than ye; why, then, do ye despise us?" Now suppose it were possible to persuade

48

His Majesty to place himself among the men of Israel and lend his authority to all our just demands?'

I found his eyes upon me, which were small but with a very piercing glance. Before I could find my tongue, being much startled by his words, he caught me in his arms, weeping many tears again, and calling me 'good brother Joyce', whispered that he had ever held me in high esteem, yea, fit to be a captain in the Hosts of the Lord. My fleshly nature trembled, part with joy and part with fear. For I understood that while on the one hand he promised me my longed-for promotion, on the other he would have me steal away the King from Holmby House. And knowing by rote the *Laws and Ordinances of War*, most rigorously enforced in our armies, I bethought me that even for stealing a sheep a man was made to run the gauntlet.

But while I thus quaked, Cromwell on a sudden ceased his weeping, and became in an instant that military commander whose swift decision was famous in the field. He spread out a map upon the table and rapped orders at me, smart and brisk.

'Put in spurs,' says he, 'and ride to Holmby, picking up upon your way five hundred men you can trust from these several garrisons. What follows I must leave to your discretion, yet I am confident that your brethren of Holmby garrison will stand by what you do.'

When he had said this, he fell a-laughing, and seeing my astonishment, told me:

'Whensoever during the war I was to win a battle, this divine impulse to mirth came upon me. Before Naseby I did laugh to such excess as if I had been drunk.'

3

Secret Memoirs of Thomas Herbert

I well remember it was the second day of June in this year of 1647, that I was bidden accompany the King to Althorp to play bowls. For I have it in my journal that there had fallen out a sharp passage betwixt Mr Dowcett, the Clerk of the Kitchen, and myself anent my diet. I having told him that it was my habit, for the preservation of my health, to take only sage with sweet butter for breakfast during this month, he had served me instead with a spiced fricassee, and my stomach being highly offended therewith, I would fain have stayed retired in my chamber. But Colonel Greaves and Major-General Brown, who were to escort the King as usual with a guard, would not excuse me from accompanying them.

We had been upon the green about an hour, when the Colonel spied some of his men in close conversation with a horseman in a red cassock, who carried a cornet furled about its staff. The Colonel hailed him, and asked what news from the headquarters of the Army at Newmarket, supposing him to have come from thence, bidding him not to be afraid to speak.

Whereupon the stranger replied, looking hard at His Majesty, that he was not afraid of any man in the kingdom. Then began he to rant in the manner of the sectaries, inveighing hot against the Parliament who would disband the Hosts of Israel, as he termed them, without their arrears of pay. To which the common soldiers of the guard said Amen, though they were of the Old Model and as such were deemed faithful in the Parliament's service.

'This fellow is one of the Agitators, I warrant you,' says the Colonel to Major-General Brown, 'who would seduce my garrison.' And straightway he gave order that there be no more playing at bowls that day, but we return to Holmby.

It chanced to be my turn of duty to lie on a pallet in the ante-room when the King had retired, a sore penance for me who have ever been most sensitive to draughts. It was long ere I could sleep, and I wondered still to see the line of candlelight beneath the bed-chamber door, and to hear the scratching of the King's quill. At length I sank into repose, but not for long. I was most rudely awakened by a clangour, as though one banged with a sword-hilt upon the outer door, and to add to this unseemly noise, the clock in the turret tolled the hour of midnight. Then there came a con-fused shouting of orders and feet running hither and thither. As I wondered in myself, all in a sweat of alarm, there came intruding into the ante-room Mr Firebrace, Page of the Backstair, his dress disordered and his manner wild.

'Here is a desperate business,' says he. 'There is one gives his name as Joyce, his rank being cornet, has surrounded the house with five hundred troopers, and says his business is with the King.'

At this there came in to us Mr Harrington, in his nightgown, and what he had to relate made me the more afraid. It seemed that Colonel Greaves, bidding his garrison stand to arms to resist Cornet Joyce, those knaves, far from obeying, flung wide the gates and embraced Joyce's troopers as their brethren in the Lord. Whereat the Colonel slipped out through the back entry to bear these strange tidings to Westminster, while Cornet Joyce swelled to such a pitch of insolence that he locked up the Commissioners of Parliament in their bedchambers, saying he had nothing to do with Commissioners, but only with the King.

'God protect His Majesty!' cried Mr Firebrace. 'There have been, so I hear, some dark whispers of late as though the fanatics in the Army would not stick at secret murder.'

Mr Harrington and I consulted together what we ought to do, while Mr Firebrace, though but a youth of humble stock, presumed to urge upon us that it was our bounden duty to defend the sacred person of the King, though it be at the cost of our lives. I was much surprised by his vehemence, for hitherto he had appeared prudent and modest, and of no great devotion to His Majesty. We had scant time to debate, for a hasty foot upon the stair warned us that this Joyce had discovered where His Majesty lay.

He beat with his sword-hilt on the ante-room door, which we had locked from within, and Mr Harrington, opening it a crack for fear lest otherwise he break it down, demanded his name and business, and withal whether he had obtained leave of the Commissioners thus to intrude himself into the royal apartments. To which he replied, thrusting open the door, that he had orders from those who cared not a brass thimble for the Commissioners of Parliament, and that speak with the King he must and would. I recognized him as the stranger who had appeared upon the bowling-green that day, suspected by Colonel Greaves to be one of

51

those firebrands termed Agitators. And he having now a cocked pistol in one hand and a naked sword in the other, I felt a fainting to seize my spirits in such extraordinary manner that, finding myself ready to swoon, I was fain to pretend that something had offended my stomach and retired to the necessary-house.

When I returned, I saw that Mr Firebrace, with more courage than discretion, had set his back against the bedchamber door, while Mr Harrington attempted to reason with the intruder, saying it was past midnight, that the King was abed, and that it was high treason for any man to enter His Majesty's apartments with a naked sword. While they argued it back and forth, there came the tinkle of a silver hand-bell from the bedchamber, whereupon I, being the senior Groom on duty, slipped within, and falling on my knee, acquainted His Majesty with the cause of this unseemly commotion. He was pensive, and said:

'I was obliged to ride a stage with this Joyce on my way from Oxford to the Scots, and it was plain from his talk that he is a dangerous fanatic. Pray tell him, Mr Herbert, that I will receive him in the morning, and not before.'

I was in a shake lest the ruffian, being crossed, should use violence to come at the King; but instead, he flung away in a great huff, muttering to himself.

It was ever His Majesty's habit to rise at five of the clock in summer, when he would fall to his religious devotions, being perforce his own chaplain. His Majesty made no remark to me upon the disturbance of the night, but when I had withdrawn the curtains and handed him his robe, he signed to me as usual to leave him to his prayers. At six o'clock I re-entered the bedchamber with Mr Harrington to assist His Majesty with his toilet, he speaking cheerfully to us anent the beauty of the day and said he would walk in the gardens before breakfast; all as though he had forgotten the seizure of Holmby during the night.

But as soon as we stepped out of doors, there was an ugly reminder of it in the shape of Cornet Joyce and his five hundred troopers, mounted as if ready to take the road. When the King appeared, Mr Joyce, as though to assert himself, unfurled the cornet he carried and began dexterously throwing it from one hand to the other, giving it many complicated twirls. Mr Firebrace whispered to me that he recognized the colours of Lord General Fairfax, a white star upon a deep blue ground. Then fell out a most extraordinary conversation, which I took care to set down in my journal that same evening.

The King: Who is in command here?

A voice from the ranks: We're all commanders.

Joyce: We've come to take Your Majesty away.

The King: Are you acting by the authority of the Parliament?

Joyce: They haven't ordered me not to do what I'm doing.

The King: Who has ordered you, then?

Joyce: The Army.

The King: Then you must have something in writing to show me from General Fairfax.

Joyce: Please Your Majesty not to ask me such questions.

The King: But indeed I must. I pray you, Mr Joyce, deal ingenuously with me, and show me your commission.

Then did Joyce grow defiant, and waving his hand towards the massed ranks of troopers, said that there was his commission. I marked an involuntary shudder seize upon His Majesty; but he said with smiling urbanity that it was as fair a commission as he had ever seen in his life, legible without spelling. And continued seriously:

'What if I refused to go with you? I hope you would not force your King. You must satisfy me that I shall be used with respect and honour, and you must release the Commissioners of Parliament before I will stir.'

At this point Major Thomlinson, who was in command since the leaving of Colonel Greaves, and who had assembled the garrison of Holmby, thus addressed them:

'You are here in the service of the Parliament. Can you stand by and see its authority flouted by one who can produce no credentials?'

On which the whole concourse of them shouted:

'All! All!'

'You cry all, all,' says Major Thomlinson, much put out, 'but I will wager not two in the company know what is happening. It is

53

plain abduction! Now let those who are willing that His Majesty stay with the Commissioners of Parliament speak.'

They responding, 'None! None!', Major Thomlinson fell into a pet and cried wrathfully:

'I would have lain down my life rather than have allowed His Majesty to be snatched from the safe keeping of the Parliament.'

'Gallantly spoken,' says Joyce with sauciness. 'But I've my orders from those who are higher in rank than you. And if three or even four parts of the Army don't approve of what I've done, I'll be content to be hanged at the head of my regiment.'

'Certainly,' the King observed, 'you must have the countenance of great men, for you would not of yourself have ventured to seize my person. However, I pardon the treason if you convey me safely to your General, and permit the Commissioners of Parliament to accompany us.'

They could come if they pleased, says Joyce; and then with an earnestness I am sure now was feigned, he begged His Majesty to believe that he would be received with every respect by the Army, and meanwhile should choose how far he pleased to travel that day. Whereat the King smiled and said:

'I am an old campaigner, Mr Joyce, and can ride as far as any man here. Let my horse be brought.'

When he thus spoke, the troopers gave a roar of exultation, bawling:

'The King and the Army!'

But under cover of this uproar, His Majesty said to me:

'Thus is mere power above all law and order; yet I hope my resolution is so fixed that no power can force me to do a base thing. These men are masters of my body; my soul is beyond their reach.'

Truce

I

Unfinished Autobiography of Cornet George Joyce

Upon our way from Holmby to Newmarket, we lay at Childerley, the house of a Malignant, and thither came Lieutenant-General Cromwell. I had been much scandalized by the lewd rout who ran out of the towns and villages to fawn upon Charles Stuart; but I could scarce believe my eyes when our new Joshua entered his presence bareheaded, kneeled to kiss his hand, rejoiced at his coming among us, and says he:

'I call God and angels to witness that I knew nothing of Mr Joyce's intent to take Your Majesty away.'

Ah, what a cruel stroke was that! But when the King asked if then I would be hanged for such a deed, Cromwell excused it, saying I was a man whose zeal sometimes outran my discretion, and then spoke lustily against the Parliament who had imprisoned His Majesty and denied him his chaplains. And afterwards sent for me in private, hugged me in his arms, told me he had prevailed with the General to have me promoted captain, and that this glorious work I had begun would bring forth fruit in righteousness. Yet he was pleased to speak in that manner he often used, resembling a smoke-screen which conceals the advance of armies, and though I knew him to be in truth another Joshua, whom no man was able to resist all the days of his life, I could not but stagger when I saw him become so courtier-like.

For when we came to Newmarket, it was by his orders (the Lord General being but a cipher) that the odious, vain and wicked mummery of a Court was restored to Charles Stuart, and his outed chaplains, who were little better than papists, given back to him. And with my own ears I heard Cromwell assure him that he was concerned only to meet the royal wishes, begging pardon for the poor rough soldiers who knew not how to behave themselves towards a prince, yet must do their best until such Malignants as

57

the King chose to name were recalled. And says Cromwell, laying his hand upon his heart:

'Whatever the world may judge of us, we shall be found no self-seekers, farther than to live as subjects ought to do, and to preserve our consciences. Men cannot enjoy their lives and estates quietly unless Your Majesty enjoys your rights, and it is for this reason I rejoice that Your Majesty is rescued from the captivity into which the Parliament presumed to place you.'

Though I guessed there was some holy cunning behind his words, yet they troubled me, and when they leaked out to our privates, there were sour looks. For Charles Stuart to enjoy his rights, said they, was not why they had fought the war. And when I said to them that now we had gotten his person into our hands, we could chaffer with the Parliament for our arrears, as had the Scots, they muttered that it was more than their arrears they wanted.

What then? said I. To which they would give me no plain answer, for I believe they guessed I was a spy placed among them by Cromwell, against whom they began to murmur dangerously. For there was grown up a mutinous spirit in the ranks, part bred by the idleness of camp life. Nor was it now only the levellers among them who said, they had as much right as their officers to dictate terms to the vanquished, of whom Charles Stuart was the chief, and who, like the fourth beast in Daniel's vision, had thought himself able to change laws and crush the Saints. The kingdom is ours by conquest, said they, for have we not borne the burden and heat of the day, suffering hardship and peril, wounds and sickness, in the Lord's own cause?

When I disclosed this camp-fire talk to my superior, Major Harrison (a worthy man, the son of a London butcher), he seemed not fretted by it, but says he:

'Never fear, good Joyce, Charles Stuart shall be brought to book for his crimes, one way or another. Sodom's sins were hardly so great, who was destroyed with fire and brimstone. But first we are to settle accounts with the House of Commons.'

On June 10th our whole force was mustered upon Triploe Heath, with orders to march on London. There we were to destroy the idols and cut down the groves in the heathen City, and to purge out those in Parliament who had gone astray like a wanton heifer, as said the prophet Hosea.

2

Diary of Colonel Jack Ashburnham

June 24th, 1647. Upon this day, to my infinite joy, I was reunited with my dear royal master at Woburn. I was obliged to travel from France in company with Colonel Will Legge, who is Rupert's spaniel, and with Sir John Berkeley, sent to H.M. with a letter from the Queen. H.M. knew him little, for he was not among those persons of quality who served H.M. before the war, being in a very private station, and his military post in the farthest corner of the kingdom. A vain, ambitious person, with great confidence in himself, and does not delight to converse with those who do not share it. We passed the whole journey quarrelling.

I learn that Woburn is but a temporary lodging, the Army marching steadily upon London, though absolutely forbidden by Parliament to approach. What the lousy redcoats will be at, I know not, but certainly their devilships at Westminster are in a fret, and these two parties of thieves falling out, honest men may thrive.

To tempt H.M. to rest content to reside with the Army, they have restored to him his favourite chaplains, Drs Hammond and Sheldon. They could do no less, their watchword being freedom of conscience; I hear on good report that there are within their ranks some hundred and four score sects, venting a gallimaufry of strange opinions, some dipping, as they term it, men and women naked in rivers, other some saying they are too spiritual to need creed, sacrament or church, and all of them whining through their nose about the New Jerusalem.

There are large promises from Cromwell (Fairfax being but a mere figurehead) that soon he will take off all restraint from H.M. who may have whom he will to be about his person. But for the nonce, his Household is the same as that appointed by the Parliament to attend him at Holmby, all of them fellows of mean birth and low fortune, or else of the underling gentry, or a company of prick-eared puritanical rascals. There is one Harrington who, with great noise but to little purpose, trumpets forth tedious pedantical discourses anent the several sorts of government that have been in Greece and Rome. His fellow Groom, one Herbert, informs us daily, as a matter of high import, whether or not he has gone to stool.

I was much taken aback when, condoling with H.M. that he had lived for months attended by such a rabble, he spoke in their defence, saying that they had used him with all civility, and that at least two among them had proved their change of heart towards him while he was yet at Holmby.

'The Parliament's Commissioners,' said he, 'denied me pen and paper, which Dowcett, appointed by them my Clerk of the Kitchen, conveyed to me underhand when he came to take orders for the dishes of the day. And Harry Firebrace, my Page of the Backstair, offered voluntarily to smuggle out letters to my wife, at which he proved himself very apt, being assisted in it by Mrs Whorwood.'

H.M. said further that he believed others thus forced upon him, now wished him well, and therefore I should be pleased to forget their past. But I having been bred up in the best company, cannot demean myself by talking with inferior persons, who are moreover vile stinking rebels. And this is one of the greatest of my master's defects, that through the candour and sincerity of his own nature he is more unsuspicious of others, and more credulous of fair pretenders, than suits with the prudence he testifies in everything else. Nothing awakens jealousy in him but gross flattery, which, when he sees anyone so servile as to use, he believes the soul that can descend to such baseness might be capable of falsehood. But those who are cunning attempt him not that way, but put on a face of fair honest plainness, with which he has been often in his life betrayed. And now he will trust those bare-faced turnabouts who float up and down with the tide of the times.

60

July 15th. We having come with the Army as far as Caversham, not a day's posting from London, H.M. prevailed with what they term the Council of Officers to permit him a visit from his children who are prisoners at St James's, the which Parliament had utterly denied him. This meeting, compounded equally of joy and sorrow, was at the Greyhound inn at Maidenhead, and thither I accompanied H.M., together with those I could well have done without, *viz.* a strong troop of horse, pretended as a guard to protect H.M. From whom, is not known, but certainly it was not from the common people, who flocked in multitudes to cheer H.M., strewing the road with flowers and sweet herbs. We had with us Fairfax, a man of a drowsy presbyterian humour, who wishes nothing that Cromwell does, and yet contributes to bring it all to pass, and that arch-hypocrite himself who, pox take him, cannot, I swear, be outdone by the Devil, either in cunning or malice.

The Princess Elizabeth, a prisoner almost ever since she can remember, is grown into a very comely maid, serious beyond her years; I recall she was born on Holy Innocents' Day in the year 1635, and is as fair and fragile as the snow which then smothered London. She, with her brother, the Duke of York, captured at the fall of Oxford, after their obeisance rushed into their father's arms, but young Harry of Gloucester, a babe scarce out of the petticoats, remained upon his knees gazing wide-eyed at H.M.

'Child, do you not know me?' asked the King. And when the innocent said 'No', my master looked very melancholic, but took the lad upon his knee and said: 'I am your father, sweet heart, and you were but an infant when we parted. It is not the least of my misfortunes that I have brought you and your brothers and sisters into the world to share my sharp trials.'

Then all the royal children burst into weeping, at which H.M. gathered them into his arms, kissing and blessing them. In truth, there was not a dry eye in the apartment, and the wettest of all belonged to that slimy serpent, Cromwell, who blubbered to me:

'It is the tenderest sight ever I beheld. No man was ever more mistaken than myself in the sinister opinion I entertained of the King, whom I now deem the most upright and conscientious man of his three kingdoms. I pray God that He will be pleased to look upon me according to the sincerity of my heart towards His Majesty.'

I pray God He'll strike you dead, thought I.

Speaking of this scene to Berkeley when we returned to Caversham, that swaggering captain-puff had the face to tell me he believed Cromwell quite converted. Berkeley fancies he obtained great influence with the rebels when he tamely surrendered Exeter to them. I warned them, he brags to me, upon what slippery ground they stood, that the Parliament, when they had served its turn, would dismiss them with reproach. Which made such an impression on them that they told me at parting, they should never forget what I had said to them. And the very high contests which have fallen out betwixt the Parliament and the Army, says he, make me confident that both sides will in the end be ready to have His Majesty as the umpire. Said I, you should have taken up the trade of almanack-maker.

July 31st. Strange happenings. On the 28th, some of the Army officers presented to Parliament an impeachment of eleven of its members. This was an arrow that the House of Commons did not expect to have been shot out of that quiver; however, the accused members, who best knew the temper of the Army, thought it safer to retire themselves. Yet the Army still pretended dissatisfaction, demanding that the Trained Bands of London be put under the command of well-affected persons (the self-same demand this mongrel Parliament made to H.M. before the war), that all members of the House be called to give account of the monies they have received from forfeited estates, and that the pay of the Army be put into a constant course.

The which so enraged Parliament that they voted, 'That the yielding to the Army in these particulars would be against their honour and destructive of their privilege', with many high expressions against such insolent presumption. And withal sent a peremptory order to Fairfax to withdraw his troops beyond a thirty-mile radius, called up the Trained Bands, and, if you please, sent an appeal for aid to their late dear brethren, the Scots. Yet notwithstanding that the cits were loud in their cries of, 'Live and die with the Parliament', Speaker Lenthall and the independents in the House left the sinking ship and scuttled over to the Army, leaving the presbyterian remnant still breathing fire.

Upon the 29th, the Army broke camp, shot out one claw to grip the Thames at Tilbury, while another seized Deptford after some bloodshed. At which the cits changed their tune, whining, 'Treat! Treat!', and Southwark made instant submission to the redcoats. Would I had been present in the House to hear that hoary rebel, Denzil Holles, futilely raging, as reported in the news-books:

'Instead of a generous resistance, vindicating the honour of Parliament and preserving the people from being enslaved by a rebellious army, we are to deliver up ourselves and the kingdom, prostitute all to the lust of heady and violent men, and suffer Mr Cromwell to saddle, switch and spur us at his pleasure. That we should fall so low as dirt, vote the common soldier his full pay, and what is worse, expunge our declaration against their mutinous petitions, and cry *peccavimus* to save a whipping! Yet even this will not do.'

In truth it will not. The main force being now concentrated upon Hounslow Heath, yesterday drove home their lesson by parading through the City and occupying the Tower. The Lord Mayor and Aldermen, like whipped curs, crept on their bellies to Fairfax in the Hyde Park, humbly promising to do whatsoever his Excellency should command, and presenting him with a gold cup, which he sullenly refused to accept, and with very little ceremony dismissed them. Meanwhile Cromwell, with a detachment of his Ironsides, strode into the Commons' House and terrorized those members who remained into repealing all ordinances made against the Army.

What will fall out next, God knows. There is much in men's mouth a quip of that buffoon, Harry Marten, one of the Commons who spares not friend or foe with his clowning:

'As the King called a parliament he could not rule, so now the Parliament find they have raised an army they cannot rule. I wonder much whether the Army have not made Agitators *they* cannot rule.'

63

August 20th. Upon the 13th, H.M. was brought here to his own house of Oatlands, where we are to remain until Hampton Court is prepared for his dwelling. And it is given out that when he comes there, all H.M.'s friends will have free access to him.

Now having overawed both Parliament and City, Cromwell and Ireton have been a-flitting during this past week between their headquarters at Putney and this house, endeavouring to wheedle H.M. into accepting what are termed the Heads of the Proposals. At the express command of H.M., I was present at these conferences, together with the ruffler Berkeley and Will Legge, though what wise counsel H.M. hopes from these, is more than I can imagine. Legge is what his friends term modest and his enemies stupid, a man distinguished for nothing but his idolatry of Rupert and an aptitude for getting himself captured during the war.

Cromwell is at his most serpent-like, and even his son-in-law, Ireton, a block of ice with the brain of a crafty lawyer, twists his features into a semblance of affability. After they had withdrawn from their first visit, H.M. remarked to us that these terms were such as had been whispered to him informally ever since his abduction by Cornet Joyce.

'A king,' said he, 'can never be so low in fortune but he adds weight to that party which possesses his person. They would have me to be their puppet ally, the Imperator of the soldiers.'

Yet though he vowed he never would consent to play that role, he would consider their terms; for with reverence I must say it, H.M. has ever been too prone to temporize and hiver-hover, fixed in his illusion that all men are reasonable. Which fatal trait in him has led some fools astray into accusing him of duplicity. The plain truth is, he has entered into no engagements, nor made an offer he was not prepared to implement if it should be accepted. But of swift decisions (except upon the field of battle) he is incapable, being wedded to the principle of looking all round a subject before he will say yea or nay. For myself, I would no more parley with these villains than with the weasel that spoils my hen-roost.

Now briefly the Heads of the Proposals are these. The Church to be suffered to retain her hierarchy and ritual, but deprived of all civil jurisdiction. What is to become of her property not already filched by the cut-purse Parliament is not said. Every function of Sovereignty other than ceremonial to be placed in a Council of State composed of 'trusty and able persons' (the prime officers and their sycophants), in whose choice H.M. to have no say for ten years, after which time they would graciously permit him the selection of three names for the filling up of vacant offices. For future parliaments, none to have a vote who have expressed by word or deed their loyalty to H.M. Five of his most faithful adherents to be exempt from pardon, the rest fleeced on a reduced scale from that demanded by Parliament in the propositions they offered him at Newcastle.

'Even supposing I accepted these proposals,' says H.M. to Cromwell and Ireton, 'what if Parliament refused them?'

To which Cromwell replied in one of those frank outbursts of his which are as startling as gun-fire flashing through thick smoke:

'If they do not agree, we will make them.'

When we were private again, H.M. spoke with some heat, saying that should he yield, it would be equivalent to abdicating, not only for himself but for his successors, all save the trappings of royalty. As for his subjects, what freedom would be theirs when parliaments were so shamelessly packed? And that which touched him nearly, was the demand to sacrifice his friends.

'But these five marked down for slaughter, Sir,' says Berkeley, 'are safe overseas.'

This moved H.M. not at all, for says he:

'I will have no man suffer for my sake, for I repent of nothing so much as my sacrificing the Earl of Strafford.'

August 31st. This day H.M. rejected the Heads of the Proposals, speaking thus:

'I have considered of these terms only because I hold it my duty to explore every avenue to peace. But of the three things I vowed never to part with at the time of the Treaty of Uxbridge, the rights of my successors are struck at, the betrayal of my friends is still demanded, and I am by no means satisfied with the measure of toleration offered to the Church.'

Upon this, Ireton dropped the mask and spoke with menace:

'Sir, we will have our desires, with or without Your Majesty.'

When the rogues had withdrawn, I besought H.M. to have a care, for I was affrighted by Ireton's threat, and I begged H.M. to consider how entirely in the power of these villains he was.

'Your Majesty acts as though you have some secret strength that I know not of,' I reproached him.

At which he smiled, and pointed towards his favourite motto which he had scratched with a diamond on the window, *Dum Spiro Spero*, 'While I breathe, I hope'.

3

Unfinished Autobiography of Cornet George Joyce

Throughout the late summer of 1647, the Lord was pleased to test me with grievous trials, tearing me as it were asunder betwixt my trust in our great Cromwell and his bowing down in the House of Rimmon.

For when Charles Stuart was removed to Hampton Court, all those bold sons of Belial who had been of his Household and armies were allowed free access to him, and I saw for myself how in the Presence Chamber, Cromwell rubbed shoulders with those whose portion was to gnash their teeth in Hell, bobbing and bowing like a jack-in-the-green. And when Parliament voted to dismiss the chaplains of Charles Stuart, what must Cromwell do but set a guard for the protection of these brother beasts of Nebuchadnezzar. So low did he fall as to make no demur when the wicked superstition of touching for the evil was revived, and the sweaty multitude flocked to it.

Some who were close to Cromwell said, he hoped still to flatter Charles Stuart, and thus induce him to approve all the righteous demands of the Army. Yet the private men staggered in spirit to hear of Cromwell's truckling to the Man of Sin, whose mother was a Hittite and his father an Amorite. It was even buzzed about our camp at Putney that Cromwell had accepted the earldom of Essex and captaincy of the Gentlemen Pensioners, while Commissary Ireton was to be Lord Lieutenant of Ireland. Our eyes were scandalized when we saw these precious Saints playing at billiards with Charles Stuart, and hunting with him and his son York. Ah, what grievous wrestlings had I with Satan, who whispered to me that far from being Joshua, Cromwell was the second beast in the Book of Revelations, who would exercise all the power of the first.

Like the prophet Daniel, I opened my window towards Jerusalem, knelt upon my knees three times a day, and besought the Lord for guidance. But I being such precious gold, it pleased Him still to try me in the fire. One moment I feared that Cromwell was falling down to worship the golden idol of Nebuchadnezzar; the next I remembered Daniel who, albeit he lived in the palace of the kings of Babylon, and was clothed in purple, yet he was set there by the Lord to make known to them their wickedness and foretell their destruction. At length the Lord took pity on me and spoke articulate, bidding me arise and learn from the very lips of Cromwell what he did intend.

He heard me out with patience, and answered that if he could obtain Charles Stuart's signature, we of the Army would avoid that great objection that would be laid against us, both by Parliament and the people, that we would impose the rule of the sword. At which I made bold to show him a tract scattered about our camp, called *Putney Projects*, in which he was denounced as a renegado and a prime Cavalier. And because he had laid his commands upon me to report men's words spoken round the camp-fire, I whispered to him that the more fiery of the Saints clamoured for a bloody sacrifice which alone could prevail with the Lord for turning away His wrath from this nation. Cromwell shot me a sharp glance, and asked what they intended by this.

[Mr Joyce's reply being most obscure, drawn from several prophecies in Scripture, it is omitted, but the sense was that some of the common soldiers were for the secret murder of the King. Ed.]

'The Lord forbid!' he groaned. 'Such a deed would rouse the whole nation against my poor godly men.'

'Sir,' I insisted, 'Master Hugh Peters preached a sermon in our camp last Sabbath, wherein he complained that men were more afraid of a dead dog than a living lion. And this the fiery Saints interpret as meaning that it would be a righteous act if they pistolled the King when he rides abroad, or otherwise took away his life.'

For a while he paced the chamber, musing aloud upon David's failure to call Joab to account for the assassination of Abner. Then, descending to profane speech, he reminded me that the Prince of Wales was safe overseas, who certainly would avenge his father's murder, wherein the French and other popish nations would assist him.

'I have been upon my knees day and night to the King,' says he, 'that he would approve publicly our occupation of London and put his signature to our proposals for the reform of government. Must I at last say, as it was written of Babylon, "I would heal Babylon, but she would not be healed"? I know not, only that I have not yet received a clear call from the Lord. I will seek Him again, brother Joyce, that He may make known to me His will.'

I perceived that the Lord had hearkened to his fervent prayers, when I heard that he was using arts to frighten Charles Stuart into escaping overseas and thus to avoid death by a private hand, a door being left open for that purpose, as you shall hear. Had he done so, it was the purpose of Cromwell to set upon the throne the child Gloucester, that the common rout might be satisfied with this toy.

Sortie

I

Diary of Colonel Jack Ashburnham

October 12th, 1647. H.M.'s children being here at Hampton Court upon a visit, I was present when he spoke strangely to the Duke of York.

'James,' says he, 'if there appears any alteration in the temper of the Army, as that they restrain me from the liberty I now enjoy of seeing you, you must bethink yourself how you may make an escape out of their power and transport yourself beyond seas. I wish you to think always of this as my solemn command.'

And further made the Duke learn by heart a message he must carry to his elder brother, which ran thus:

'I command you never to yield to any conditions that are dishonourable, unsafe to your person, or derogatory to regal authority, upon any considerations whatsoever, though it were the saving of my life.'

When the Duke had retired, I expressed my astonishment to H.M. that he should speak as though expecting some sinister fate. Who told me, that several times this past fortnight he had found placed in his chamber writings in an unknown hand, warning him that he was in danger of being made away with privily.

October 16th. This day the King's children were taken back again by their jailer, the Earl of Northumberland. H.M. complained to his own jailer, Colonel Whalley, that the Princess Elizabeth had been much disturbed during her stay, by reason of the brutish talk and laughter of the guards posted in the Long Gallery, and prayed it might not happen again. Whereupon Whalley (who is Cromwell's cousin and heretofore has played the same courtier-like role), turned saucy, and said it would not happen again because the Army had resolved to permit H.M. no more visits from his children. And in the same impudent manner, reminded H.M. it was time he renewed his parole to abide with the Army.

When the dog had gone about his business, Berkeley was urgent with H.M. that he should not renew his parole, knowing what fine scruples H.M. has anent breaking any pledge.

'Though Cromwell still swears he will hazard his life to restore Your Majesty,' says Berkeley, 'I sense the same ominous change in him as we marked just now in Whalley. Several times of late he has let fall hints to me as though Your Majesty is in peril from the fanatics in the Army, and I cannot but remember that Putney, their headquarters, is but six miles distant. If Joyce should abduct Your Majesty a second time, I much fear it would not be as a hostage.'

For once I was fain to concur with Berkeley, and became instant with H.M. that he should think of his escape overseas, which I could contrive, being a man of resource. H.M. was very pensive, and as is his fatal habit, must needs spend time probing the question.

'It is true,' said he, 'that I dread nothing so much as secret murder, and not only because of the natural horror of it. It would enable my enemies to blacken me after my death, and perchance put forth the libel that I laid violent hands upon myself. Yet I am convinced such a villainy is far from the mind of Cromwell, both as a Christian and a rational man. My person is precious to him, for as has been plain since my seizure by the Army, he craves the authority of the Crown to buttress the rule of the sword.'

'Which authority Your Majesty has refused to give,' Berkeley reminded him.

Then said I, with a flash of inspiration:

'It may be that only by winking at the deeds of violent men can Cromwell maintain his control over them. Your Majesty has seen tracts and sermons printed of late wherein Cromwell is denounced as a renegado. For God's sake, Sir, think upon making your escape.'

All which seemed to weigh with H.M., yet he would go no further than refusing to renew his parole to abide with the Army.

October 20th. Cromwell came upon one of his visits, and spoke blubberingly against the violence of the firebrands in his ranks. Then, as is his habit, he ceased boo-hooing, and blurted forth his real thoughts. Whole regiments, he cried, were become forcing-beds of levellism, and this threatened to destroy all discipline, for they would no longer obey their own officers. (And the cur might have added that their egalitarian theories are odious to him, who is one of the richest landowners in England.)

Then, again bespattering the floor with his tears, he said that his cousin Whalley could not answer strictly for his guards here, any more than could he himself for their comrades at Putney.

October 22nd. These two days past, neither Cromwell nor Ireton has waited upon H.M., and there is a rumour that the fanatics in the Army would have them outed, as turning Cavalier.

After dinner, H.M. sends for one Huntingdon, major in Cromwell's regiment of horse, who of late seems to have grown so attached to H.M. that several times he has hinted to me he had thoughts of laying down his commission. Says H.M. to him:

'I beg you to be plain with me, sir. Do you consider that Mr Cromwell remains the same in heart as by his tongue he has so oft expressed himself in my regard?'

Huntingdon appeared much startled, and begged that he might delay his answer to the question till tomorrow.

October 23rd. H.M. at his dressing, when word was brought that Major Huntingdon was in the out-room and craved permission to speak. H.M. dismissed all his attendants save for myself and Berkeley, and in comes Huntingdon, much agitated.

'I roused Mr Cromwell from his sleep last night,' says he, 'and besought him to be open with me concerning his intentions towards Your Majesty. He struck himself upon the breast, and swore he would do whatever he had promised to restore Your Majesty, imprecating heaven that neither himself nor his wife and children might ever prosper if he failed in his word, for that he would stand by Your Majesty were there but ten men left to assist him.'

'Nay,' said I, 'here is over-much protesting.'

Huntingdon took a turn or two about the room, gnawing his

73

lip, as though he knew not how far to speak his secret thoughts. Then says he:

'I obtained Mr Cromwell's solemn promise that if he should change his mind, or anything fell out to hinder his good intentions, he would give timely notice to Your Majesty. Yet I cannot but warn you, Sir, that he is a subtle man who governs himself by other maxims than the rest of the world. I confess I suspect him most when, as of late, he repeats constantly that his course must be set by the will of the Lord, that he must seek the Lord day and night, and is ready to obey the divine commands. For I cannot but wonder whether by such revelations as he saith he receives from God, he often justifies himself for what he secretly wills.'

Then did both Berkeley and I renew our entreaties to H.M. that he take himself out of such hands while there was time, reminding him of the vastness of this palace, which has fifteen hundred rooms in any of which an assassin could be lurking, of the writings he had found warning him of some bloody attempt upon his person, and of the hints Cromwell had let fall that Whalley could not answer for his own guards. H.M. promised to consider of it, for he will do nought hastily.

November 1st. Myself and Sir John Berkeley were this day summarily dismissed by Whalley, who refused to give a reason for it. We came no farther than my own house at Thames Ditton, where I at once began to lay my plans, as the chartering of a ship to lie off Southampton and relays of fast horses thither, in case H.M. can contrive to escape from Hampton Court. Will Legge, being permitted to remain with H.M., acts as our go-between. Pray God my master will prove resolute to save himself in this extremity!

2

Secret Memoirs of Thomas Herbert

On a morning early in the November of 1647, I was much surprised to hear the summons of the King's hand-bell when he had but just commenced his long devotions. So punctual was he at these that nothing, even of importance, would make him shorten them. I entered the bedchamber hastily, fearing he might be sick. He held in his hand a paper which he showed me, saying he had found it between the leaves of his prayer-book, and asking if I knew how it came there, for it had not been in the book last night. It was as great a mystery to me as to the King, and neither of us knew the hand which, said His Majesty, he thought to be disguised. I took a copy of this letter:

'In discharge of my duty I cannot omit to acquaint Your Majesty that my brother was at a meeting last night with eight or nine common soldiers of the Army, who in debate of the obstacle which most did hinder the speedy fulfilment of their desires, did conclude it was Your Majesty, and so long as Your Majesty doth live you would be so, and therefore resolved to take away your life. And to that account they were assured that Mr Dell and Mr Peters (two of their preachers) would willingly bear them company, for they have often said in their sermons that Your Majesty is but a dead dog. My prayers are for Your Majesty's safety, but I do much fear it cannot be whilst you are in those hands. I wish with all my soul that Your Majesty were at my house in Broad Street where I am confident I could keep you private till this storm be over, but beg Your Majesty's pardon and shall not presume to offer it as advice. I am Your Majesty's most dutiful subject, E.R.'

I was so stricken with horror that I was fain to clutch at the table to prevent myself from swooning. But the King, though somewhat pale, retained his calm, and says to me that he believed the letter to come from some prominent citizen. (For there was great discontent in the City since its brutish treatment by the soldiers.)

It would be the morrow or the day after the finding of this anonymous letter, when Colonel Whalley came to the King in great perturbation, and showed His Majesty an express he had just now received from Mr Cromwell at Putney. It ran:

'Dear Coz Whalley, there are rumours abroad of some intended attempt upon His Majesty's person. Therefore I pray you have a care of your guard, for if such a thing should be done, it would be a most horrid act.'

'Alas!' groans Whalley, 'that such a crime should be so much as thought of by any that bears the character of a Christian!'

The King gave him a considering look, and says he coldly:

'I cannot but wonder, sir, at this sudden care for me, after you have dismissed my most faithful attendants without reason given.'

Colonel Whalley was huffed, protesting that he was appointed to safeguard His Majesty and would die at his feet in his defence. Then he said something of which I thought little at the time, but which since has drawn me to credit what the Cavaliers assert, namely that Mr Cromwell, for his own ends, was frightening His Majesty into making his escape, leaving a door open for that purpose.

'I showed Your Majesty this express,' says Whalley, 'only that you may be assured, though menacing speeches come frequently to your ear, that we senior officers abhor the thought of so villainous and bloody a deed. I shall take care to double my guards after supper tonight; but they being here purely in Your Majesty's defence, *I shall give them strict orders that they are not in any way to presume to interfere with Your Majesty's movements.*'

As I have remarked before, His Majesty was much devoted to an exact routine. Since his coming to Hampton Court, it was his invariable custom on Mondays and Thursdays to retire into his bedchamber at two hours after noon to write letters, there being no longer the least restraint laid upon his correspondence. Between five and six he came forth for public prayers with his chaplains, and afterwards went to supper.

The apartments he occupied in this ancient palace (which was liker a village than a single house) all opened out of one another, terminating in the backstair, at the head of which Mr Firebrace, the Page, had his little room. Upon one side of these apartments, having access to them, ran the Long Gallery where the guards were stationed. Several of these chambers were untenanted, but that upon the west of the bedchamber was occupied by Mr Nicholas Oudart, a Belgian, formerly in the employ of Sir Edward Nicholas, Secretary of State, but now in the service of His Majesty.

Thursday, November 11th, was a day of such drenching rain that His Majesty was unable to take his usual exercise abroad. Old

Mr Maule and I were the Grooms on duty, and our place was in the ante-room upon the east. But when the King retired at two of the clock to write his letters, he says to me with what I deemed then to be only his native kindliness (but since suspect another motive):

'If the guards will not annoy you, do you stay in the Long Gallery. For I have observed that when the wind is strong from the north as it is today, it makes the chimney in the ante-room to smoke, which will be sure to bring on your cough, Mr Herbert.'

So we sat down by one of the fires in the Long Gallery, Mr Maule and I, and to entertain the old gentleman I rehearsed to him the history of my fluxes and distempers, telling him of the care I took to preserve my health by purging every Friday, and utterly refraining from taking a bath in this month of November. Thus we passed the time pleasantly enough until four o'clock, when His Majesty rang his bell to ask for candles.

At half past the hour, he rang again for snuffers; and that was the last sight I had of him till we were reunited in the Isle of Wight.

At five o'clock, the Commissioners of Parliament, my Lords Pembroke, Denbigh and Montagu, came into the gallery with Colonel Whalley, ready to escort His Majesty to prayers. I thought the Colonel to seem nervous, and supposed it to be on account of the bloody threats of which he had before spoken. But the truth would seem to be, he had a part to act written for him by his cousin Cromwell, and he would have made but a poor stage-player. I drew his attention to the whines of His Majesty's greyhound bitch, Gipsy, and at her scratching on the inside of the bedchamber door, but he paid no heed to me, making somewhat strained conversation with the Commissioners.

At six o'clock my Lord Pembroke began to fret, saying he had an appointment with a bottle of choice claret, and wondering testily what kept the King so long at his correspondence. Whereat Whalley entered the chamber of Mr Oudart to consult him, who said, he happened to know that His Majesty had a particular letter he wished to write to his daughter, the Princess Mary, in Holland, and no doubt but this was the reason for the delay.

It was not until the clocks struck seven that Whalley suggested to us that His Majesty might have been taken ill, and bade Mr Maule enter the bedchamber to see. But Mr Maule replied that he had received the strictest orders from the King not on any account to disturb him until he rang. In any case, says he, the bedchamber door which opened on the gallery was bolted as usual on the inside. Down bends Whalley to the keyhole, but could see nothing; while all this time the dog within was at her scratching and whining.

'Bless me,' says Whalley, as though visited by an inspiration, 'I wonder if there is not another way into the bedchamber.'

Which remark startled me, seeing that the Colonel had been His Majesty's warder here for more than two months past. He sent for Mr Smithsby, Keeper of the Privy Lodging, and as though he were a perfect stranger to Hampton Court, inquired of him the design of the royal apartments. Smithsby made him a look as though he thought he jested, but patiently described how they lay, beginning at the backstair.

'The backstair!' cries Whalley, clapping a hand to his brow. 'Upon my soul, I never thought of that!'

So down the main stair we must go, the whole party of us, then through a labyrinth of galleries and towers, until by this circuitous route we ascended the backstair to Mr Firebrace's little chamber, but he had absented himself. On our progress towards the bedchamber, we found all the doors unbolted, and the apartments empty; only when we came into the ante-room, there upon the floor lay His Majesty's cloak.

'Lord save us, this looks ill!' groaned Whalley. 'Sure His Majesty would not have stepped outdoors without his cloak on such a night. Can it be that some villain has abducted him?'

Then did my Lord Pembroke, who was now in a high choler, positively order Mr Maule to go into the bedchamber, who returned to say that he found the room empty save for the dog, and on the table four letters lying. He had presumed to glance at the inscriptions, and there was one directed to Colonel Whalley.

Thereat we all rushed in, and examination made of these letters. One, which lay open, was the paper signed 'E.R.', shown to me by His Majesty, and since suspected to have been writ by Cromwell himself to affright the King into going away. His Majesty wrote nought to Colonel Whalley save to say he had been so civilly treated by the Colonel, that he could not fail to acknowledge his courtesy, and to ask that certain pictures might be disposed of in the manner herein directed. There was a postscript which made me marvel how the King could care for such trifles at this time; he wrote he had almost forgot to request that the bitch, Gipsy, be sent to the Duke of Richmond.

Of the other two letters, one was addressed to the Parliament and the second to its Commissioners. My Lord Pembroke then and there read aloud the latter, which same removed from me the dread lest His Majesty had been abducted. I took a copy, which ran thus:

'I call God to witness with what patience I have endured a tedious restraint which, so long as I had any hopes that this sort of my suffering might conduce to the peace of my kingdoms, I did willingly undergo. But now finding by too certain proofs that this my continued patience would not only turn to my personal ruin, but likewise be of much prejudice to the public good, I thought I was bound, as well by natural as political obligations, to seek my safety by retiring myself for a time from the view both of my friends and enemies. Let me be heard with freedom, honour and safety, and I shall instantly break through the cloud of retirement and show myself to be *Pater Patriae*.'

Colonel Whalley was now, or perchance feigned to be, in a hot passion. He summoned Firebrace and Oudart, and roundly accused them, with ancient Mr Maule, of being the instruments of spiriting His Majesty away, assuring them that their heads should fly for it. Then must he send an express to Cromwell at Putney, desiring to know what he should do. Back comes the order to make close search of every room in that huge palace, in case His Majesty might be hidden away there.

Which seemed to me so strange and irrational, after what the King had written to the Commissioners, that I was at a nonplus.

79

3

Diary of Colonel Jack Ashburnham

November 11th, 1647. Berkeley and I were at the riverside with two spare horses as soon as it grew dark, and waited in an agony until, beyond my expectations, my dear master landed from a rowboat with Will Legge ere it had turned six of the clock. Marvellous to relate, they had found no let or hindrance from the moment when Legge, concealed in the ante-room, had tapped upon the bedchamber door very softly soon after half past four. Only in the haste and agitation of those first few moments, H.M. had dropped his cloak and durst not return for it. But this, perchance, proved fortunate, since the guards, seeing him but in his suit and without boots, would not suspect he would venture abroad on so foul a night.

Thus they had passed swiftly through the untenanted apartments, being met at the head of the backstair by Firebrace, who was in the secret, as was likewise old Maule. Thence by way of that long series of buildings which terminate in the water-gate. Guards they met in plenty, but none hindered them; I suppose they thought H.M. to be taking some indoor exercise, and they had been instructed by Whalley not to presume to interfere with H.M.'s promenades within the palace.

'And yet,' says Legge, 'I could not but think it strange that at the water-gate there were no sentinels at all.'

I bade him leave such profitless musings, our present need being haste, for certainly there would be an immediate hue and cry after H.M. when he did not emerge from the bedchamber at his usual hour. I informed H.M. that my confidential servant had chartered a ship which even now stayed for us off the coast of Hampshire, and that I had relays of fast horses all along the way. As he was mounting, he asked what news from London.

'Much discontent,' said I. 'The cits, like rural swains, begin to mutter that their shepherds at Westminster have sheared them nearer than their sheep, yet will not bestow so much tar upon them as will preserve their buttocks from the flies.'

'Pondering upon the anonymous letter I found within my prayer-book,' says H.M., 'I have come to the conclusion that the writer is Mr Edmund Rigby, a great merchant, who entertained me before the rebellion. And I am minded to accept of his invitation to lie private at his house in Broad Street.'

Good God! here was the same whimsy which had seized upon him after we left Oxford. All three of us joined our voices in imploring him to lay aside so fantastical a notion. Were there not strong detachments of the redcoats quartered in London and Westminster, and had not the City shown of what craven spirit she was when she made submission to them in July? So at length (I sweating lest at any moment there come pursuit) H.M. was persuaded to ride towards Bishop's Sutton where we were to find my first change of mounts.

November 12th. All last night we rode through the New Forest, H.M. acting as our guide in the stormy dark, he having so often hunted here. But although he had yielded to our pleas that he venture not into London, we found to our consternation that he was set against escaping overseas.

'A king who willingly absents himself,' says he, 'must lose the respect of his people. It would be given out that I had abdicated, and God knows what mischief might befall if that were said.'

'What, then, is Your Majesty's pleasure?' I asked him.

'My desire,' says he, 'is to find some secure retreat whence I may reopen negotiations with the Parliament.'

From my long acquaintance with him I knew it was useless to argue, and so chewed upon the matter as we rode. Presently I said that if H.M. desired some secure retreat, what better than the Isle of Wight, whose inhabitants were stoutly loyal? Needs must Berkeley raise objections, reminding me that it had a Roundhead Governor, Colonel Hammond, who having married Hampden's daughter was kin to Cromwell, that he had served in the rebel armies since the beginning of the war, and that he had an uncle who was their Master of Ordnance.

'Do you think I am ignorant of this?' I retorted. 'But Robert Hammond has another uncle who is one of His Majesty's favourite chaplains. Moreover, this Robert said in my hearing that he had begged from Parliament the Governorship of the Wight because he wished to dissociate himself from the perfidious actions of the Army towards His Majesty (those were his very words). At least the Wight may prove a safe temporary retreat, being full of hidden creeks whence His Majesty can slip away to France if need arises, and Hammond's garrison at Carisbrooke consists but of twelve veterans who have passed their military career under former royalist Governors.'

It being now broad day, and we fearing at any moment to be overtaken by the hell-hounds, H.M. said he would go down the east side of Southampton Water to Titchfield, where he knew the dowager Countess of Southampton would shelter him. He would take Legge as his companion, and Berkeley and I should cross to the Wight.

'But,' says H.M., 'you are on no account to disclose my present whereabouts to Hammond unless you can obtain his solemn pledge to receive me as his guest and not as a hostage. Take with you, pray, this copy I made of the "E.R." letter to show him, and make sure he understands that I am fleeing, not from the Parliament, but from lawless assassins who sought my life.'

So I came with Berkeley down the west side of the water to Lymington, but here we find ourselves storm-bound.

November 13th. The seas somewhat subsiding, we crossed this morning to Yarmouth on the horse-ferry, being very disagreeable in each other's company. For Berkeley was still set against the venture, out of jealousy because I had proposed it, and passed the whole journey crying down Hammond, pestering me with what I already knew, as that he was but a spark of seven-and-twenty, had been given a regiment by his cousin Cromwell, and had it not been for this kinship would certainly have been condemned to death by a court of war for killing a brother officer in one of his rages.

'This hot temper of his,' says Berkeley, 'is matched only by his greed. He has feathered his nest from Cavalier estates, not resting content with the huge dowry brought him by Hampden's daughter. And after our men had held him prisoner for a while at Basing House, where he was most honourably entertained, needs must he dun Parliament for £1,000 of public money for the inconvenience he had suffered. I would not trust a dog into his keeping, much less the sacred person of our master.'

We encountered the subject of our quarrelling as we were upon our way from Newport to Carisbrooke, he riding to the town upon some business. As soon as we espied him, says Berkeley to me, since you have such misplaced belief in him, do you open to him our business. So I accosted Hammond, and told him briefly that H.M. had left Hampton Court in a very private manner to escape assassination by fanatics, withal showing him the copy of the 'E.R.' letter. I thought he would have swooned!

'Oh gentlemen!' cries he, 'you have undone me by bringing His Majesty into the Wight – if indeed you have brought him. If you have not, pray let him not come!'

Seeing my blank looks, he began to say that he was entangled in a most painful conflict of loyalties, being on the one hand a faithful subject of H.M., and on the other owing his appointment to the Parliament. But anon, seeming to recover his composure, he grew very fervent in his expressions of loyalty to H.M., saying further he believed the King had made choice of him as a gentleman of honour and fair honesty, and swearing that he would by no means fail H.M.'s expectations. Then he asked, where was the King? To which I replied I might not tell him unless I had his solemn promise to behave towards H.M. as became a loyal subject. Whereat he swore roundly that he would receive H.M. with that honour and reverence which was due to his Sovereign Lord, and begged that he might be conducted by us to acquaint the King in person with his readiness to serve him.

I agreed, but only on the condition that none accompany us. Upon our way to Cowes, Berkeley renewed his grumbles in my ear.

'In my opinion,' says he, 'this is a slippery customer who will steer no straight course. As for his verbal promises, did not His Majesty receive the self-same before he most unwisely entrusted his person to the Scots?'

'Pish,' says I, 'why do you fear? We are two to one, and if Hammond proves false, we may easily secure him.'

But I began to stagger in my confidence when, as we were waiting for a boat, Hammond insisted that Captain Baskett, Governor of Cowes Castle, make a fourth in our company. In all our passage across the Solent, Berkeley and I quarrelled apart.

'You have told me a dozen times,' says he, 'that you know His Majesty much better than I do, and therefore I will not see him before you have satisfied him with your proceedings.'

I said I would certainly take that upon me. But when I came to H.M. at Titchfield and related the business, for the first time since I made my bow at Court as a lad he looked upon me with a cold countenance, echoing Hammond's words, 'You have undone me!' This put me in an anguish, for it seemed to me as though H.M. suspected I had betrayed him. I threw myself at his feet, weeping like a wench. Hammond had given his word, said I, to perform all that could be expected of a good subject, and had I not consented to his coming over with us, without doubt he would have dogged us with his spies.

'Yet if error there has been,' cried I, 'I'll sheathe my sword in Hammond's bowels ere he can do Your Majesty any mischief.'

'Do you think I would consent to murder?' says H.M. very sharply. 'You speak like a child, Jack. It is too late to think of anything but going through the way you have forced on me, and to leave the issue to God.'

I was somewhat cheered when Hammond was presented to H.M., for he behaved himself with all due reverence, renewed his former promises with warmth, and swore that he would preserve H.M. at the cost of his own life, enlarging much upon his pure intentions, honour and honesty. Yet H.M. seemed wary of him, and cut him short by bidding him remember it was H.M. who was to be the judge of what was honourable and honest in Hammond's conduct.

Hammond taking wine with me alone, he condemned roundly the fantastic giddiness of the Agitators and levellers, of which he was sure the Grandees of the Army (a new high-flown title the prime officers have bestowed upon themselves) were quite free. I

84

am related, says he, to the chief among these Grandees, and know them for men of honour.

November 14th. H.M., and we attendant on him, crossed to the Wight in Hammond's boat last evening, and this morning we rode to Carisbrooke, seeing its tall grim keep rear up above the trees of Parkhurst Forest several miles ere we reached it. Says Hammond:

'I must confess that at my first coming here to take up my appointment, I found the aspect of the castle harsh. But I can assure Your Majesty that the improvements made by Sir George Garey, when he was Governor in the days of Queen Elizabeth, have rendered it surprisingly comfortable within.'

'This is not my first visit to Carisbrooke, sir,' says H.M. 'I dined at the castle when I was Prince of Wales, and afterwards made several shots with the ordnance.'

Which remark seemed to upset Hammond, who perchance remembered how excellent a soldier H.M. had proved himself in the late war. Nor did he appear best pleased with the rapturous reception accorded H.M. by the twelve old men who formed the garrison. However, he was eager to describe what arrangements he proposed to make so that the King be lodged in proper state. The Great Hall, says he, could be used as a Presence, since it had access by way of the backstair to a spacious bedchamber above. As for necessaries such as plate, carpets and hangings, until these could be sent from Hampton Court, he begged H.M. graciously to make use of the Governor's own, poor and unworthy though they were.

But indeed they proved far otherwise. For this is a very rich and pampered spark who denies himself nothing.

December 1st. To my great joy, and Berkeley's discomfiture, the Wight is like to prove a very secure refuge for H.M. The chief gentlemen of the Island hasted to him to kiss hands, and Hammond makes no demur at his dining at their several seats and hunting in the forest. For the guards posted at the three main crossing-places to the English coast, Hammond excused it reasonably enough on the score that some of the bloody assassins from whom the King fled might try to creep over.

His chaplains, and all those attending upon him at Hampton Court, have received passports from the Parliament to come to him, to whom he remarked with a smile that they had done well if they could have brought Hampton Court with them, for in truth this castle has a melancholy air hung about it.

H.M. had scarce taken up residence when he sent new proposals to Parliament, stooping so low as to offer to abandon control of the militia during his lifetime, provided only that this should be without prejudice to his successors. Likewise an Act of General Oblivion, with a request that he be permitted to come to London in safety, there to negotiate in person with the two Houses.

Berkeley being sent at the same time with letters to Fairfax and Cromwell, asking their support in obtaining a treaty, we pass our time very pleasantly here.

4

Letter from Sir John Berkeley to the King

The Garter Inn, Windsor. December 5th, 1647.

May it please Your Majesty, I send my cousin Henry with this, which I beseech Your Majesty to decipher without delay.

As soon as I arrived at Windsor, where the Grandees of the Army have their headquarters, I waited on them; but though I sent in a message that I was the bearer of letters from Your Majesty, they presumed to make me stay a full hour in an out-room ere they would receive me. When at length they did, General Fairfax said ungraciously that he would forward Your Majesty's letters to the Parliament, 'in whose service we are', while both Cromwell and Ireton saluted me very coldly.

I was perplexed by this reception, and sent my servant to desire my old acquaintance, Scoutmaster Watson, to call on me, who made a midnight tryst at the backside of the inn.

'On the day after the King landed in the Isle of Wight,' he told me, 'there was like to have been a mutiny. A general rendez-vous of the Army being ordered at Cockbush Field near Ware, Harrison's and Lilburne's regiments came with papers in their hats, demanding the right to elect their own officers, and accusing Cromwell outright of forsaking the good cause. Then did Cromwell spur in among them with drawn sword, arrested three ring-leaders, and at a drum-head court of war made them draw lots, he who drew the billet marked with a D. being shot to death upon the spot, while the other two were imprisoned. Thus was the Army taught to know its master.'

I said to Watson I could not understand what all this had to do with my own cold reception just now.

'Cromwell,' says he, 'likewise has been taught a lesson. Mutiny can be put down by terror, but can be ensured against only by good-will. Since the threatened mutiny at Cockbush, he knows that if he cannot bring the fanatics in the Army to his sense, he must go to theirs, a schism being evidently destructive.'

'I cannot credit,' said I, 'that Cromwell would wink at assassination, in particular since it is whispered that he affrighted the King into escaping from it.'

Then did Watson say, wonderfully apeing Cromwell's unctuous style:

'He acknowledged in my hearing that the glories of the world had so dazzled his eyes that he could not discern clearly the great work the Lord was doing, and said that he was now resolved to humble himself and desire the prayers of the Saints, that God would be pleased to pardon his self-seeking and bowing down to idols. These arts, together with comfortable messages to the two mutineers clapped up after Cockbush, have reinstated him in the affections of his poor godly men.'

I could not but laugh at Watson's mimicry, but he cut my mirth short by adding:

'There's talk of sending eight hundred picked men to the Wight to secure the King's person; I dare think no further. If His Majesty can escape, let him do it without delay. As for you, I must warn you that Ireton is pressing for your arrest.'

87

Postscriptum. Being still resolved to fulfil my mission, I wrote to Cromwell, reminding him that I was sent with a letter from Your Majesty which required an answer. He replied in a verbal message by Colonel Cook, that he durst not see me, as this would be dangerous for us both. I was to assure Your Majesty that he would serve you as long as he could do it without his own ruin, but Your Majesty must not expect that he should perish for your sake. I implore you, Sir, lose no time in putting yourself beyond seas.

5

Diary of Colonel Jack Ashburnham

December 7th, 1647. After supper, H.M. sent for me to his bedchamber and showed me a letter he had just deciphered from Berkeley; upon the reading of which I said that Berkeley was an alarmist and always had been so.

'My opinion of him is otherwise,' said he, 'but certainly I am not minded to take his advice on this occasion. For though Parliament has not accorded me the courtesy of acknowledging my proposals, Hammond tells me they are sending Commissioners hither with terms of their own.'

December 20th. There arrived this day the Commissioners, who presented H.M. with four Bills, making it plain, God damn them, that these are but the first of their demands. A sip disclosed what bitterness the draught would contain.

1. The militia to be vested in Parliament for twenty years, after which time its future to be debated by the two Houses.   2. A total abolition of episcopacy, with a refusal to tolerate the Prayer Book even in H.M.'s own Household.   3. H.M. to take upon himself the blame for all the bloodshed in the war, and acknowledge that Parliament had been necessitated to fight 'in its just and lawful defence'.   4. H.M. to put his signature to the proscription

and plunder of his friends, seven of whom are now marked down for slaughter.

On the heels of these Commissioners came some from the Estates of Scotland, the same who several times had conferred with H.M. at Hampton Court. They make H.M. a million promises, a coin that nation always abounded with and made most of its payments in. Their guardian angels were in company with them, a gaggle of ministers; and by the way I hear there is a new term coined for their pharisaic rantings, which is 'cant', after one of their rabbis, Andrew Cant of that ilk.

The Earl of Lauderdale confessed to me that there is widespread reaction towards H.M. in Scotland, the common sort being disgusted with their Judases who sold him.

December 23rd. These two days past have been occupied with conferences between H.M. and the two sets of Commissioners, at which I was present. With those of Scotland, all turned upon their damnable Covenant, but now they will sugar the pill. H.M. is asked to agree that presbyterianism be established in England for the space of three years, after which the question of religion to be debated by an assembly of divines in which H.M. may nominate twenty members. I expected him to swallow it down without much grimacing, for he has offered somewhat on the same lines before. But said he:

'I take you all as my witnesses that I do not bind myself in any way to forward presbyterianism in England, nor will I consent that the Covenant be imposed, during the stipulated three years, on any of my English subjects who conscientiously object to it, and I must insist that within my own Household the Anglican ritual be left undisturbed.'

To these qualifications the Scots gave consent, pledging themselves further that if the Parliament and Army would not agree to a general disbandment and a personal treaty with H.M., they would invade England on his behalf. Though I hate the Scots right heartily, I could not but remark to H.M. that these were by far the best terms offered him since the end of the war. It being plain that the Kirk, and its high priest, Argyll, would prove the greatest

89

obstacles, H.M. has written personally to that squint-eyed Marquis, beseeching his concurrence which would ensure a united Scotland.

December 24th. H.M., having been permitted but four days to consider the monstrous demands of Parliament, this morning rejected the Bills, the Scotch Commissioners being present and declaring their dissent from the same in the name of the whole kingdom of Scotland. H.M. pressed the Parliament's Commissioners hard yet once more that he be allowed to come to London to negotiate in person; but says he:

'Neither the tedious and irksome condition of life I have so long suffered, nor the apprehension of what may befall me, shall make me change my resolution of not consenting to anything which my conscience forbids.'

And he told them further that having fulfilled the offices both of a Christian and a king, he would patiently await the pleasure of Almighty God to incline the hearts of the two Houses to consider their Sovereign's counter-proposals and to compassionate their country's miseries. The Lord forgive me if I blaspheme, but I think it more likely that what will incline them to a treaty is this new threat from their one-time dear brethren of Scotland.

December 28th. A black day, which began fair. H.M. signed the Engagement, as 'tis called, with the Scots, and took farewell of both sets of Commissioners, those from Parliament being escorted by Hammond as far as Newport.

While he was absent, back comes Berkeley, with news of troops of the Old Model being landed in the Wight to make H.M. a close prisoner.

'It is now or never, Sir,' says he. 'For the moment you have liberty to ride abroad, and I beseech you seize what may be your last chance of freedom. I have a ship waiting off Southampton, and see there,' says he, pointing to the vane on St Nicholas's Chapel, 'the wind is in the right quarter for her to sail.'

Both the King and I were infected by his frenzy, and so horses ordered as though for hunting, and I began to draw on H.M.'s boots. Yet as I did so, I heard him give an exclamation, and following the direction of his eye, perceived that even in these past few minutes the weather-vane had veered into the north-east, which would render Berkeley's ship land-bound. H.M. smiled strangely, and says he:

'I believe it is the finger of God.'

In the afternoon, Hammond returns from Newport, and straightway sends for me, with Legge and Berkeley. He seemed clean crazed in his wits, ranting at us like a Tom o' Bedlam:

'The Commissioners of Parliament have commanded me to double my guards, lock the gates, keep His Majesty a strait prisoner, and dismiss you three gentlemen forthwith.'

Nothing we could say would move him. It was with much ado that we so far prevailed with him as to permit us to take farewell of our master, which must be done, he swore, in his presence. So we went with him to H.M., who demanded the reason for our dismissal.

'The Commissioners of Parliament,' blustered Hammond, 'have laid their orders upon me in consequence of Your Majesty's rejection of the four Bills. I am commanded to send away such of Your Majesty's servants as I see fit, and to take other precautions for Your Majesty's remaining in my custody.'

The King, with a heightened colour, told him that 'custody' was an ill word to use.

'Did you not engage your honour,' asks H.M., 'to behave towards me as a loyal subject and an honest gentleman?'

'I said nothing to that purpose,' answers Hammond, which lie made me itch to bury my sword in his guts.

'My chaplains did not appear at dinner to say grace,' the King said to him. 'Are they likewise dismissed?' And when the rogue's silence gave consent, H.M. grew the more indignant, saying: 'You of the Army pretend to liberty of conscience; shall I have none? You use me neither like a Christian nor a gentleman.'

Whereat Hammond bade farewell to manners, and shouted like a froward child:

'I'll speak to you when you are in a better temper! Sir, you are too high!'

H.M. laughed outright (which is rare with him) and says:

'My shoemaker's fault. My shoes are of the same last. Shall I have liberty to go about and take the air?'

'No, I cannot grant it,' yelps this cur. 'There's plenty of air within the castle walls.'

H.M. told him he was an equivocating gentleman, then turns to us to take farewell. Under cover of my weeping, I whispered to him to bend all his thoughts upon escape, pledging myself to retire no farther than the Hampshire coast, and reminding him that one, John Newland, a merchant and member of Newport Corporation, had offered to keep a boat hidden in Wootten Creek, but ten miles from Carisbrooke, in case H.M. might find a use for it.

As we rode through Newport, too sorrowful even to fall out among ourselves, one Captain Burley, formerly H.M.'s Governor of Pendennis Castle, came forth from his house with a drum, bawling to the townsfolk that H.M. was a close prisoner, and that they should aid him in a rescue. These supine swains but gawked at him, and up comes Mayor Read, a vile crop-pate, with his officers. Monstrous to relate, we heard him tell Burley that he would be sent to Winchester assizes, there to be tried for levying war *against* the King!

Isolation

I

Narrative of Henry Firebrace

Since your noble Lordships of the Privy Council have laid an absolute command upon me to give an account of what I know of His Majesty's sufferings during the time when he was in the Isle of Wight, I must obey. I fear 'twill be but a naked, undressed narrative, for I am ignorant of the rules of writing histories, yet at least it will be as full of truths as words.

I was bred to the trade of scrivener, and writing a neat hand I was received into the service of my Lord Denbigh. His lordship being one of the Commissioners of Parliament appointed to receive the person of the King at Newcastle, when His Majesty was surrendered by the Scots, I accompanied my master thither, and was informed by him that I must now exchange my post as his secretary for that of Page of the Backstair. I must confess I had no relish for my new appointment, for though I meddled not in politics, I had espoused the cause of my noble patron, who was on the parliamentary side during the war, and besides which the duties of a page were altogether unknown to me and I was sure would prove disrelishful.

Your Lordships are earnest with me that I should inform you why it was I offered my poor services to the King. Wanting the faculty of expression, I am hard put to it to answer, only that it was himself, and not his cause, which drew me to him, for high matters of State I did not understand. And in this I was not single, for it is now well known how many plain modest men inclined towards him on personal acquaintance, yea, even those who had fought in the field against him. After some weeks' attendance at Holmby, I was so wrought upon by the dignity of the King's carriage, and the great kindliness he used towards his humbler servants, that I grew so that I really did desire to do him any service that might be within my modest means.

His Majesty was not forward or over-credulous of the

professions of a person he knew so little as I, and who, he was aware, would not be suffered to be about him if I were thought to have a kindness for him. However, after longer observance, and sometimes speaking with me whilst he was walking in the gardens among others, His Majesty began to believe there was sincerity in what I professed. And at length confided to me that what racked him most sore, was the being cut off from all correspondence with his wife. This touched me near, for I was then deep in love with her whom afterwards I married, and I considered how it would be with me if I could not exchange letters with my sweetheart. Therefore I made bold to say to His Majesty that I thought I could contrive to convey his letters out of Holmby, if he would be pleased to trust me with them.

At first he was wary, lest I had offered this service on purpose to trepan him. Likewise was he in extreme labour lest his letters to Her Majesty miscarried, since the Parliament had published to the world his cabinet of private papers seized after his defeat at Naseby-fight. Not, said he, that he would blush for anything writ in these papers, yet he must deplore the state of things when letters between husbands and wives were stolen, read, and brought in evidence. I would fain know, says he, him who would be willing that his letters to his wife were made into public prints.

So at the beginning he gave me what proved to be only blank papers, to test whether I were honest or not; but anon entrusted me with real letters, which I was to pass on to Mrs Jane Whorwood, his laundress, who contrived to convey them to the Queen overseas. In no short time the Commissioners of Parliament grew suspicious and searched her, and albeit she slipped the letter she carried behind the arras, it was discovered ere His Majesty could find it, and Mrs Whorwood dismissed. Thus for the time my poor services must be laid aside.

I was acquainted by His Majesty with his intent to make his way out of Hampton Court, but took no active part therein. It was not until the beginning of the year 1648 that I was able to be of some further modest assistance to the King. Your noble Lordships, who understand these high matters, may be pleased to pardon my ignorance of why was passed by the Parliament the vote of Non-

Addresses after the Commissioners had left the Isle of Wight in December, 1647. The result I saw with my own eyes, which was, the cutting down of His Majesty's Household from thirty to a bare sixteen, and the dismissal by Governor Hammond not only of gentlemen of quality, as Sir John Ashburnham and Sir John Berkeley, but even of Mr Babbington, the barber, whereafter His Majesty refused to be shaved or to have his hair trimmed. All visitors were denied him, and now he must not step outside the castle walls.

I pray your Lordships pardon this unworthy comparison, but I was reminded of a thrush my mother kept in a cage when I was a lad, how it beat its wings against the bars, and presently thereafter died. It was the wettest spring ever I remember, and day after day the King would sit at his barred window, having none about him save such persons who were placed there by those who wished him ill, and therefore chose instruments as they thought to be of their own principles. My heart was wrung with compassion for him, though I could not enough admire the patience with which he sustained such isolation. He read much, delighting in the works of the poets, and to while away the tedious long days he translated from the Latin several learned works upon theology, and wrote likewise those pious meditations of his own, since given to the world under the title of *Eikon Basilike*.

At length I could endure the sight of his silent suffering no longer, and so I hit upon the device of what we afterwards termed the chink.

Now when Mr Hammond purged the Household, he appointed four Conservators who were constantly to wait upon the King, two at a time, except when he was in his bedchamber, when they were to bring their pallets close against either door which gave access to it, thus keeping His Majesty a strait prisoner within. For a month and more I took care to wind myself into the good graces of one of these Conservators, Mr Thomas Herbert, who, though I believe he had acquired some kindness towards the King, was passing timid and certainly would do nothing to offend the Parliament who had appointed him. Mr Herbert complained constantly, that His Majesty retiring so early into the bedchamber, the Conservators were obliged to sup from a tray outside his doors, which arrangement, said Mr Herbert, offended his delicate stomach.

'Sir,' said I to him one day, 'when you are one of the Conservators on duty, would it please you if I took your place at the door while you supped comfortably with the other gentlemen?'

He said in truth it would, explaining to me at great length the state of his health. On the first evening when I was his substitute, I tapped on the bedchamber door, very softly lest I be heard by the Conservator against the other entry, at the same time whispering my name. His Majesty opening to me, I begged the honour of doing him some humble service, such as he had allowed me to perform at Holmby. He seized my hand, and thanked me as though I had offered to lay down my life for him (as in truth I would have done, so much was my devotion increased).

'Sir,' said I, 'it is not safe to open the door, for someone might surprise us talking. Therefore I design, with Your Majesty's permission, to cut a small chink in the panelling of the wall, through which we may not only converse, but pass papers if they be folded very small. Upon the least noise, Your Majesty may let fall the arras on your side, which will quite conceal the chink.'

The King being delighted by my simple plan, thereafter for some weeks, whenever it was Mr Herbert's turn of duty, I both passed and received letters through this small slit. To transmit them to their several destinations I must needs have assistance, and by discreet probing I discovered that several of the Household among the lesser servants had come to share my devotion to His Majesty. I cannot well express what it was in him which drew forth this love, even as it were against their will, in those who had been against him. I have heard it said that he was stiff and cold in his carriage towards his great subjects; however that may be, with lowly men he was liker a father than a master, interesting himself in all our petty affairs, even when he was reduced to extremities. He had a royal memory, in so much that he would inquire after the welfare of our wives and children by their names; and so great a courtesy that if obliged to disagree with another, would be sure to say, 'By your leave, I think it otherwise', and give his reasons. And what touched me to the heart was, when any of my endeavours for him failed, he would thank me as heartily as if they had succeeded.

Among those I found won over to His Majesty was Mr Richard Osborne, appointed Gentleman Usher on the recommendation of my Lord Wharton, a hot stickler for the Parliament. Mr Osborne contrived a neat ruse for smuggling letters in and out. For he, holding His Majesty's gloves during dinner and supper, would secrete a note in one of the fingers. Likewise was there Mrs Wheeler, his laundress, and her maid Mary, who concealed correspondence in His Majesty's clean linen. Their complice was Mr Dowcett, Clerk of the Kitchen; it being his duty to attend every day to inquire what His Majesty would please to eat, he arranged a simple cipher language. As for example, if he said, 'I hear there is fresh sparrowgrass in Newport', or 'Artichokes are late this season', it was a sign that His Majesty carefully inspect his clean neck-bands or shifts to find a paper tucked therein.

I must not forget Mrs Jane Whorwood, who sent messengers disguised as coney-catchers and pedlars; nor Mr Hopkins, Master of the Grammar School at Newport, who introduced into the castle a scrub-woman, so ignorant she could not read nor write, yet with such mother-wit that she played go-between to admiration. But since I have promised that this bare, awkward narrative shall speak plain truth, I must presume to say that during this period of his close imprisonment, His Majesty was far too trusting, and ready to keep intelligence with anyone who offered to serve him. For the sake of swiftness, he would have his letters to his friends abroad transmitted through the public post, inscribed from a merchant in the Wight to another in France. Withering, the post master at Newport, sent all such letters on to the Committee of Parliament who sat at Derby House in London, as we learned too late. There were others, too, who alack proved false, though I know not their names to this day.

In his secret correspondence, His Majesty wrote either in cipher or else in a neat, old-fashioned clerkly hand quite unlike his own, on common paper, which must be folded so small to go through the chink or in the finger of a glove that the creases in it made tedious reading. Thus through the various channels I have mentioned, a correspondence was maintained with Sir John Ashburnham and Sir John Berkeley, who still stayed near the Hampshire coast, and with one, Colonel Bamfield, who was striving to arrange the escape of the young Duke of York from St James's Palace, for whose safety His Majesty was most painfully concerned.

It was some time early in this year of 1648 that there was made known to His Majesty through the news-books (which Governor Hammond never failed to bring him, they being the mouthpiece of his enemies) the fate of Captain Burley, who had incited the townsfolk of Newport to attempt a rescue of the King in the previous December. He had been tried at Winchester, 'twas said by a packed jury, and suffered the full penalties of high treason. On reading this, His Majesty saith to me that it was designed to strike terror in others who wished him well, and then spoke these words:

'As I have leisure enough, so I have cause more than enough, to meditate upon and prepare for my own death. For I know there are but few steps between the prisons and the graves of kings.'

This put me in an anguish, for I understood him to mean that he feared Carisbrooke's narrow cage would serve better than Hampton Court for that secret murder which he ever dreaded. So now I could not rest until I had somehow contrived to open the door of his cage. Musing upon it, I thought it not at all impossible to accomplish. I founded my little stratagem upon the fact that Mr Hammond set no sentries in the base-court of the castle; and the next time I had access to the chink, I acquainted His Majesty with what I had in mind.

If, said I, he could come forth from his bedroom window by a cord, he could cross the base-court to the ramparts upon the southern side, where at one point there was a drop of but twelve feet. Thence a natural gully in the earth sloped steeply to the counterscarp, over which two gentlemen, being on horseback, could easily assist His Majesty. They, having a spare horse with them, would escort him the ten miles to Wootten Creek, where Mr John Newland kept his boat.

I was perplexed and disappointed to find His Majesty not

very enthusiastic anent my plan, and supposed he deemed it too full of hazards. It may have been so; yet I must crave your noble Lordships' pardon if I say, that since I have had leisure to muse upon this period, I am sure he was never whole-hearted in this or other devices for his escape from Carisbrooke. I would not so presume as to pretend to know his secret thoughts; only because I had grown to love him dearly, I sensed in him a sharp conflict, as if his natural instinct to regain his freedom warred with what he considered his duty to remain.

However that may be, he gave me leave to go on with my stratagem, the which I did, taking great care to keep it as simple as I could. The two gentlemen I picked on to be lurking below the counterscarp were Mr Osborne, before mentioned, and young Mr Edward Worsley, heir to Gatcombe, one of the principal seats in the Wight. Those who stayed near the Hampshire coast were advertised to provide a ship, and Mr John Newland pledged to keep his lusty boat ever ready in the creek. The only danger I foresaw was from the sentries who paced the ramparts, and to overcome this, I enlisted the services of Captain Silius Titus, appointed by the Parliament His Majesty's Equerry.

He had fought upon the Parliament's side, as had several others in the Household, all through the civil war, and done good service. But on hearing of the fate of Captain Burley, he fell into a rage, said to me it was a very mockery of justice to condemn a man for high treason who had attempted to serve the King, and that were there to be another war, he himself would fight upon the King's side. His tongue being somewhat free, I did not disclose to him the whole of my plan, only that on such and such a night as I should advertise him, he ply the sentinels with wine and ale, pretending it was his birthday.

Still one thing troubled me, and that was, whether the bed-chamber window was wide enough to allow His Majesty to pass, the new bars there reducing the space between the mullions to but seven inches. I proposed with a file to cut one bar; His Majesty objected that Hammond might spy it, and said, he had made trial by putting his head through, and he had heard that where a man's head can go, he may wriggle his body after. I liked it not, but did not presume to suggest to him, who was so prudent and methodical a gentleman, that we settle the matter by procuring a rule and measuring His Majesty's frame.

All things were thus prepared and every man well instructed in his role. The night I chose was that of March 20th, it being moonless. When I judged that the Conservators on duty would be asleep, I came beneath the bedchamber window and tossed a small pebble against the glass as a sign that all was quiet. I heard the casement open, and waited to assist His Majesty's descent. But then to my grief and horror came a groan, and I knew that, too late, he had found himself mistaken, he sticking fast between his breast and shoulders, while I on the ground could not come to his aid.

Yet at the instant before he endeavoured to come out, he mistrusted, and tied a piece of his cord to a bar of the window within, by means of which he forced himself back, not without pain. So soon as he was in again, to let me see (as I had to my grief heard) the design was broken, he set a candle in the window, the sign we had before agreed on. Now I was in labour how to give notice to Mr Osborne and Mr Worsley, which I could find no better way to do than by flinging stones from the place upon the ramparts where I should have let the King down. Which proved effectual, so that they went off, and no discovery made.

After this I applied to Mrs Whorwood in London that she should send me files and *aqua fortis* to make the passage more easy. But ere they came, a letter from the Committee at Derby House arrived for Mr Hammond, to direct him to have a careful eye on those about the King, for that they had discovered there were some who gave him secret intelligence.

2

Correspondence of Colonel Robert Hammond

(From the Derby House Committee to Colonel Hammond)

London. March 23rd, 1648.

Sir, this day we received dispatches that some forces of the Army in Wales being ordered to disband, their commander, Colonel Poyner, has most villainously resisted, seizing Pembroke and joining to himself other disaffected troops in the neighbourhood. This is like to prove the spark that touches off the gunpowder, for we have advices that all up and down the country there is serious disaffection, some presuming to say that Parliament has no longer any legal right to levy the monthly assessment of £150,000, since they by the vote of Non-Addresses have in effect deposed the King. Even those we deemed our sure friends are joining with Malignants to rise in arms against the Parliament, and we hear that in Scotland the Duke of Hamilton is mustering an army to invade us.

Even as we write, word comes that a portion of the fleet has revolted, and is sailed away to Holland to the Prince of Wales. In a word, these poor kingdoms are like to suffer again a bloody civil war, unless the Lord be gracious unto us.

Sir, we have good intelligence that there are those about the King who would snatch him from your protection, though we cannot come by their names. There is a plot to fire the castle by means of a great heap of charcoal that lies near his lodging; and upon that tumult he is to make his escape. The King has a bodkin with which he will raise the lead of the iron bar at his window, to put in *aqua fortis* and so eat away the iron. There is a plain fat man gone from Portsmouth to carry the mercury-water, and there is a ship rides off the coast of Hampshire to waft the King to Holland. Mrs Whorwood is aboard her, a tall, well-languaged gentlewoman with a round visage and pock holes in her face. The King is to change clothes with a fisherman or some such person.

Sir, it has pleased the Parliament to double your pay, and to vote you £6,000 over and above your expenses.

*　　　*　　　*

(From Colonel Hammond to the Derby House Committee)

Carisbrooke Castle. March 28th, 1648.

My Lords and Gentlemen, your Honours' letter put me in a frenzy, and I beseech you send me more troops who may guard this coast lest the revolted ships come hither.

I wonder much what black arts the King practises if he has in truth seduced from their trust any who were appointed by the Parliament as persons of approved integrity. I at once dismissed Mr Cresset as the most like to be a traitor, since both his father and brother died fighting in the King's armies. The rest of the Household I summoned to my presence, and well groped them that I might make some discovery of what other serpent lurks among them; and he being suspicious in his answers, I dismissed Captain Burroughs, the Gentleman Harbinger. On the honesty of the others I would stake my salvation.

It irks me sore that I must now take upon myself the duties of the two who are outed, and I humbly beseech Parliament that I may receive their salaries.

*　　　*　　　*

(From Lieutenant-General Cromwell to Colonel Hammond)

Windsor. April 25th, 1648.

Dear Coz Hammond, comfort thyself with the reading of the Epistle of James, wherein will be shown thee that if thou dost persevere to the end, thou wilt be made perfect.

We are now to march against the perfidious Scots who, like Ephraim, have made a covenant with the Assyrians. The Lord will pour out His wrath upon them, for we shall meet them like a bear that is robbed of her whelps, and devour them like a lion. In order whereunto our prime officers met together to seek the Lord. On the first day Colonel Axtell prayed large two hours, confessing the sins of the nation in a wonderfully pathetic manner. The second day, Colonel Hewson, Colonel Ewer and Colonel Pride preached each two hours, with much heart-searching that we might discover for what sins the Lord was again chastising His Elect. Upon the third, Major Goffe, scarce able to speak for weeping, saith it had been revealed to him by the Spirit that it was neither the sins of the Army nor the sins of the Parliament which had again provoked the Lord, but the sins of the King. And asked therefore for a resolution that if the Lord be pleased to bring us home in peace, we would call the King to account for all the blood he has shed. To this we each and every one said Amen, and Major Harrison closed with a short prayer.

Intelligence came to the hands of a very considerable person that the King attempted to get out of his window, and that he had a cord of silk whereby to slip down; but his breast was too big and the bar would not give him passage. This was done in one of the dark nights of March, the guards having some quantity of wine in them. The same party assures that there is *aqua fortis* gone down to remove that obstacle which hindered, and that the like design is to be put in execution on the next dark night. The person that was to help the King from his window was Mr Firebrace; the other person doubted is Captain Titus.

The Lord endue thee with truth and judgment in the inward parts.

*　　　*　　　*

(From Colonel Hammond to the Derby House Committee)

Carisbrooke Castle. May 1st, 1648.

My Lords and Gentlemen, it being my ambition faithfully to perform all obligations laid upon me by the Parliament, upon advice that the King had attempted an escape I dismissed both persons suspected, Mr Firebrace and Captain Titus, telling them that they might whistle for their wages. The which I hope the Parliament will be graciously pleased to place to my account, I having to perform their duties.

The next morning at about two of the clock, I entered the King's bedchamber very softly, to make search of his desk and pockets. But he heard me, and stepping from his bed was so wrathful as to box my ear, then snatched from me the papers I had found, flinging them upon the fire. I was fain to lay a hand upon his person in order that I might pluck out the papers, which he prevented, and in the scuffle His Majesty had the misfortune to hurt his face against a corner of the table.

This is the plain truth, which I hasten to tell your Honours, lest my unfriends say, I used unseemly violence with the King.

Today I removed His Majesty to the house of my Chief Officer, Captain Rolph, which stands upon the left of the gate and close against the curtain wall. To reach His Majesty's Presence and Bedchamber, it is necessary to pass through Mr Rolph's own quarters; and I need not to remind your Honours how trusty a person this is, he having been long in the service of Lieutenant-General Cromwell before the war.

As an additional precaution, I have dismissed Mrs Wheeler, the laundress, and her maid, both of whom I suspect of passing notes to the King. I would stake my life on the fidelity of those remaining, in particular Mr Osborne, a person of discretion and zeal. None but those eight to whom the Household is reduced, and my officers, have access to His Majesty, for I will not count Chapman, the Porter of the castle who carries coals for the King's fire, a decayed ancient and very moon-calf.

I assure your Honours that I shall not permit the King to be snatched from my care, as I hear his son the Duke of York has been spirited away from St James's by one Bamfield, and I suppose gotten over to France.

*　　　*　　　*

(From Colonel Hammond to the Derby House Committee)

Carisbrooke Castle. May 29th, 1648.

My Lords and Gentlemen, I am scarce able to write, being prostrate with grief and mortification.

Upon receipt of your Honours' warning, received by me on

the 5th of this month, that despite all my precautions a new con-
spiracy was hatching to snatch the King away, I constructed a platform built out on supports beneath his windows, setting thereon
a guard of three soldiers. I once more summoned all the remaining
attendants of the King to my presence, subjecting them to a very
sharp interrogation, at the end of which I was satisfied with their
innocence. I read them a sermon on the perils of the hour, the
whole of Kent having risen against the Parliament, and there being
strong rumours that the revolted ships are sailing to the Wight with
the Prince of Wales in command, to wrest the King from the
protection of his loving Parliament.

Judge then my anguish when, a week since, Mr Rolph (whom
I have promoted to the rank of major) came to me and told me
this tale: That Mr Osborne, and likewise Mr Dowcett, Clerk of the
Kitchen, had been plotting underground and had seduced three of
my own soldiers with bribes and fair words. When these three
should be on duty together upon the platform on the next dark
night, they were to assist the King's descent to the counterscarp,
Dowcett having helped him from the window, and Osborne with
one Worsley, a gentleman of substance in the Wight, to be waiting
with horses beyond the wall. And what filled my cup of bitterness
to overflowing, the maggoty-headed idiot, old Chapman, who is up
and down all day to tend His Majesty's fires, with a file has been
cutting through a bar at his leisure, if you please, cunningly filling
up the gap with clay.

I thought I would have lost my wits by such disclosures, but
Mr Rolph hastened to assure me that all was not lost. Two of the
sentinels seduced had repented of it, and had confessed the wicked
plot to Rolph, and that the date chosen was this night just past.
Then Mr Rolph was earnest with me that I should take the King in
the very act, for this, says he, will expose to all the world the King's
duplicity, who would sneak underhand from the protection of his
faithful Parliament and captain once again the Malignants now
risen throughout his realms.

My Lords and Gentlemen, I do protest upon my honour that I
suspected nothing sinister in Major Rolph's suggestion, for though
he was but a serving-man in the household of my cousin Cromwell,

he is too much a Christian to set his hand to any unlawful act. It is true that last night he lurked beneath the platform with a cocked pistol, but he has sworn to me that this was only that he might fire into the air if he required assistance.

And as it fell out, it was not he who fired, but the third sentinel, one Floyd. For he, suspecting a change of heart in his comrades, and alarmed moreover by the presence of Mr Rolph skulking beneath the platform, took it into his wicked head that he himself was being used as a decoy to lure the King to his death. Therefore, just as His Majesty was about to come forth from his window, Floyd shot off his musket as a sign it was not safe.

I sent at once a party of musketeers to ambush Osborne and Worsley, but in the darkness they got clean away. Dowcett and Floyd I arrested, and this morning yielded to Major Rolph's entreaties that Floyd be shot to death by a firing-party for his crime. I do beseech your Honours that a reinforcement be sent me of tried and trusty men, for I feel myself encompassed with traitors, and know not on whom I may rely.

Parley

I

Secret Memoirs of Thomas Herbert

I was afflicted with head-rheums and was aguish all over my body during the summer of 1648, which was cold and wet, and the Chief Officer's house at Carisbrooke, whither His Majesty had been removed, proved very discomfortable. Mr Hammond having dismissed so many of the Household, he doubled the duties of those of us who remained. There were constant alarms as if the King should escape, but of such complots I was quite innocent; for though I heartily wished him well, and pitied his strait imprisonment, I stayed faithful to the Parliament who had appointed me in this service.

There was a very fierce spirit grown up in the Army against the King at this time. Until His Majesty's refusal of the four Bills, no man had mentioned his person without respect and duty, and only lamented 'that he was misled by evil counsellors'. But upon his rejection of these four Bills (which in truth would have made him less than the least of his subjects), every soldier's mouth was opened against him with the utmost sauciness and licence, each striving to exceed the other in the impudence and bitterness of his invective. And the friends of the Army in Parliament got passed a vote of Non-Addresses, wherein, after a most scurrilous catalogue of reasons, they bound themselves to hold no more communication with His Majesty; declaring further that any man who presumed to address his Sovereign would incur the penalties for high treason.

His Majesty was more damped in his spirits at this time than ever I knew him before or since. I asked him, did he think that the new war which raged throughout his realms would be to his advantage, to which he answered No. For those who had risen were disunited save in a common detestation of the Scots, being some Cavaliers, others old Parliament-men, with a good many of the common folk, for truth to tell, this was a popular revolt. The local leaders issued their own commissions, not being able to obtain any from the King, and this made for confusion and rivalries. Likewise had they no strongholds, nor a commander round whom to rally; though there was a rumour as if the young Prince of Wales was with the Scotch army, which caused His Majesty keen anguish for the safety of his Heir.

Yet it seemed as though this second civil war was like to benefit His Majesty in another way. For it called out of the House of Commons all the military members, and the presbyterians being again in the majority, they rescinded the vote of Non-Addresses, and at the beginning of August sent three Commissioners to Carisbrooke to invite the King to enter into new negotiations, limited to forty days, in the town of Newport.

I being present when His Majesty received these Commissioners, recorded in my journal what he said at meeting:

'I look upon treaties as a retiring from fighting like beasts, to debating like men, whose strength should be more in their understanding than in their limbs. But,' said he, 'a blind man is as fit to judge of colours, as I am to treat concerning the peace of the kingdom, seeing I have been for half a year so strictly confined.'

At which they told him, he was to be at Newport in the same freedom and state as at Hampton Court, and should have all his advisers about him. Which proved but a half-truth, I am sorry to say.

During this month of August, we had advices that all the principal risings were put down, and that Duke Hamilton, though he had thirty thousand men, quartered them at such a distance from each other that the van was fifty miles from the rear when Cromwell struck at the centre near Preston, and totally routed them. And here I must note to my sorrow, there was a new barbarous spirit which distinguished the Army in this second civil war. For the Scotch prisoners were plundered to their very shifts ere they were sent as slaves to the Plantations, and had the remainder counter-attacked, Cromwell had given orders for the butchery of four thousand of his captives.

Nay, even the good General Fairfax seemed infected by this new savagery. He had absolutely refused to march against his fellow presbyterians, the Scots, but having starved the town of Colchester into surrender upon promise of quarter, what must he do but execute its commanders, Sir Charles Lucas and Sir George Lisle, upon the spot. And that which touched the King nearly was the frightfulness perpetrated upon a former humble adherent and companion on his journey to the Scots in '46. I mean Dr Michael Hudson who, having raised a troop in his native Northampton-shire, was driven to bay in a moated manor there, and surrendering was flung over the battlements, his hands cut off as he clung to the stonework, and knocked on the head while he paddled in the moat with his bleeding stumps. 'Tis said that one of his captors went so far as to cut out his tongue and have it salted as a trophy of his barbarous deed.

And ere I leave so disrelishful a subject, I must set down what fell out concerning Major Rolph. Mr Osborne, who was for a time His Majesty's Gentleman Usher at Carisbrooke, appeared at the bar of the House of Commons and accused Major Rolph of a de-sign to murder the King, in which accusation he was supported by Mr Dowcett, Clerk of the Kitchen. Both these men swore that Rolph, who took them to be of his mind, confided to them how on an occasion in May of this year, he had waited almost three hours beneath the platform built outside His Majesty's windows, with a good pistol to fire at the King if he came out.

But Mr Rolph being tried at Winchester by that same corrupt Justice Wilde who had condemned Captain Burley, he directed the jury, 'that there was a time indeed when intentions and words were treason, but God forbid it should be so now. How did anyone know but that these two men, Osborne and Dowcett, would have made away with the King, and that Rolph charged his pistol to preserve him? Or perhaps they would have carried him away to engage the kingdom in another war. They were mistaken who be-lieved the King to be a prisoner; the Parliament does only keep him safe to prevent the shedding of more blood'.

And so the Grand Jury returned an *Ignoramus* on the bill, and Major Rolph, having £150 for compensation, returned to his duties at Carisbrooke. To the much misliking, I believe, of Governor

Hammond, who all along suspected him to be set there by his old master, Cromwell, as a spy upon the Governor.

*   *   *

It was in the first week of September when, all things being in readiness, His Majesty rode into Newport to begin negotiations for a treaty, he having given his parole not to depart during the forty days thereof, and twenty days after it should be concluded. Mr William Hopkins, Master of the Grammar School, had the honour to entertain His Majesty, his school-house being situated in St James's Street on the road to Cowes. This Mr Hopkins, I learned afterwards, had turned ardent for the King since His Majesty's coming to the Wight, in so much that he, his wife and their son George, were full of fantastical schemes to raise the Island gentry, surprise Carisbrooke, and place Governor Hammond under arrest.

I was quite forgotten and felt something of jealousy when we came to the Grammar School, for there met us a flock of His Majesty's old attendants, his reunion with whom was very joyful. But there was weeping likewise when they saw how changed was his appearance. From the time when Babbington the barber was taken from him, his hair and beard were untrimmed and shaggy, and were both now all grey; and his dress ill befitted his rank.

'Whilst I was at Carisbrooke,' I heard him say to Mrs Wheeler, his laundress, 'they kept me two months under a want of linen, which though it distressed me, I scorned to give them the pleasure to complain to them anent it.'

Yet he had taken such care to be sparing in his diet and observe regular exercise about the castle, that his health remained unimpaired, and he carried himself with the same majesty as he was used to do. And it soon became evident that his mind had not been permitted to rust during his solitary confinement, and that his intellectual faculties were as acute as formerly.

Some days after his coming to the Grammar School, there arrived the Parliament's Commissioners, who hired every room of the Bull inn in the High Street, overflowing into houses on either side. They waited on His Majesty the day after, he being so gracious as to permit me to be present, since one of them was my

114

noble kinsman, the Earl of Pembroke. He received them in the large schoolroom on the first floor, now become his Presence, and after compliments exchanged, he uttered this reproach:

'Though I am again accorded the honours of a king, I find there are guards set about the house, and whenever I ride out I am dogged by a troop of horse.'

The Commissioners answered with a stale put-off, *viz.* that it was only to protect his person from violence. But when he told them he had made choice of his advisers in the coming negotiations, they answered with something of a sneer that since he had always desired a personal treaty with the Parliament, it should be so in sober earnest, and therefore no man on His Majesty's side might take part in the debates. The best he could wring from them was, that his advisers might stand behind a curtain where they could hear what was said. When the Commissioners were taking their leave, my Lord Pembroke said to me apart (with a great oath) that by fair means or foul he would force the King to come to terms, for the Army had resolved to abolish the House of Lords after they had deposed His Majesty.

Strange to relate, the principal of His Majesty's friends, that is to say, the Duke of Richmond, the Marquis of Hertford and the Earls of Southampton and Lindsey, were earnest with him that he should grant whatever Parliament demanded at the outset, and waive the formality of studying each clause. For if Cromwell, they said, who was now in Scotland, on his return were confronted with a treaty signed and sealed betwixt the King and Parliament, he would not venture to withstand their combined authority. But to these pleas the King was deaf, saying with something akin to horror:

'My lords, you cannot be serious. To bind myself to a general and implicit consent to whatever they shall desire, were a blind obedience as never was expected from any man, much less of a king by his subjects. This were as if Samson had consented, not only to bind his own hands and cut off his hair, but to put out his eyes, that the Philistines might with more safety abuse him.'

And so began this abortive treaty. The proceedings took place in the Town Hall, commencing each day at nine of the clock, and being resumed after dinner. I was present, attending on my Lord Pembroke, he and his fellow Commissioners sitting on either side of a long table, His Majesty being in a chair of estate, and his advisers behind a curtain on the backside of it. The terms offered proved to be but the four Bills dressed up in other language, from which His Majesty had dissented in December. And some of it was very ill language, for the Commissioners were reinforced by several fiery ministers, one of whom presumed so far as to tell His Majesty that if he did not consent to the making away with the Church of England, he would be damned. To which he answered:

'My conscience receives little satisfaction from these pious threatenings. I pray you give me more religious and rational arguments than soldiers carry in their knapsacks.'

All, both friends and enemies, were in admiration at the King's nimble wit and logical debating; and upon a day I taking wine with my Lord Pembroke and Sir Harry Vane, the former says to me:

'The King is wonderfully improved.'

'No, my lord,' I made bold to say, 'it is your lordship who has too late discerned what he really is.'

'As for me,' says Vane, 'I have been much deceived in his character. For I ever considered him a weak man, but now that I find him to be of great parts and ability, he is the more dangerous.'

Many concessions did His Majesty grant, as may be read in the public records. Even to the consenting, against his better judgment, to the preamble (which unless granted they would not treat at all), wherein he was required to agree that the two Houses had been necessitated to enter into a war for their just and lawful defence. Though he observed that this would be to naturalize rebellion, and proposed instead a general Act of Indemnity, he was persuaded by his friends to yield, for otherwise, said they, it would be given out that he had refused to secure the Parliament, and all who had adhered to them, from a prosecution for high treason under the Statute of Treason of King Edward III. Yet he still insisted that this preamble be not binding if the treaty as a whole were broken off.

As concerning the militia, their darling, the Commissioners

116

demanded power to raise what forces they pleased in future, and likewise to impose taxes to maintain them by such ways and means as they thought fit. This monstrous power, which would give Parliament authority over all subjects, and the disposal of the fortunes of all men of what degree soever, without limitation, they would have for the term of twenty years. And when the Commissioners rejected His Majesty's attempt to curb the extravagance of their demand by inserting into it a clause whereby no subject be compelled to serve as a soldier against his will, save only in the case of foreign invasion, he being almost as weary of the importunities of his friends as of the malice of his enemies, gave his consent. For his own advisers pressed him hard to yield, as the only means of uniting with the Parliament against the Army, their common foe.

But he was not to be moved by any man either to forsake the Church or to sacrifice his friends. Both these touched him so near that he vowed he would much more willingly die than yield.

Towards the end of the negotiations, none but myself and Sir Philip Warwick, one of his secretaries, being by, he spoke thus:

'Is not this treaty like the fray in the comedy, in which a player says there has been a fray and no fray, for there have been three blows given and I have had them all. For observe whether I have not granted absolutely most of their propositions and only limited a few of them; and consider whether they have made me one concession.'

And he went on to make a prophecy:

'They will ask so much, and use it so ill, that the people of England will one day be glad to relodge the power they have taken from the Crown where it is due. I wish,' says he, 'that I had consulted nobody; for then, where in honour and conscience I could not have complied, I could easily have been positive. God knows that I have gone to the limit of concession only that my people may clearly discern how much of my right and dignity I would sacrifice for their peace. But instead I fear I have the more enslaved them.'

I observed then that His Majesty was weeping, the biggest drops that ever I saw fall from a human eye; but recollecting himself he turned presently his head away, for he was loth it should be discerned.

Each evening when we returned to the Grammar School, His Majesty sat late with his secretaries, arranging the notes taken of the day's debate and drafting what he intended to say upon the morrow. And when this business was completed, he would sit up into the small hours of the morning, engaged upon a letter he designed that Sir John Ashburnham carry over to the Prince of Wales, together with copies of all the papers which had passed during the treaty.

2

Part of the King's last letter to the Prince of Wales

By what you read enclosed, you see how I have laboured in search of peace, what I conceded and what withheld. To deal freely with you, I feared from the first it would prove a mock-treaty. For a grand maxim with the Parliament has been always to ask something which in reason and honour must be denied, that they might have some colour to refuse all that was in other things granted. I have never heard that all the propositions in a treaty must be swallowed whole. If some be harsh or rough, they may be made fit by wise treaters for an acceptable agreement; if others be unpassable, they may be rejected. Yet those who have come to me to treat from the Parliament, through all these years, have no power to debate but only to impose.

I know not but this may be the last time I may speak to you, for I am sensible into what hands I am fallen. And yet, I bless God, I have those inward refreshments the malice of my enemies cannot perturb. I have learned to busy myself by retiring into myself, and therefore can the better digest what befalls me. It is some lessening the injury of my long restraint when I find my solitude has produced something useful to you, that neither you nor any other may hereafter measure my cause by the success, nor my judgment of things by my misfortunes. Which I count the greater by far because they have lighted upon you and others whom I love, of whose unmerited sufferings I have a greater sense than of my own.

I had rather you should be Charles *le Bon* than *le Grand*, good than great. I hope God has designed you to be both, having so early put you into the exercise of affliction. If He gives you success, show the greatness of your mind rather to conquer your enemies by pardoning than punishing. If He restore you to your right upon hard conditions, whatever you promise, keep. Do not think anything in this world worth the obtaining by foul and unjust means.

These men who have violated laws which they were bound to preserve, will find their triumphs full of troubles. I have conflicted with different and opposite factions (for so I must needs count all those that act not in any conformity to the ancient and settled laws of these kingdoms, established in Church and State). No sooner have they by force subdued what they count their common enemy, but they are divided into so high a rivalry as sets them more at defiance against each other than against their first antagonists. Thus all the lesser factions at first were officious servants to presbytery, till time and military success, discovering to each their peculiar advantages, invited them to part stakes, and leaving the joint-stock, pretended each to drive for their own party, to the undoing not only of Church and State, but even of presbytery itself, which seemed at first to have engrossed them all.

I have observed that the devil of rebellion does commonly turn himself into an angel of reformation, and the old serpent can pretend new lights. They raise a war and christen it 'the Cause'; when their conscience accuses them of sedition, they stop its mouth with the name of parliamentary privilege. They cry out 'necessary taxation' when they would rob and sequester, and with religion as their watchword they crucify the Church. You may hear from them Jacob's voice, but you shall feel they have Esau's hands.

Time will dissipate all factions, when once the rough horns of private men's covetous and ambitious designs shall discover themselves, which were at first hidden under the pretence of pious zeal. The English are a sober people, however at present infatuated; and they will feel it at last to their cost that it is impossible these men should be really tender of their liberties who use their King with such severe restraints, both divine and human. Let, then, no passion betray you to any study of revenge upon those whose own sin and folly will sufficiently punish them in due time. But as soon as the forked arrow of rebellion is drawn out, use all princely arts and clemency to heal the wound, that the smart of the cure may not equal the anguish of the hurt.

It is all I have left me now, a power to forgive those who have deprived me of my wife, my children, and my royal rights. And I thank God I have a heart to do it. Be confident, as I am, that the most of all sides who have done amiss have done so not out of malice, but misapprehension of things. You will have more inward complacency in pardoning one than in punishing a thousand. If you saw how unmanly and unchristian the implacable disposition is in my ill-wishers, you would avoid that spirit.

Nor would I have you to entertain any dislike of parliaments, which in their right constitution, with freedom and honour, will never diminish your greatness, but rather will be as interchangings of love, loyalty and confidence between a prince and his people. This black parliament had not been so, however much biased by faction in the elections, if it had been preserved from the insolence of a mean sort of men who made riots and tumults. Nothing can be more happy for all than in fair, grave and honourable ways to contribute their counsels in common, enacting all things by public consent. We must not starve ourselves because some have surfeited of unwholesome food.

How God will deal with me as to the removal of these pressures and indignities which His justice, by the very unjust hands of some of my subjects, hath been pleased to lay upon me, I cannot tell. But if you never see my face again, and God will have me buried in such a barbarous imprisonment and obscurity (which the perfecting of some men's designs requires), wherein few hearts that love me are permitted to exchange a word or look with me, I do require and entreat you, as your father and your King, to confer all love, respect and protection on your mother, my wife, who has been content, with incomparable magnanimity and patience, to suffer both for and with you and me. And for these weather-tossed kingdoms, I pray Almighty God that He will be pleased to make you a harbour unto them.

If mine enemies shall destroy me (for I know not how far God may permit their malice to proceed, and such apprehensions some men's words and actions have already given me), let my memory ever live in you, as of your father who loved you, and once a king of three flourishing kingdoms, whom God thought fit to honour not only with the government of them, but also with the suffering many indignities and an untimely death, while I studied to preserve the rights of the Church, the power of the laws, the honour of my crown, the liberties of my people, and my own conscience which, I thank God, is dearer to me than a thousand kingdoms.

I know God can, I hope He will, restore me to my rights; I cannot despair either of His mercy, or of my subjects' love. At worst I trust I shall but go before you to a better kingdom, which God hath prepared for me, through my Saviour Jesus Christ, to whose mercies I commend you and all mine.

Farewell till we meet, if not on earth, yet in heaven.

3

Correspondence of Colonel Robert Hammond

(From Major Thomas Harrison to Colonel Hammond)

Windsor. November 20th, 1648.

Sir, we of the Army are exceeding wroth that this synagogue of Satan called the Parliament are so led along by their father the Devil that they would make a treaty with the Man of Sin, only because they still hanker after the fish and the garlic and the melons of Egypt. They have forgotten the word of the Lord to Moses: When the Lord thy God shall deliver them before thee, thou shalt smite them and utterly destroy them, nor show mercy unto them. By which is meant that not only Pharaoh, but his seed likewise, growing up in wickedness, shall continue with shortness and be confounded with the fierceness of the wrath of God.

Now the Lord General Fairfax being still sat down before Raglan Castle, that sink of iniquity, and Lieutenant-General Cromwell not yet returned from destroying the outworks of Babylon in the North, our prime officers (who may be likened to the ancients of Israel gathered together by Moses) have consulted together, and this day presented to Parliament a Grand Remonstrance. For God stirred up the hearts of some honest soldiers to petition us that we no longer provoke Him, but offer a sacrifice which shall go up as a sweet savour in His nostrils.

That precious Saint, Colonel Ewer, presented the Remonstrance, discoursing at large upon the 8th chapter of the first book of Samuel, wherein the children of Israel demanded a king, to their own undoing. Descending to profane language, he gave the heads of the Remonstrance thus: That there be no further proceeding with the Treaty of Newport, and that the Parliament return to their vote of Non-Addresses. That public justice be done upon the principal actor in the late war. And because the whole house of Ahab must perish, that a peremptory day be set when the Prince of Wales and the Duke of York be required to appear and make satisfaction, which if they refuse, they be proclaimed traitors.

Upon which reading, the members made that kind of hum which commonly shows that the House dislikes a motion. When this was stilled, Colonel Ewer urged them with tears to be true to the good cause, and bring delinquents, without partiality, to condign punishment, to make inquiry for the guilt of the blood that has been shed in both wars, and to execute justice lest the Lord smite us with pestilence and famine. For, said he, it is commanded that we make no league with the Canaanites, but put them all to the sword.

Yet these Parliament-men, like a washed sow, return to their wallowings in the mire, and are set upon making terms with Beelzebub and throwing us, the Saints, for him to mangle. Wherefore it is the earnest desire of the Army that you take good care to secure the Man of Sin. He being now in too public a place, it were good if you conveyed him back to Carisbrooke, where his person may be disposed of by what means soever seem good to you, who shall be held scatheless.

* * *

(From Colonel Hammond to Commissary Ireton)

Carisbrooke Castle. November 22nd, 1648.

Dear Coz Ireton, I must needs complain to you in the absence of his Excellency the Lord General, of the insulting letter I have received from Major Harrison, who insinuates that I should take some desperate and unlawful means to secure, as he terms it, the person of the King. Nay, he goes so far as to hint at secret murder, the which from him I do not much wonder at, seeing he is a butcher by trade.

Sir, I am a gentleman of honour, and I am outraged to be thought capable of turning assassin. Moreover I must remind you blunt that I was appointed custodian of His Majesty by the Parliament, and not by the Army, and therefore take no orders regarding the disposal of his royal person save from the two Houses, who are at this instant concluding their negotiations with the King.

* * *

(From Commissary Ireton to Colonel Hammond)

Windsor. November 24th, 1648.

Dear Coz Robin, I am very sure you wrong good Major Harrison in what you write. His care is only lest the King take himself underhand from your charge, as is all too evident he has attempted during the time he has been in the Wight. And he being now in so public a place where he is surrounded by his adherents, it is feared they may find means to spirit him away.

I do not deny that it was the Parliament who appointed you, and the Lord forbid that I should tempt you from your allegiance to the Houses, though they be only a sort of generation of men who through accident bear the sway. Yet pray remember you are an officer of the Army, in whose care the King was until he took himself privily from Hampton Court. It was for the public ends that you did receive your trust, and I do appeal to your conscience to whom you owe most faith, the backsliding Parliament, or those whose judgments and affections are now clean contrary to them? I hope you will not give yourself up to a delusion of an air of honour, and mere form and shadow of faithfulness to the neglect of the reality or substance.

All our prime officers here long to see you, that you may be assured of the tenderness we in the Army have towards you, and that we may remove your vain scruples. Will you not, then, give us the happiness of a visit to headquarters?

*　　*　　*

(From Lieutenant-General Cromwell to Colonel Hammond)

From the camp before Pontefract. November 25th, 1648.

Sweet Robin, my bowels are moved for thee in the heavy burthen the Lord hath been pleased to lay upon thee at this season. But thou must remember that the Lord hath spoken plainly and is not to be trifled with. What manifest signs He hath given to show which betwixt the Army and the Parliament enjoys His favour! Let not thy fleshly nature ensnare thee. If thou shouldst reason that thy allegiance is either to the carnal Parliament or to the capital and grand author of all our woes, thou wouldst be guilty of grave sin.

Would that I might see thee and that we might seek the Lord together. But this Malignant garrison is resolved to endure to the utmost extremity, expecting no mercy, and indeed it shall receive none. With Samaria it hath stirred up our God to bitterness; its men must perish by the sword, and its women be dashed to death upon the ground.

The peace of our Lord Jesus Christ be with thee.

4

Secret Memoirs of Thomas Herbert

The days permitted for the negotiations being expired, the Parliament's Commissioners came to take farewell of the King.

Some of His Majesty's friends were hopeful that so great concessions as he had made would move the Houses to give him leave to come to London, and then, said they, the concluding of the treaty would afford opportunities for the softening of that which was most harsh in it, and what His Majesty urged as matter of conscience would find reverence.

The King himself most earnestly begged the Commissioners that since he had yielded so much of his own just rights to give satisfaction to the Parliament and peace to the realm, they would be a means that he might be pressed no further, since the few things he had denied had so near relation to his conscience that, to retain its peace, he could yield no more. And desired them to use the same eloquence and ability by which they had prevailed with him, in representing to the two Houses the sad condition of the kingdom, if it were not preserved by this treaty.

There was much in the mouths of all men at this time a Grand Remonstrance presented to Parliament by the firebrands in the Army, wherein, in most unseemly language, they demanded that the King 'be brought to justice', yea, and his two elder sons with him. In taking leave of the Commissioners, His Majesty made plain to them he knew of this threatening Remonstrance, speaking thus:

'My lords, you are come to take your leave of me, and I believe we shall scarce ever see each other again, but God's will be done. I am fully informed of the whole carriage of the plot against me and mine; but nothing so much affects me as the sense I have of the sufferings of my subjects and the miseries that hang over my three kingdoms, drawn upon them by those who, under pretence of justice, violently pursue their own ends. My lords, you cannot but know that in my fall and ruin you shall shortly see your own.'

It would be a day or two after the Commissioners had left, that Colonel Hammond presented himself to the King, having about him a funereal air. He spoke somewhat wild, saying he was a gentleman of honour, with hints as if he had been approached to act otherwise. Then said he, there were positive orders brought him from the Lord General Fairfax to repair to the Army's headquarters at Windsor, the which he durst not disobey. I found it in my heart to pity Mr Hammond, so distraught was he. The truth is, he was a young gentleman who doted on his ease, and he had begged the Governorship of the Wight so that here he might reign as a petty viceroy while waiting upon the outcome of the quarrel betwixt the Army and the Parliament. In a word, he had retired himself on purpose to avoid trouble, yet it had pursued him.

He informed the King that his orders had been brought him by that same Colonel Ewer (I believe a hackey-coachman before the war) who had presented to Parliament the Grand Remonstrance, and that Ewer was appointed by the Army to be Governor of the Wight in his room. But this Mr Hammond would by no means stomach, distrusting such a ruffian, and was insistent that Ewer accompany him to headquarters. Meanwhile, said he, he had forwarded to Parliament the General's letter to him, that they might see he was but obeying the command of his superior officer, which was far from his choice.

And further informed His Majesty that he had appointed his own deputies at Carisbrooke to order affairs in the Wight till his return. Two were of the Island militia, Captain Hawes and Captain Boreman, and the third was Major Rolph. His Majesty liked not the appointment of Rolph, for despite his acquittal upon trial, there was still suspicion that he would have pistolled the King on an occasion at Carisbrooke. I think Colonel Hammond liked it neither, but was in some fear of Rolph, or rather of his former master, Cromwell, who still lingered before the petty garrison of Pontefract.

Hard upon the heels of Mr Hammond, there left us also many of the King's friends. Some, as my Lords Hertford and Southampton, went to attend to their own affairs. Sir John Ashburnham was for Holland, to carry His Majesty's letter, of six sheets all written in his own hand, to the Prince of Wales. This was a most forthright gentleman, and I set down in my journal a remark he made to me anent the treaty Commissioners:

'They are like the beggar with the cocked pistol in the fable, who cried, "Charity, for the love of God".'

But the Duke of Richmond, His Majesty's cousin, a very gentle, modest man, and my Lord Lindsey, remained at Newport, though the King had given them leave to depart with the rest. For albeit there came heartening news at this time that the Parliament had rejected the Grand Remonstrance by sixty-seven votes, these noblemen were very uneasy about the safety of the King. This on account of a rumour that a strange person, thought to be an officer of the Army, had been seen riding to Carisbrooke Castle, much muffled up as though he would conceal his identity.

5
Narrative of Henry Firebrace

The last two days of November in the year 1648 are branded on my mind, full as they were of alarums. The very elements seemed to give warning of some dire deed, with raging winds and torrential rain, and the nights pitchy dark.

After supper on the 29th, His Majesty retired into his bed-chamber at the Grammar School, to write a letter to the Queen, bidding me come for it at eight o'clock. But long before that hour, I was affrighted by glimpsing soldiers prowling round the house with cocked pistols. I made so bold as to give upon the bedchamber door that special knock which intimated to the King that I had urgent news to report. When he opened, I cried on God to preserve him, for that I feared some dismal attempt upon his person, imparting to him what I had seen. I cannot without tears recollect how he laid his hand upon my shoulder, saying in most kindly fashion:

'Honest Harry, be not thus afraid. You know that Hammond has appointed three deputies in his absence. These will be trebly diligent, and it may be have set a threefold guard here.'

But what with the raging of the elements and the glimpse I had got as it were of evil spectres prowling, I had fallen into a frenzy of terror, and I fell to imploring him after this fashion:

'Ah, Sir, I much fear you are deceived. For God's sake think of your safety. There is still a door of hope open; the night is dark and I can bring you privily into the street and thence conduct you to

Wootten Creek, where Mr Newland has a good boat always ready and a stout heart to serve you. Commit yourself to the hazard of the sea rather than trust your person in the hands of these merciless villains who I fear this night will murder you.'

'Harry,' says he, 'this is wild talk. I do not fear, and even if I thought there was any danger, I should be reluctant to go because of my parole.'

Then he bade me wait while he finished and sealed his letter, which he gave to me to carry to the post office. I was groping my way along the street, when a hand was clapped upon my shoulder; but even as I supposed myself under arrest, a voice I recognized as that of Mrs Jane Whorwood bade me hold my tongue.

'If it were known I was in the Wight,' says she, 'I should go to prison or pot, and am content with either, so I convey my news to the King.'

Not a word more would she speak until we were clear of the houses on the road to Cowes, and then said she in that deep voice which was liker a man's than a lady's:

'I would not trust a messenger, so urgent are my tidings. And to give you a foretaste of them, know that Hammond was no farther on his road than Farnham when he was arrested by Colonel Ewer and conveyed to the Army headquarters as a prisoner.'

'Upon what charge?' said I.

'For not rendering such ready obedience to orders as was required,' said she. 'I suspect he refused to set his hand to some vile deed or wink at it being done by others.'

Then she told me that this very day, as soon as it was dark, two thousand soldiers had been ferried to the Wight under the command of Lieutenant-Colonel Cobbett, who himself was now at Carisbrooke, his men being disposed up and down the Island to keep the inhabitants from stirring, and some being those strange soldiers whom I had spied skulking round the Grammar School with their pistols cocked. All this Mrs Whorwood bade me relate to the King without delay, she herself being intent upon seeking out our old acquaintance, Mr Newland, to make sure his boat was manned in case His Majesty could contrive to reach it.

Such disclosures were like a leaden weight upon me as I

128

hasted back to the Grammar School. They must be made known to the King, thought I, by some gentleman of influence with him, and therefore I tapped upon the door of the oak parlour, for I knew the Duke of Richmond to be within. I found his Grace in company with the Lord Lindsey and Colonel Edward Cook. I hesitated to give my news in the presence of one who was of the Army, but he, seeing my distraught looks, said to me:

'Mr Firebrace, I will withdraw if you have something secret you wish to impart to my lords. Only I swear to you, that if it concerns His Majesty's safety, I am content that the uniform I wear be dyed a deeper crimson with my own blood in his defence.'

Then did I blurt out my news, to which all three gentlemen listened aghast, and carried me at once abovestairs to the bedchamber, where His Majesty was at his devotions. When the tidings had been made known to him, he asked Colonel Cook if he had heard of this great force of soldiers being brought into the Wight.

'Sir,' says the Colonel reproachfully, 'had I heard of it, I would not have failed to advertise Your Majesty. That on so foul a night this huge force should be shipped across the Solent portends something extraordinary. At supper-time I saw Major Rolph enter the Bull inn; I will go to him, and as his superior officer demand to be informed of the situation.'

Now from this point there is much that I do not know of my personal knowledge. But the particulars were written down for me at my request by Colonel Cook (since deceased), while they were fresh in his memory, and so I include them in my narrative.

*   *   *

The Colonel hastened to seek out Rolph, whom he found abed. In reply to his question, was there a design to seize the person of the King? Rolph feigned ignorance, saying it was impossible for him to know what were the present purposes of the Grandees at Windsor. But then, contradicting himself, he says that Cook might assure the King he should have no disturbance this night. Whereat Cook pressed him hard, urging that there must be some extraordinary design afoot, considering that in such extremity of weather a great body of men should be ferried to the Wight. Why, says Rolph pertly, he and his fellows had been on duty here so long, it was more than time they were relieved. And says again, the King may rest quietly this night.

'If,' says Cook, suspecting the repetition of the words, 'this night', 'you do receive orders to remove His Majesty, shall I be so timely acquainted with them that the King be not surprised with their execution?'

Rolph replying, with a saucy grin, that would be only to have a due respect for His Majesty, the Colonel was convinced that he was lying, and hurried back to the Grammar School. Says he to the King, I am acquainted with one man who will not answer me with a put-off, and that is Captain Boreman at Carisbrooke. At first His Majesty would not give him leave to ride thither, out of his princely consideration, saying that he would not expose Cook to the foulness of the ways on such a night. It took much persuasion ere His Majesty agreed, in these words:

'Well, you are young and healthy, and I do hope you will receive no hurt and that I shall live to reward you.'

This Colonel Cook repeated to me with emotion, saying it was no wonder His Majesty conquered men's hearts, so grateful was he for the most trifling service, and no matter what his plight, loth to expose his servants to any hazard.

So the Colonel took horse, and setting his face against the gale, groped his way through the pitchy dark to Carisbrooke, where he sheltered in the gatehouse, bidding a corporal of the guard bring Captain Boreman to speak with him there. But instead there came a curt order from Lieutenant-Colonel Cobbett to proceed to the Chief Officer's house, where was Cobbett himself in company with some dozen prime officers. It was with much ado that the Colonel wrung from Cobbett permission to exchange a few private words with Captain Boreman, to whom he expressed his astonishment, Boreman being a Deputy Governor.

'I am,' says the Captain bitterly, 'liker a prisoner in my own garrison, and these officers have threatened me with instant death if I so much as whisper to my militiamen.'

It was plain to Cook that the man was in actual fear of his

life, and though he would fain do his duty by the King, durst not disclose all he knew. He swore he had not heard of a design to seize the royal person, yet confessed he thought it not at all unlikely.

Back comes Cook to Newport, it being now between eleven of the clock and midnight. His apprehensions were much increased by finding that during his short absence, some of the sentinels about the Grammar School had been set within it, ay, even close against the bedchamber door, where His Majesty was like to be suffocated with the smoke of their musket-match. Being senior in rank to the officer of the watch, Colonel Cook positively ordered him to move his sentries to a more seemly distance. Which being done, before he went in to the King, he saddled two horses, secreting them under a little penthouse near the Grammar School, but six miles distant from the mouth of the Medina, to reach which there would be no necessity to pass through the town.

When he had told his story, both the Duke of Richmond and the Lord Lindsey agreed with him that a new and desperate complot was imminent, and the only question was, could His Majesty yet escape? The King said, such a thing was not possible, and that should it miscarry, it would only exasperate the Army and drive them to extremities. But his friends were resolved to save him even without his leave; and the Duke of Richmond asked Colonel Cook, who was drying his saturated clothes at the fire, how he had passed to and fro. Why, says Cook, I had the password. Do you believe, the Duke asks him, that you could get me out? I have no doubt of it, says Cook.

So his Grace puts on a dark cloak, and went out with Cook into the street, repeating the password whenever they were challenged, and back into the bedchamber again. It could be done with ease, they assured His Majesty. Colonel Cook was most particular in his account of what followed, because it was in the nature of a mystery to him, and so remained. For, said he, the King was of so keen an understanding, ever maintaining that reason was the divinest power; yet upon this occasion he urged an argument against reason, *viz.* that he could not break his parole.

Upon this the Duke of Richmond reminded him that his parole had been given to Colonel Hammond as representing the

131

Parliament. Likewise that it was a two-sided agreement, entailing his liberty to walk abroad, whereas the Army had violated the promises made to His Majesty by setting guards even at his door. While the Duke was thus urging him, His Majesty sat beside the fire with his head resting on his hand; and instead of replying to his Grace, he says abruptly:

'Ned Cook, what do you advise?'

The Colonel was much startled, and demurred at offering his advice when His Majesty had here two members of his Privy Council.

'You are a plain, honest man, and a soldier,' says the King. 'I command you to give me your opinion.'

Then did the Colonel reply in the form of questions, thus:

'Suppose I should tell Your Majesty that the Army designs suddenly to seize your person? Also, that I have the password, horses in readiness under a penthouse hard by, which may carry you the six miles to Mr Newland's boat, myself likewise desirous to attend Your Majesty, though it be to my utter ruin, and the foulness of the night as it were fitted for our purpose, so that I can see no difficulty in the thing? All these particulars are the true state of the case, and all that remains is for Your Majesty to resolve what you shall do.'

The King kept silent for a while, looking into the fire with an expression exceeding pensive. He had but to speak the word, and the door of his prison would fly open and his long captivity be at an end. And if I may presume to speak so, to whom he had deigned to show his heart, I am sure he must have seen in the glowing coals the face of his beloved wife, that face which, unless he took this last chance of escape, he might never see again in this world. Yet at length he seemed to brace himself, and says he:

'They have promised me, and I have promised them. They asked and received my parole to abide here till the treaty be concluded. I will not break my pledged word.'

All three gentlemen were at a nonplus, imploring His Majesty to lay aside such scruples, withal reminding him that he had given no parole to violent men who had said openly in their Grand Remonstrance that they sought his life.

'Sir,' pleaded his Grace of Richmond, 'you did not hesitate to escape from Hampton Court, where your peril was but as a shadow to this ugly substance.'

'I had withdrawn my parole ere I went away from Hampton Court,' says the King.

And then, looking on a sudden strangely cheerful, he said that now he would go and take some rest.

'Which, Sir,' says Cook mournfully, 'I fear will not be long.'

I suppose that something in the Colonel's manner made His Majesty suspect he knew more than he had disclosed; though it was not so.

'Ned,' says he, 'what troubles you? Tell me.'

Whereat Cook fetches a deep sigh, and says it was His Majesty's extreme peril and his unwillingness to evade it.

'Never let that trouble you,' says the King, still cheerful. 'Were it greater, I would not break my word to prevent it, for there is nothing so goes against my conscience as to violate a pledge.'

The Duke of Richmond remained with His Majesty to assist him to undress, while the Lord Lindsey and Colonel Cook returned to the lodging they shared in the town. But they went not to bed, for notwithstanding Rolph's specious promises, they feared the King would be seized without warning. Yet all things were carried with such suddenness and quiet that they heard not the least whisper until the King was taken.

*   *   *

Now do I return to my own experiences. Ere he lay down upon his pallet in the bedchamber, the Duke sent for me and bade me lie in the ante-room to be at hand if he needed me. The which I did right willingly, often starting awake and longing for the light of day. But it was still full dark, being about the hour of seven, when a knocking on the ante-room door brought me to my feet. There leapt into my mind that dreadful fright when Cornet Joyce stole away the King from Holmby, and upon my soul I looked to see that ruffian when I opened the door. But instead there was Mr Mildmay, the Gentleman Usher, who said that some officers of the Army were very desirous to speak with the King.

133

I closed the door again, but durst not lock it, and tapped upon that of the bedchamber. On my whispering my news to his Grace, he said the King was sound asleep, having retired so late, and that these personages of the Army must stay till he woke. But even as the Duke was speaking, in rushed Lieutenant-Colonel Cobbett and Major Rolph who, without any reverence, bawled at the King that they had orders to remove him. And as if it were in truth a repetition of what Cornet Joyce had acted, when the King inquired whose orders, they would give no plain answer, but said, the Army's.

'To what place?' asked His Majesty.

'The castle,' says Cobbett.

' "The castle" is no castle,' His Majesty says sternly. 'I command you to name it.'

After a short whispering together, Rolph replied with a sinister leer:

'Hurst Castle.'

I saw the King recoil as from a blow, and heard him murmur:

'You could not have named a worse.'

The Duke then stepped forward and bade both the intruders withdraw while His Majesty dressed, but this they sullenly refused, saying they had orders to stay close to the King's person, and so far forgot their manners as to seat themselves in his presence. Plucking up courage, I asked His Majesty if he would not eat ere he went on that long journey. His answer still rings in my ears, for they were almost the last words I heard that blessed royal martyr speak:

'Honest Harry, I thank you for your care of me, and I will gladly take breakfast from your hands.'

I ran to prepare some viands, but coming to tell His Majesty they were ready, to my horror I found him being hustled down the stair by those bloodhounds, who never before had gone so far in rudeness. The King kept his composure, asking if he were not to have any of his own servants with him. To which the wretches replied, 'Only such as be useful'. His Majesty named scarce a dozen, being so gracious as to include 'Honest Harry Firebrace', as he termed me; but this would not do, they would have only Mr Herbert and Mr Harrington. To which the King objected that Mr Herbert had been abed these past three days with an ague, and he did not know whether he would consent to attend his master to so bleak a place.

At the stair-foot, I fell upon my knees in an anguish of weeping to kiss my dear master's hand, yet even this they prevented, still thrusting him forward with a 'Go you on, Sir'. And so to his coach which was set close against the street door. Then must Major Rolph, upon whom lay strong suspicion that he would have pistolled the King at Carisbrooke, most impudently, with his hat on, step into the coach beside His Majesty. But the King, with great courage, rose up and thrust him out again, saying sternly:

'It has not come to that yet. Get you gone.'

Taken unawares, Rolph missed his footing and fell upon his back in the road. Whereafter, cursing most frightfully, he mounted the King's led horse and rode by the coach side, stooping to shout vile abuse through the window. His Grace of Richmond was permitted to attend upon our master for scarce two miles, when he was made to take his leave.

I could have added much more to what I have writ, but think I have sufficiently tired your noble Lordships. I shall conclude only with this; that if I had ten thousand lives and had spent them all (as I should willingly have done) to have preserved that great prince, I had been more than amply recompensed in his last act of kindness to me. For ere he took leave of the Duke of Richmond, he was pleased to give his Grace particular charge to recommend me to the Prince of Wales, still naming me 'Honest Harry Firebrace'.

135

Bombardment

I

Secret Memoirs of Thomas Herbert

Towards the end of November in the year 1648, my old distemper of rheum was very sharp, so that I was confined to my bed. In this state was I, when a command was brought me, with the like to Mr Harrington, that we attend the King who was to take a journey. What was our horror when, coming to the Grammar School, we saw His Majesty being hustled into his coach by Army officers, one of them Major Rolph, and the other a stranger to me, who was Lieutenant-Colonel Cobbett. What it portended, I could not tell, only the weeping of the Duke of Richmond and of His Majesty's lower servants made me suspect that here was some desperate business. The more so when, upon our setting forth, the coach was quite hemmed in by a strong guard, all of them with cocked pistols.

His Majesty said nought to Mr Harrington or me in explanation of the mystery, but to divert us asked us to guess our destination. Which we could in no wise do, for what with the darkness of the day and the twists and turns we took along by-roads axle-deep in mire, we confessed ourselves at a loss. Only afterwards I learned that because Cobbett was fearful of attempts at rescue (though two thousand soldiers were now in the Wight to keep the inhabitants from stirring), he would not venture on the direct route from Newport to Yarmouth, but took us through Calbourne and over the Yar by the bridge there to Freshwater Isle, the extreme west point of the Wight.

Northwards of Freshwater we made a temporary halt at a decayed strength named Worsley's Tower, long uninhabited, and here, still fasting, we stayed while a boat was fetched from Yarmouth. His Majesty was so good as to express regret that I had not been warned, in my sick condition, whither we were bound, for, said he, it was to the most dismal fortress in all his dominions. We were like to have been drowned ere we reached it, for the seas were so rough that the crossing of the Solent in an open boat took near upon three hours.

The blockhouse where at last we landed was built by King Henry VIII upon the hard sand called the Hurst, opposite Worsley's Tower, and thus they commanded between them all the shipping which entered the Solent by the Needles. Though never properly maintained, Hurst Castle was occupied by the Parliament's forces throughout the civil war; but it was of so vile and unwholesome an air that the common guards there had to be changed very frequently for the preservation of their health. The blockhouse, a huge, twelve-sided tower, loomed up above us like some threatening fate; and upon the lowered drawbridge on the seaward side, His Majesty's new jailer awaited us, at whose appearance my heart sank into my hose.

His name was Ayers, a rag-picker, I believe, before the war, but like so many others in the New Model Army, rapidly promoted from the ranks to high command. Nothing at all of his face could be seen, except his eyes, which glared ferociously through a bush of black whisker like a beast from its lair. In his hand he grasped a halberd, and he was armed besides with a long basket-hilted sword. No reverence made he to the King, but strutted and scowled in desperado-fashion, clanking his bunch of keys.

Once within, we had to grope our way by the feeble flame of a lanthorn, for even at bright noon the sun does not penetrate into Hurst. We climbed a spiral stair which wound through the heart of the blockhouse, and I began to suspect that I was in the grip of nightmare, nor did the ensuing days dispel this illusion.

Carisbrooke Castle, forbidding though it was, seemed a veritable paradise in comparison with Hurst. The chambers were but as caves contrived in the thickness of the walls, the furniture set kimkam here and there, the grease from the candles standing in great pools, with other sluttish negligences. All the accommodation His Majesty had for his victuals was a nasty court of guard, where a sutler dressed his meat most abominably. The bleak air of the sea made the whole castle so damp, that His Majesty's hat-case and everything of leather would be each day covered with mould. And albeit the walls were six yards thick, yet it rained through the cracks in them, and then one might sweep up a peck of saltpetre, which stood in a perpetual sweat upon them.

This put me into a flux and feverish distemper, and being forced to table with the ruffian Ayers, he offended my stomach even worse than did the meats. But His Majesty making the best shifts he could with things as he found them, I was soon ashamed to be complaining.

I had lived close to him now for near upon two years, and through strange twists of fortune, seeing him now courted and caressed, now hidden away in obscurity, and but lately managing single-handed treaty propositions which were liker a drench poured down his throat, than a draught which might be fairly and leisurely tasted. I was aware that the conditions of Hurst Castle must be a torment to a gentleman so fastidious and sensitive; and moreover he let fall some hints that he verily believed he had been brought here to suffer at the hands of an assassin. Yet in all these vicissitudes there was somewhat within him which remained the same; I know no better word for it than fortitude.

Let his enemies maltreat him as they would, still he for his part would preserve his health by regular exercise, and his intellectuals by reading and by that debate which was ever a delight to him. Nor would he, however low he fell, put off the king, but must have his shift handed so, and his meat, though he scarce tasted the vile stuff offered him at Hurst, served on the knee. From his present exercise he excused me on account of my delicate health. For now his promenade was limited to ploughing ankle-deep through shingle along the two-mile causeway which joins Hurst to the mainland near Milford. Daily at a set hour he would take this walk, wherein not one tree or blade of grass softened the stark prospect, his ears affronted by the ceaseless scream of the sea-fowl and by the tumult of a fierce tide, and his nostrils by a most foul stench which came off the mud flats.

Mr Harrington was his companion on these melancholy promenades, they being dogged at each step by three or four soldiers. When there was not a sea-fog, His Majesty diverted himself by identifying the rig of vessels plying betwixt Cowes and the Needles. I have before mentioned that Mr Harrington was ardent for the republican form of government, and he stuck stoutly to his views. Yet he confessed to me during this period that if anyone could change him, it was King Charles, and that if a monarch we must have, there was no man on earth more fit to wear a crown. Anon he grew so warm in his admiration of the King that he fell to praising His Majesty in the presence of Governor Ayers. With the result that he was called on by Ayers to recant, and refusing, was summarily dismissed.

Thus was I left His Majesty's sole attendant and companion during the remainder of our stay at Hurst; and I wondered what was become of my rheum, and how my feebleness seemed cured as by a miracle.

2

Unfinished Autobiography of Cornet George Joyce

The unregenerate Parliament were debating the treaty they would make with the Man of Sin, when news reached them that he had been clapped up in Hurst Castle by the Hosts of the Lord. A madness seized them, in so much that they voted unanimously that the Army be declared traitors unless they released Charles Stuart, and that an impeachment for high treason be drawn against Lieutenant-Colonel Cobbett and other prime officers.

Whereupon orders were issued that we break camp and march again on London. And on that very day there was a sermon preached which rejoiced our hearts, for it was by Master Hugh Peters who was close in the counsels of Cromwell and knew his mind. Master Peters took his text from Deuteronomy, wherein the Lord made known to Moses that the time was ripe when the children of Israel should cross over Jordan and possess the Promised Land. He spoke pityingly of Moses (by whom he intended the Lord General Fairfax), for that his eyes should not see this goodly land, for to Joshua, our great Cromwell, was appointed the work of destroying the heathen Canaanites.

It was the first day of December when we, by whom I mean the regiments containing the choicest Saints, marched into the City of Westminster, where we occupied Covent Garden, Durham House, and those sties of uncleanness, James's and Whitehall. The lewd rout of the people cried to us as we marched, 'A king! A king!', whereupon a private in our ranks hoisted an old sack upon a pike-head, telling them that they should have a king, though it be one of clouts. These ingrates were as insensible of their true champions as were the Israelites, and as eager for their idol as they for their golden calf. And so witless had become those who sat in the Commons' House that despite the encompassing of them by the Saints, still would they tempt the Lord, carrying without a division the wicked resolution 'that the answer of the King to the propositions offered him at Newport was a ground to conclude a treaty with him'. Their deaf ears heard not the word of the Lord, that Og, King of Bashan, was delivered into our hand and must be slain, yea, and his issue, that Israel might possess the land.

At James's was I quartered, mine eyes offended by worldly pomp, but my spirit much refreshed by the wonderful ways of the Lord, who exalted the humble to lie in the bed of princes. Here also was lodged Commissary Ireton, to whom we all looked for guidance until Joshua should come again among us, who was then upon his road from the North. That evening, Commissary Ireton invited some prime Saints to sup with him, among whom was myself, and Colonel Pride, by-named by the ribald Cromwell's Drayhorse, because honest Thomas Pride had pursued the trade of drayman ere he received his call to fight in the Lord's armies, and it was to Cromwell he owed his command. Also there sat at meat with us Mr Henry Marten, a worthy person, and although somewhat loose-living, a staunch friend to Israel.

We lamented much that those who sat in Parliament were become as unserviceable oxen that carted the Ark, turning to right or left and not keeping upon the narrow way to Bethshemesh. Says Mr Ireton, we have not thoroughly purged out the old leaven from among them. And Colonel Pride, clapping a hand upon his sword-hilt, demanded to know what we had journeyed so far through the wilderness to obtain, if now a majority in the House would turn

143

right-about, and restore the Man of Sin. Says Mr Marten, with a little smile:

'Your hand, my good honest friend, is upon the touchstone that can solve all. Ay, the sword can do all things, even to the turning of a majority into a minority.'

Then he grows solemn, and says that the poor besotted people of England elected certain members who had proved unworthy, and that we, the people's true protectors, must come to their aid, ensuring that those who had forsaken the good cause did not enter the Parliament House next day to conclude their evil treaty with Charles Stuart. And with that Mr Marten whips from his pocket a list, telling us that since he had sat in this parliament from its first assembling, he was well acquainted with the secret opinions of each man therein.

With a pen he drew a black cross beside more than two hundred names, leaving less than fifty who, avowed he, were true patriots and friends of the Army. Colonel Pride seemed affrighted by so huge a purge, and asked what pretext he could use to debar two hundred gentlemen from entering their own House. But Mr Marten had an answer pat on his tongue:

'That none might be permitted to sit but such as continued faithful to the public interest.'

Whereat Commissary Ireton was pleased to nod his head, saying nought but by his manner well approving. Ere we retired that night, Colonel Pride bade me pick from among my horse soldiers those I knew the most to enjoy the Lord's favour, to reinforce his foot regiment next day.

Very early on the morrow, we marched across the Park into the Palace Yards, where the Westminster Trained Bands kept guard about the Parliament. But as at the sound of trumpets the walls of Jericho fell down, so did these men drop their halberds and flee incontinent. According to orders given me, I permitted to pass through the Palace Yards all those members who came; but when they sought to enter the Commons' Chamber, they found stationed at the door thereof Colonel Pride, with a naked sword in one hand and a list in the other, who turned back those beside whose name

144

was the black cross. I felt a holy mirth to view their indignation, and to hear their loud cries of 'Privilege!'

'Your privilege,' says Colonel Pride, 'is to go home, and those that will not, must be locked in the Court of Wards under a strong guard.'

By whose authority did he do this thing? they demanded. To which he answered short, I have orders. Those members suffered to remain, not at all approving this purgation, sent out the Mace to fetch their excluded colleagues, but says Colonel Pride to the Sergeant-at-Arms:

'You may take that pretty toy back where it belongs, for I have something here which is no toy, I warrant you,' brandishing his sword.

Next day our great Joshua returned to London and took up his lodging at Whitehall, lying in Charles Stuart's own bed. We the officers who had partaken with Colonel Pride in his purge, waited upon him and described our proceedings, whereat he wept bitterly, protesting that he had known nought of it, seeing that he was absent when it was done.

'My bowels,' saith he, 'are moved for these my good friends in the Parliament. But the interest of honest men is the interest of the nation, and those only are honest to whom the Lord shows favour.'

By which I understand him to mean that clearly the Lord had not shown favour to the majority of those who sat in the Commons' House.

Now would Joshua bestow a notable blessing on the City of London by making her the permanent quarters of the Saints. He demanded of her the sum of £40,000 in return for the favour that we refrain from plundering, to be given to us as part of our arrears of pay. Which money was very churlishly yielded, for the souls of the citizens were become so tanned with sin, even like a piece of neat's leather, that some presumed to murmur against us as we marched through the streets. They were a stiff-necked people, and the wrath of the Lord waxed hot against them, bold sons of Belial by the daughters of Anak, whose mouth was full of cursing. Yet would we return good for evil by requisitioning the Companies'

Halls and removing therefrom offensive and superstitious decoration, a blemish on the City and affrightment to the very heavens. Their steeple-houses we purged likewise, that they might become fit billets for our godly soldiers, and we stabled our horses in Paul's.

Ah, how I rejoiced to hear it said that all popish and profane trade signs would shortly be replaced by pious ones, the play-houses and bear-gardens closed, the maypoles burnt (which were nought but heathen images), and sundry ale-houses suppressed. For these taverns, saith Cromwell, are the very bane of the nation, because men indulge in lewd and disaffected talk over their ale. And weeping afresh, he said in my hearing:

'We grieve for this famous City of London, through which we marched only to let them see that their destruction (if they perish) will be of themselves, not us.'

And now like all the kings of Canaan when the Hosts of Israel had passed dryshod over Jordan, the hearts of both Parliament and City failed them, and those who did not flee, made submission. And we were ready to say with Joshua to Achan, Because thou has troubled us, the Lord trouble thee. For we knew that we could not possess the land in safety, nor stand against our enemies without, till we had stoned to death this new Achan, the Man of Sin.

In the Council of Officers (wherein I, being now a captain, had my seat) there was debate as how best we might please the Lord in dealing with him, and three factions emerged among us. The first would have him deposed and kept alive in a close prison, saying, he might afterwards be made use of. And his son could pretend no right while he lived. The more forward of the Saints, as Colonel Hewson and Major Harrison, would have his life taken by poison or such other way as would make the least noise. For which there were hands ready enough to be employed.

Cromwell liked not this, for, said he, it would come out, and even as the five kings of the Amorites leagued together when Jericho and its king were destroyed, so might the Kings of France and Spain aid Charles Stuart's son. To which answer made that the Hosts of Israel set their feet upon the necks of these five kings, and afterwards hanged them upon gibbets.

The third party carried it (whose principal was Commissary

146

Ireton), that he be brought to trial as a public malefactor, which would be most for the honour of Parliament, and would teach all kings to know that they were accountable and punishable for the wickedness of their lives. And, says Ireton, if he be tried and condemned in the name of the people, these should rest satisfied.

3

Secret Memoirs of Thomas Herbert

After Mr Harrington's dismissal, I bade defiance to my health by accompanying the King upon his exercise, for I could not in conscience permit that he be left without a companion, inconsiderable though I was. And marvellous to relate, I took no hurt from it.

Upon a morning in the second week of December, there fell one of those clammy sea-fogs so frequent here; and it was only by the crashing of feet through the shingle that we were aware of someone approaching. The intruder upon our promenade was Governor Ayers, who came to inform His Majesty of that outrage of all parliamentary privilege known as Pride's Purge. His glee made worse what he related, he exulting that this was but a further proof that God was on the side of the Army. Whereat the King replied, as to some child's boasting:

'The prosperous winds that oft fill the sails of pirates, do not justify their piracy, nor signify the approval of heaven. I am sure success can never prove the justice of any cause, for otherwise you must call those just who crucified our Saviour.'

When Ayers had taken himself off, I expressed to the King my horror and bewilderment. I supposed, said I, that this wanton violence must be intended to obstruct the Treaty of Newport, and I wondered much to see the Parliament so chastised by that military force they themselves had raised.

'Do you not perceive,' asked His Majesty, 'the real purpose in this forcible debarring of all in the Parliament who would make a treaty with me?'

'That the Army may dictate their own terms to you, Sir,' I ventured.

The mist obscured him from me, and it was as though a phantom spoke from it these fateful words:

'The Army intends my death.'

I drew near to him, all a-tremble, for I supposed he referred to those threats of secret murder which had constrained him to absent himself from Hampton Court. And truly, thought I, if so black a deed were contemplated, this isolated blockhouse, veiled so often in a vapour, and he with no attendants save myself, was a fit scene for it. But His Majesty, as it were musing aloud, continued:

'That I must die as a man is certain. That I may die a king by the hands of my own subjects, a violent, sudden and barbarous death, in the midst of my kingdoms, in the strength of my years, my friends and loving subjects being helpless spectators, my enemies insolent revilers and triumphers over me, is so probable in human reason that God has taught me not to hope otherwise as to man's cruelty.'

These words of his increased my terrors, and I began to weep. He smoothed my shoulder, begging me to take comfort, and saying:

'My long and sharp adversity, I thank God, has so reconciled me to those natural antipathies between life and death which are in all men, that the common terrors of it are dispelled, and the special horror of it much allayed. And truly my enemies have left me little of life, but only the husk and shell, which their further malice can take from me, for they have already slain me by piecemeal and bereaved me of all those earthly comforts for which life itself seems desirable to men. And in particular those comforts of dearest relations, which are as the very life of our lives.'

Yet speaking such sad words, he did not seem sad in himself, but as a man who meditated. Or rather I should say, as one who armed himself for some great conflict, since from this time forward I remarked a new strength and resolution in him. One fear alone he confessed he had not overcome, and that was of a sudden and secret attempt upon his person.

It was on the night of December 17th, near three weeks after our coming to Hurst, when I, asleep upon my pallet in the slit of

148

room which served as ante-chamber, was awakened by the ringing of my master's silver bell which, with his two watches, ever reposed beside his couch. When I hasted to obey the summons, I saw by the night-light the King sitting up, his head bent sideways as though he listened.

'I have heard,' says he, 'the grinding and clanking which accompanies the raising of the portcullis and the lowering of the drawbridge upon the landward side, and likewise the noise of a horse. It is an unseasonable hour for any man to ride hither, and I will dress, for I will not be surprised in my bed as I was at Newport.'

When I had assisted him to put on his clothes, he bade me endeavour to get news, and therefore I tapped upon the door, which was locked on the outside. The sentinel opening to me, I told him I must speak with Governor Ayers (though I confess I was mortally afraid of that desperado). I found him hunched over one of the fires in the vast circular apartment, smoking a foul pipe. Summoning my courage, I inquired of him who it was who had come to Hurst in the night-time. He snarled at me very rudely to mind my own business, withal reminding me how it had fared with Mr Harrington.

'I thank you, sir, for your friendly advice,' said I, much as one might seek to placate a wolf. 'But His Majesty has commanded me to inquire who has come and for what purpose.'

For a space he did but glower at me through his great bush of whisker, but at last says short that it was Major Harrison, the occasion of whose visit would be known speedily. Returning to the King with this information, I observed his features to sharpen, and he exclaimed:

'So it has come to this after all!' Then, seeing my blank looks, he said with more discomposure than I ever marked in him before or afterwards: 'Do you not know that this Harrison is one of those fanatics I was warned intended to assassinate me at Hampton Court? To my knowledge, I have never seen him in my life, nor did him any injury, but this is a fitter place than Hampton Court for such a crime. Herbert, I trust to your care; pray go and make further inquiries.'

Such trust lent me a desperate courage, and when I returned to Ayers I took a high hand with the ruffian. I was one appointed by the Parliament, I told him, to be responsible for His Majesty's safety, and it would go hard with me ere I failed in my charge. This time I brought His Majesty what I deemed to be good news; Harrison was come to remove him to Windsor, which had always been his favourite royal seat. He was silent a space, regarding me with an expression I could not interpret. And when at length he spoke, I was at a loss to understand him.

'I know well, Herbert,' says he, 'what this removal portends. That I may be destroyed, as with greater pomp and artifice, so with less pity, it will be but a necessary policy to make my death appear as an act of justice done by subjects upon their Sovereign, though they know that no law of God or man invests them with any judicial authority without me, much less against me.'

I would have made bold to beseech him lay by such fantastical fears, but there was no time to debate the matter. For now Major Harrison presented himself to say that he was ready to escort the King upon his road to Windsor. So for the last time we walked down that long spit of shingle to where a troop of horse was drawn up upon the mainland, with a coach for the King. We drove through the New Forest to Winchester where, though threatened with indictment for high treason, the Mayor and Aldermen came in their robes to greet His Majesty. And a great multitude of all sorts, dispossessed clergymen, country squires and mechanics, knelt in his path with loud cries of 'God bless you', and prayers for his safety.

That night we lay at Farnham, and the next day at my Lord Newburgh's house at Bagshott. Upon our last stage to Windsor, who should meet us but Mr Harrington, who, crying out with joy to see His Majesty, was being beckoned into the royal coach, when Major Harrison prevented it, unless Mr Harrington would pledge his oath not in any way to aid His Majesty, which he stoutly refusing, he was placed in custody. This I mention as an instance of that blind devotion which the King had the secret of attracting, even in hot republicans.

When we came to Windsor, the folk were not content to shout and pray for His Majesty, but fell to pelting his guards with brickbats and filth. Whereat the soldiers opened fire, killing several, and with my own ears I heard Harrison mock them, he who had been a butcher in civilian life, with:

'Bleat, bleat, foolish sheep!'

At our entrance to the castle, we found kneeling in the gate-house his Grace, the Duke of Hamilton, who had lain here a prisoner since he was captured after Preston-fight. Weeping so much that he could scarce articulate, he cried to the King:

'My dear, dear master!'

On which the King, tenderly embracing him, replied, not without that dry humour which on occasion salted his speech:

'I have been so indeed to you.'

More they would have spoken, but immediately were parted, for there were strict orders made that they should not be permitted to converse. His Majesty was lodged in his own apartments near the keep, looking across the valley of the Thames, his warder being Colonel Witchcote, an austere gentleman but courteous. During this first week, His Majesty enjoyed some shadow of his old pomp, being served on the knee, his chair of estate set up in the Presence, and the Assay, the testing of his food for poison, observed. But no chaplains were allowed him, and upon Christmas Day, arraying himself in his richest garments, he read the service of the Church of England to his attendants with great solemnity, having passed the forenoon in private prayer. How his enemies spent that festival, was shortly made known to him.

For on the morrow, when he was taking his favourite promenade along the terrace on the north side of the castle, myself being in attendance, there approached my noble kinsman, the Earl of Pembroke, who saith he had secret business to impart, but that I, being as he was pleased to call me, a gentleman of discretion, might remain to hear it. I am sorry to say that his lordship's breath gave evidence that he had been baiting the bombard, as the vulgar term hard drinking, but perhaps on this occasion it was to give himself Dutch-courage.

'It may be that Your Majesty has learned from the news-books,' began my lord, 'that upon the 20th of this month, Parliament re-affirmed the vote of Non-Addresses, and summarily quashed the whole of the Newport negotiations with Your Majesty.'

'Parliament?' the King repeated, whereat I saw my lord flush, for after Pride's Purge those few of the Commons who were permitted by the Army to retain their seats were often hard put to it to form a quorum, and by the common sort had been nicknamed the Rump.

'And yesterday,' my lord continued, 'the Commons appointed a Committee to consider how to proceed in a way of justice against Your Majesty.'

The King remarking, with sad humour, that it was a strange manner in which to celebrate the anniversary of our Saviour's birth, my lord began to hector, saying that His Majesty was blind to the danger he was in. For, says he, there was talk as if Parliament, or rather the Army Grandees who now ruled all, would set up a High Court of Justice to try His Majesty, which would be but a show, for they were already agreed upon a verdict. His Majesty seemed not at all astonished by so monstrous a device, but rather as if he had expected some such thing. Says he:

'These gentlemen seem ambitious to merit the name of my destroyers, imagining they then fear God most when they least honour the King, who alone has the right to appoint judges. The taking away of my character by a pretended trial, is but a necessary preparation to the taking away my life. First I must be made to appear to my subjects neither fit to reign nor worthy to live; by exquisite methods of cunning and cruelty, I must be compelled first to follow the funeral of my honour, and then be destroyed.'

Having spoken thus, he would have continued his promenade, but my lord followed him, and in a lowered voice disclosed that he had not come merely to warn His Majesty, but bore a confidential message from Cromwell who, saith he, more than any man in England, held His Majesty's life in the hollow of his hand.

'I'll speak blunt, Sir,' my lord went on. 'Cromwell is a great believer in the text, "All that a man hath he will give for his life". He durst not approach Your Majesty direct, lest he fall under suspicion of playing a double game, as he did at Hampton Court. But I am empowered by him to say to you that if you will make a virtue of necessity, you may have not only your life but your throne.'

His Majesty making no comment, my lord told him that in return for these favours, all he had to do was to give his consent to the

Heads of the Proposals offered him by the Army Grandees at Hampton Court. Then the King made answer instantly, in ringing tones:

'Rather than lend the prestige of the Crown to the rule of the sword and the ruin of the Church, I am content to die. I am well prepared to give my life as a sacrifice for my people's liberties. I thank God I have armed myself against the fury of desperate men; I have a breast to receive their arrows and a heart to sustain them with patience. And now, my lord, you have our leave to withdraw.'

Upon the very next day, Colonel Witchcote presented himself to His Majesty with glum looks, saying he had orders from the Parliament to purge the King's Household, take down the chair of estate in the Presence, and serve his meals standing. His Majesty bore these indignities with his wonted patience, and because he would not have his meat handed by soldiers with their caps on, ate in private, waited on by myself. He spoke little to me at this time, seeming much withdrawn into himself, and spending longer than usual at his devotions. I for my part took added care to set down whatsoever he was pleased to say to me; for though the notion of trying our Sovereign Lord was so monstrous and unparalleled that I could not believe it would ever come to pass, yet I could not but be aware that some dread crisis was approaching.

I had the boldness to say to His Majesty that the offer conveyed to him by my Lord Pembroke was a thing inexplicable to me; whereat the King smiled, and said that he for his part understood it very well.

'Pluck off the pious vizard Mr Cromwell wears,' says he, 'and you will see a man exceeding shrewd. He knows that if I am done to death, it is his forehead that will bear the brand of Cain; and that for the remainder of his own life he will have reason to fear vengeance by a private hand or invasion from abroad, where happily my two elder sons are safe out of his reach. Thus will he be obliged to expose himself to all the world as a mere military despot, and tax an already exhausted kingdom to maintain his armies at full strength.'

Anent the taking away of his royal state, he said but this:

'I have oft been told how my grandmother, the Queen of Scots, was deprived in the same manner of all regal ceremony after sentence of death had been pronounced upon her. Yet in my own case, it seems they cannot stay for such formal sentence.'

In all which words, His Majesty seemed never to doubt that he would be done to death by his own subjects.

4

Diary of Colonel Jack Ashburnham

December 28th, 1648. Desperate to be near H.M., I ventured over from Holland last night, and find London as infested with red-coats as a dog with fleas. The damnable cheap dye I bought to disguise myself has turned my hair the colours of the rainbow, so am fain to heat my head with a periwig and pass as a Frenchman. Went to Fulham, where I thought to lodge with Bishop Juxon who, strange to relate, is permitted still to reside in his palace, though the Church of England is pulled down about his ears. They say it is because he is so holy a man, but I would say rather he is liker a sheep than a shepherd.

'God save me, sir!' he bleated, 'I cannot harbour you here, for you are one of those exempt from pardon.'

He warned me that I lay naked to the spite of any man who chose to bring an information against me, and that the town was full of spies, but I answered that I was ever ready to try for a hanging, so I might serve H.M. God pity him! they say he has none about him now but soldiers and the lickspigots of the Army. Have hired a lodging in Jackanapes Yard on the south side of Fleet Street, whence I may retreat into the sanctuary of Alsatia among the bullies and the cut-throats if the hunt for me grows hot. I design to contact those of the honest party who lurk up and down the liberties, and from them hear such intelligence as is not to be found in the hackney railing pamphlets and licensed news-books. Already I learn that one, Dr Hackluyt, a dispossessed clergyman, contrives still to print his *Mercurius Melancholicus,* though 'tis often suppressed.

154

Today that heap of nastiness, the Rump, passed an ordinance setting up a High Court of Justice, if you please, to try our Sovereign Lord, belching forth most abominable lies and accusations. This new monstrous language puts all men at a stand, nor can we imagine a way to oppose a crime so hellish. The common sort perceive too late that the sceptre is exchanged for the sword, there being scarce a house in the City not lousy with redcoats.

December 29th. The arse-parliament is mortified at the outset. For the Judges named to preside over this mockery of a court have refused, though hitherto but tame enough, pronouncing the ordinance to be totally illegal. Likewise did Mr Elsing, Clerk to the House since 1640, straightway resign in disgust. From *The Moderate Intelligencer* (a presbyterian sheet, writ by a tailor named Dillingham), I learn that there was an unexpectedly hot debate upon the ordinance, even this half-quarter parliament having objectors within it. Then did Cromwell arise and speak thus:

'If any man hath carried on the design of deposing the King and disinheriting his posterity, he should be the greatest rebel and traitor in the world. But since the providence of God has cast this upon us, I cannot but submit to His will.'!

January 1st, 1649. Their damnable ordinance sent up to the things called Lords who, though ordinarily nowadays they number but seven, assembled to the strength of fifteen. The Speaker, Lord Denbigh, said he would be torn in pieces ere he consented to so unlawful a measure, and it was unanimously rejected. But they, like a French skirmish, are fiery in the onset but very tame in the retreat, for immediately they adjourned and scuttled away into the country. All this vexing to his high devilship, Cromwell, and not made sweeter when, according to the news-books, twenty out of the forty-six Rumpers declined to sit in his mock court.

January 4th. Damme, I begin to hope that their High Court of Injustice will be still-born. They named a hundred and fifty persons to compose it, yet the most, from fear or conscience, have refused. I find that few among the common people credit that it is anything more than an insubstantial pageant, designed to strike terror in H.M. and bring him to grant the Army's demands.

The Rump forced to desperate straits, this day resolved, 'That by the fundamental laws of this kingdom, it is treason for the King to levy war against the Parliament and people of England. That all just power originates in the people, and that the Commons of England are thereby invested with all sovereign authority to pass any laws they choose without consent of King or Lords.' Whereupon they padlocked the door of the Peers' Chamber; and I hear some wag has chalked upon it, 'This House to let. For permission to enter apply to the Army.'

January 5th. My hopes are cuckolded. For having established single chamber government at their pleasure, the Rump have turned their fiendish ordinance into an Act, with a most scurrilous preamble wherein H.M.'s guilt is taken for granted and his condign punishment explicitly provided for. They have found it necessary to lop down their Court of Injustice from a hundred and fifty to a hundred and thirty-five, nominating 'godly men' promiscuously, which will prove in effect, the Army officers and a raff of nobodies who may hope to gain preferment by accepting.

'Tis clear the licensed news-books have received orders to blacken H.M. and make him odious to the common sort. As for example, this from *The Army's Faithful Scout* (writ by that trumpet of sedition, Henry Walker, once arraigned for high treason but pardoned by our too clement master): 'The King is cunningly merry. We find his discourse of late very effeminate and talking much of women, which he is sure for the most part to bring in at the end of every subject.'

My eyes weep blood for my poor master. The young Princess Elizabeth is reported to be sick with grief at Syon House, and he not permitted to see her. And likewise is he debarred from all correspondence with her who has been the cause of most of our troubles, I mean his wife on whom he dotes too much.

5

Letter from the Queen to the French Ambassador in London

The Louvre. January 6th, 1649.

Monsieur de Grignan, the state to which my lord the King is reduced has brought me to the resolution of imploring from the two Houses and the General Fairfax, passports to go to him in London, my only desire being to die for him, or at least with him, nor can I live without being restored to his side.

I dare not promise myself that they will accord me the liberty of coming, though I have humbled myself in the dust in my letters to them; I wish it too much to assure myself of it at a time when so little of what I desire succeeds. But if by your negotiations these passports can be obtained, I shall deem myself beholden to you till my last hour.

I have promised the Parliament not to bring with me any that may be suspected or obnoxious. In truth, my present destitution is such that I must beg from M. le Cardinal the charges for my own journey. I am obliged to keep my little daughter Henriette in bed for warmth, since our last faggot has been burned. Were it not for a surprise visit of M. de Retz, my good old friend, we had not eaten today.

M. l'Ambassadeur, I write to you upon my knees, not as a queen, nor yet as the daughter of Henri le Grand, but as a wife upon whom this dreadful hour is closing in. For the love of Jesu, help me. I shall add no more except to assure you that I am the most miserable woman in the world, Henriette Marie, R.

6

Mercurius Melancholicus (unlicensed)

January 8th–17th, 1649.

Before I come to intelligence, take note that I got into St Margaret's on Sunday last, when twenty of the Commons came to see Hugh Peters play the buffoon in the pulpit, they being quite hemmed in by the redcoats, some of whom squatted on the pulpit steps. Hugh would not be tied to a text, but began upon Moses leading the Israelites out of Egypt, which he applied to the Army Grandees whose design, said he, is to lead the people from kingly bondage.

'But how must this be done?' quoth our jack-pudding. And then clapping his hands before his eyes and leaning his noddle on the cushion, he lay in a brown study for half a quarter of an hour. Then starting up on a sudden, 'Now,' says he, 'I'll tell you what hath been revealed to me. There is no way for us to get out of Egypt than by rooting up monarchy, and this, I say, not only here, but in France and the other kingdoms about us, the Lord having a great work to finish throughout Christendom, and this Army are they that must do it.'

Then skipping through his bible, he began on a fresh tack.

'It is a very sad thing,' says he, 'that this should be a question among us, as amongst the old Jews, whether our Saviour Jesus Christ must be crucified or that Barabbas, the oppressor of the people, should be released. But I tell you, it is a question. I have been in the City, which may be compared to Jesusalem at this conjuncture of time, and I protest those foolish citizens, for a little trading and profit, will have Christ' (pointing to the redcoats) 'crucified, and this great Barabbas at Windsor released.'

After which, embracing and kissing those soldiers who sat upon the pulpit stair, he fell upon his knees and groaned:

'Oh Jesus! what shall we do now? Noble gentlemen of the House of Commons, you are the Sanhedrin, the grand council of the nation, therefore you must be sure to do justice, and it is from you we expect it. Do not prefer the vile Barabbas, murderer, tyrant and traitor, before these poor hearts, who are our saviours, who have the precious name Emmanuel writ upon the bridles of their horses.'

With other such expressions and antics, fitter for a playhouse stage than a pulpit.

Now for intelligence. The Lord General Fairfax sent the Queen's letter requesting passports to the Parliament, who would not so much as open it, nor that which Her Majesty addressed to the two Speakers, because so long ago as 1643 they had voted her guilty of high treason.

A list published of those who have accepted to sit in the High Court of Justice, who yet fall far short of the hundred and thirty-five named. Many are kin to Mr Cromwell, the rest fanatic colonels or corrupt adventurers. As Michael Livesey, nicknamed Plunder-Master of Kent, Sir Thomas Mauleverer, a convicted horse-thief, Henry Marten, justly termed by His Majesty that ugly whore-monger, Gregory Clement, a merchant who lined his pockets with £40,000 entrusted to him by the Parliament, and other such fit to make up a rogues' gallery. Even Mr Sidney, a hot republican, and likewise Sir Harry Vane, who hath spoken openly that the King should be deposed, have refused to sit among such raff. I have it from a gentleman of credit who was present in the Painted Chamber during their deliberations, that Mr Sidney told them blunt:

'The King can be tried by no court. No man can be tried by this court.'

Whereat Cromwell in a fury replied:

'I tell you, we will cut off the King's head with the crown upon it.'

They have been upon debate whether they would have both the Sword and the Mace when they come to the trial in Westminster Hall, and resolved to have both upon the table (albeit the Mace still bears the Royal Arms), since the Sword alone would betray their true character. For the Great Seal, they have made a new one, whereon is pictured the House of Commons only, and the legend, *The first year of freedom by God's blessing restored*. An acquaintance of mine, taking his morning draught in the Hell tavern at Westminster, wondered aloud how they could use the word 'restored'. Mr Marten being by, says he in his ribald fashion:

'There is a text in Scripture which has often troubled me, concerning the man who was blind from his mother's womb, but at length his sight was restored to the sight which he should have had.'

Upon the 9th, one Edward Denby, appointed their Sergeant-at-Arms (though if rumour lies not, the only arms he hath ever used heretofore are pistols to hold up men upon the highway), rode into Westminster Hall escorted by six trumpets and a troop of horse, to proclaim the setting-up of the High Court of Justice; and in the afternoon performed the same ceremony in Cheapside, the people hearkening in silence with glum faces.

Next day, those in the Painted Chamber shrank to forty-five, though all those named and residing within twenty miles of London, have received peremptory summons to attend. We hear they have appointed four counsel, two of whom straightway sent excuses that they were sick. Of the others, Isaac Dorislaus is a Dutchman and a renegado, who once held office under the Crown, and John Cook, an ancient man, is fitter to wear the Tyburn-tippet than the long robe, he having twice fled the kingdom to avoid criminal charges. They would have some great man to be Lord President, but finding none, are fain to appoint Mr John Bradshawe, who was never a member of Parliament nor yet heard of outside a townlet in the North where he was mayor. But he is high in the esteem of our present masters, because in a speech delivered to the jury at Chester last June, he declared that, 'This man, who calls himself King, is more cruel than Nero.'

On the 12th, no more than thirty-eight, and Cromwell in a passion. Bradshawe came, and is given the Dean's house in Westminster for himself and his posterity, with the confiscated estates of the Lord Cottington to maintain his new pomp. Yet it seems that though much puffed-up with his pre-eminence, he forgets not his safety, demanding a military bodyguard wheresoever he goes. And a milliner of my acquaintance tells me, he has received from President Bradshawe an order for a new fashion in hats, *viz.* one bullet-proof of iron, covered with black velvet, which I fear will cause the learned noddle to ache.

By dint of threats, the number in the Painted Chamber rose to fifty-eight upon the 15th, so now they debate the charge, Major Harrison, he that was a butcher, and Lieutenant-Colonel Axtell, a grocer's prentice ere he put on the red coat, beseeching counsel to blacken His Majesty all they could. Who I believe need no urging.

This day, the 17th, a pill without sugar presented to the Lord General (who is but Cromwell's stalking-horse) in the shape of a protest signed by the ministers of fifty-eight London parishes. They refrain not from telling what threats they have received to make them concur with the pretended High Court, not from his Excellency but from officers speaking in his name. And despite the close censorship, I have it on good authority that they are resolved to get their protest printed.

These be the presbyterian preachers who sounded the trumpet loudest through the war, but who preach now as furiously against all wicked attempts and violence upon the person of the King, urging the obligation of the Solemn League and Covenant (by which they have involved him in all the danger he is in), since those who subscribed it swore to defend the King's person and authority.

7

Secret Memoirs of Thomas Herbert

Throughout the first half of January, His Majesty stayed as much cut off from the world as at Hurst. Yet they not at all suspecting me to have any kindness for him, I was permitted upon occasion to go into the town, where to my great astonishment I met with Mr Firebrace, who told me he had a little company about him of such as had done their best endeavours to succour His Majesty when he was in the Wight. As Mrs Whorwood, Babbington the barber, one Dowcett who was some time of his kitchen, and several more.

I was in a fret lest they sought to entangle me in complots, but found they had quite despaired of spiriting the King away, being concerned now only to convey to him such intelligence as they learned from the unlicensed news-books. They much lamented that *Mercurius Melancholicus*, a royalist sheet, was suppressed again, yet its author, Dr Hackluyt, contrived to hide his printing-press and purposed to appear under the new guise of *Mercurius Pragmaticus*. Mr Firebrace would have me carry such news-books to the King, but I durst not do it, for there was a new proclamation made by the Parliament thus:

'Every person that buys an unlicensed book or pamphlet whatsoever, though but a sheet of paper, is to pay his fine, 40/- a piece. And every person who presumes to print without the *imprimatur* of the licenser is hereby warned that the penalty is imprisonment.'

Therefore I disclosed to the King by word of mouth such news as Mr Firebrace and his friends gave me. When I told him that Her Majesty had entreated Parliament that she might come over to him, but had been refused, he exclaimed:

'I thank God for their cruel kindness, which ensures my wife's safety!' And weeping, turned away his head.

On the morning of January 19th, who should come to Windsor but that same Major Thomlinson, now a colonel, who had been second-in-command of the garrison at Holmby. He was of the Old Model Army, who were for the most part gently bred, whereas those of the New Model were like beggars on horseback, leapt up from keeping an alehouse tap, or cobblers, night-soilmen, and such like. Colonel Thomlinson saluted the King very courteously, and informed him that a coach-and-six stayed below to carry him to St James's, I being still permitted to attend him. 'Twas plain that Cromwell was in a fret lest the common sort made tumults, for our coach was encompassed by a strong force of soldiers and we drove on the whip through Brentford and Hammersmith. A gentleman happening to glimpse His Majesty through the window doffed his hat, and was thrown by the redcoats, horse and all, into the ditch.

On arrival at St James's, His Majesty found himself subjected to a new and most vile persecution, namely, that of sentries intruded into his bedchamber both day and night, as if he were some felon in the Condemned Hold at Newgate. Colonel Thomlinson abhorred it, but it was Colonel Hacker, and not he, who commanded here, and who insisted that he had received such orders and must observe them. Yet so jealous was he of these his janizaries, lest they be wrought upon, as so many of his party had been by the influence of that innocent prince, that he caused the guards to be changed constantly, the same men never suffered twice to perform the same monstrous duty.

His Majesty would neither undress nor go to bed under such rude surveillance, but sat in an armchair beside the fire, and I do not think he closed his eyes during that bitter night. As for me, I brought my pallet into the bedchamber in case there was aught I could do for His Majesty's easement, but alack there was nothing, for I could not even prevail with the soldiers to forbear smoking their pipes, though I told them that tobacco was a weed the King particularly detested.

After dinner next day, in comes Colonel Thomlinson, who raged against Hacker's treatment of the King, but His Majesty excused it in these words:

'He is one of those, common in armies, who understands nothing but to carry out his orders, and this blind obedience, rather than malice, makes him put such odious restraints upon me.'

Then Thomlinson disclosed that he must now carry His Majesty in a sedan-chair across the Park to Whitehall, whence he was to go by water to Westminster Hall. The King smiled and said, he would hazard a guess that this route had been picked upon to avoid demonstrations in his favour. But if that were so, his enemies were disappointed; for when we stepped into the barge at the Privy-stair, we saw the river almost filled with boats, wherein men and women cried and prayed for the King. The very watermen who rowed the barge refused to keep their caps on, though threatened sore by mad Hugh Peters who, wearing the George and Garter he had stolen from his Grace of Hamilton, came with us in the role of high priest about to offer sacrifice.

'Your idol won't stand long,' he bawled to the people. 'We'll whisk him away, I warrant you, now we have him. He shall die the death of a traitor by order of a court which all must look upon with reverence, for it doth resemble the court of Saints that shall judge the world.'

I knew not whether to be more affronted by his profanity or

shocked by his shameless admission that verdict had been passed before trial. For the people, all they answered was, 'God save and bless the King', with dolorous sighs and lamentations. And had it not been that he was encompassed by barges filled with redcoats, I verily believe the folk would have snatched His Majesty away.

We landed at the water-gate of Cotton House, which forms part of the Palace of Westminster, where we stayed till the court was ready to sit. And here I must record what I learned afterwards from an acquaintance of mine, Sir Purback Temple, a worthy gentleman. He, having bribed the custodian of the Painted Chamber to secrete him in a space behind the arras there, was witness to what fell out when the King landed. Those assembled were debating hot as to whether or no they would permit His Majesty to keep his hat on in Westminster Hall, when there sounded through the window a roar of voices shouting, 'God save Your Majesty!' At which Cromwell ran to the casement, looking down upon the King as he walked through the gardens. Sir Purback, peeping at Cromwell through a hole in the hangings, told me he turned as white as the wall, and cries he to the others:

'My masters, he is come, he is come! And now we are to do that great work that the nation will be full of. Therefore I desire you to let us resolve here what answer we shall give the King when he comes before us, for the first question he will ask us will be, by what authority we do try him.'

To which none made answer presently. Then, after a little pause, Henry Marten rose up and said:

'In the name of the Commons in Parliament assembled, and all the good people of England.'

There were divers made objections, one, whom Sir Purback could not see from his concealment, demanding how they could rationally answer thus, seeing that they had pulled out the majority of the Commons on purpose to bring His Majesty to trial. And for the people, were they not at this precise moment acclaiming the King? But there being no further time for debate, they were fain to rest satisfied.

8

Diary of Colonel Jack Ashburnham

January 20th, 1649. These three days past I have flitted up and
down among the King's friends in London to try if we could not hit
upon some device for rescuing H.M. But find them sunk in despair,
they saying it is better to be quiet than busy to so little advantage.
And in truth I must confess that all honest men are become like oxen
shackled in the slaughter-house, unable to stir. Yet I resolved to get
into Westminster Hall, that at least H.M. may see not all his friends
have forsaken him and fled.

Were I not so sick at heart, I could make merry with the searching and double searching of the vaults beneath the Hall last night,
with what guards they set upon the leads and at every window, and
ten foot companies constantly patrolling. The public interest, which
is for ever on their vile tongues, and in which they profess to be
acting, is quite plainly not to the public taste.

I having well oiled the palm of the fellow who keeps Bodurdo's
gallery on the right side of the Hall, came thither early to get a good
seat, observing among the company several masked ladies, of whom
more anon. The vipers had been at great pains to stage this hellish
farce with pomp and pageantry, that they might cozen the populace
into deeming it a true High Court of Justice, what with crimson-
covered benches for the Commissioners, and a raised chair of velvet
for their little puppet Bradshawe, Lord President. But the effect
spoiled by the multitude of redcoats, who were musketeers under the
command of Daniel Axtell, of Hewson's regiment, that shitten
knave himself, a one-eyed cobbler, being among the judges, if you
please.

Scarce had I taken my seat, when those fiends who were to be
both judge and jury entered by the southern door in pompous state.
Bless me, they reminded me of nothing so much as the boys who
used to loiter round the door of the playhouses, in the hope that the
stage-manager, being short in his hirelings, would invite them to

'Come and be a devil', and so they might see the play for nothing by walking on. These rogues had gotten themselves pikes of cere-monial length from the Tower, who marched under the command of Colonel Fox, a tinker by trade, and there was a rout of bare-headed messengers, ushers and clerks. I was fain to stuff my fist into my mouth lest I guffawed at the sight of Bradshawe, all spruce in a new black satin gown held up by train-bearers, yet so incommoded by his bullet-proof hat that he could scarce turn his noddle.

Much confusion when the sixty-seven pitiful sottish beasts should choose their seats upon the benches, for there ought to have been a hundred and thirty-five. I marvel they did not go out into the highways and hedges and compel beggars to come and keep the benches warm. The common sort not yet admitted, but could be heard clamouring outside the north door. When the crier had made an Oyez for silence, their pestilent commission was read, after which there was a roll-call, each rogue to rise and answer to his name.

Now here fell out an incident which certainly will be omitted in their muzzled news-books. 'Tis clear the crier had been instructed to hasten on to the next name after he had pronounced that of the Lord General Fairfax, since it is well known that he has refused to have any part in the hellish business, and skulks in his house in Lincoln's Inn Fields. But ere the crier could speak the next name, a woman's voice in the front of the gallery wherein I sat said loudly:

'Not such a fool as to be here today, nor ever will be.'

I never thought to bless a she-rebel, for so this lady is, being none other than Fairfax's wife. She was of a very noble extraction, one of the daughters of Horace, Lord Vere; but having been bred in Holland, she had not that reverence for the King as she ought to have had, and so unhappily concurred in her husband's entering into rebellion, never imagining what misery it would bring upon the realm. But now, it seems, she abhors the work in hand, and has done all she can to hinder her husband from acting any part in it. As for him, out of the stupidity of his soul he has been all along out-witted by Cromwell, and made a property to bring that to pass which could very hardly have been otherwise effected.

Would I had the pen of a Shakespeare that I might describe the result of her words! Bradshawe gobbled like a turkey-cock, while all his colleagues looked like so many bladders suddenly pricked. I could hear them whispering, what was to be done? They could scarce arrest the wife of their Lord General. I suppose their one comfort was, the common folk were not there to say Amen to her words. She, having made her protest, solved their problem for them by sallying forth from the gallery with her female friends.

Then did one Denby, their Sergeant-at-Arms, endeavour to pick up the Mace that he might fetch H.M. from Cotton House. But whether it was his guilt overcame him, I know not; at any rate he trembled so much that he near dropped the Mace, and Fox and his pikemen were sent in his stead. When I saw my dear master enter from the Cloisters, my vision blurred with tears, and for a while he was hidden from me.

I was ever more ready with the sword than the quill, yet if I had the prettiest pen that ever walked on paper, I could not worthily describe how he looked. He wore that plain dark dress he ever affected, though rich in stuff, with the blue ribbon of the Garter on his breast and the Star embroidered on his cloak. His hair and beard, all grey, were neatly trimmed, and he was hatted. His expression neither wrathful nor sad, but stern enough, and his step as brisk as ever. From the outset he was careful not in any way to recognize the pretended court, making no bow to Bradshawe, though before I wept I had observed him incline his head most courteously to Colonel Thomlinson who brought him to the door.

Nor was he in any haste to be seated but, appearing perfectly at his ease where all were a-fidget, he surveyed the scene, with a slight raise of his eyebrows at the massed redcoats, and a keen glance from face to face along the crimson benches. Most there were unknown to him, and I'll swear the villains were glad that it was so, they being intent on regicide and the Prince of Wales safe overseas. By H.M.'s pallor and under-shadowed eyes I guessed he had not slept, and now have learnt the devilish reason for it, they intruding their hell-hounds into his bedchamber. Yet truly I have never seen him more composed, nay, not when he entertained foreign envoys in this very Hall in the days of his prosperity.

I had brought my tablets with me, resolved to write down what passed, for I knew there would be much left out of the printed accounts. After H.M. had seated himself in an armchair set within a kind of dock, and another Oyez made, Bradshawe opened thus, being somewhat flustered, I suspect, by the strong echo which there is in the Hall:

'Charles Stuart, King of England, the Commons of England in Parliament assembled, being sensible of the evils and calamities that have been brought upon this nation, and of the innocent blood that has been shed, which is fixed upon you as the principal author of it, have resolved to make inquisition for this blood, and according to the debt they owe to God, the kingdom and themselves, and according to that fundamental power that is vested in them by the people, to bring you to trial and judgment. Therefore they have set up this High Court of Justice, where you are now to hear your charge, upon which the court will proceed according to justice.'

Then Cook, one of their counsel, offered the charge to the clerk to read, but H.M. having, it seemed, somewhat to say in reply to Bradshawe, touched the attorney gently on the shoulder with his walking-cane. Whereupon the silver head of the cane fell off and rolled upon the floor, which made me shudder as at an ill omen. None of those mannerless oafs offering to retrieve it, H.M. himself stooped, and placed it in his pocket. *Nota bene*. There is a rumour buzzed wherein the wretch Hugh Peters is said to have tampered with the cane in order to discompose H.M. But if so, his malice missed its mark.

The charge I will not set down at length, a most tedious gallimaufry, its author being sure to use ten words where one would have sufficed, and to drag in constantly the refrain 'in the name and on behalf of the people of England', whose clamour for admittance, by the by, intermixed with lusty shouts of 'God save the King', was like to have drowned the oration. I observed H.M. to smile when he was accused of leaguing with a foreign power, by which they meant Duke Hamilton and his Scottish loyalists. The impudence! when twice has Parliament intrigued with the Scots to invade this realm, and once openly invited them.

The uproar without growing so furious that there was danger folk might storm the doors, they were at length admitted, but could see little because of the ranks of redcoats hemming them in on every

168

hand. Directly H.M. began to speak, they grew as quiet as mice. And here I must note a curious thing, remarked on by all: that his life-long impediment in speech seemed altogether to have left him, and he spoke with perfect ease and fluency. In what he said, he made clear from the outset the stand he was resolved to take, which was to expose this High Court in its true colours. Thus he spoke:

'First I would know by what authority I am called hither before I will give answer.' (I observed Cromwell, who sat at Bradshawe's side, beat one fist into the other palm, as though this were just what he had feared.) 'I was not long ago in the Isle of Wight, where I entered into a treaty with the two Houses of Parliament. Now I would know by what authority (I mean lawful, for there be many unlawful powers in the world, robbers on the highway and pirates at sea) I was carried thence, and was since brought from place to place till I came here. That I would fain know.'

Bradshawe replied pert that if H.M. had listened to the charge he would have known that it was by the authority of the Commons in Parliament assembled, on behalf of the people of England by whom he was elected King. Which stupid lie H.M. rebutted by reminding him that England had been an hereditary kingdom for near these thousand years. Then said he sternly to the rest of the villains:

'Remember I am your King, your anointed King, and what sin you bring upon your heads by these illegal proceedings. Think well upon it, I say, before you go from one sin to a greater. I have a trust committed to me by God, the which I never will betray. I am entrusted with the liberties of my people, and I do stand more for those liberties than any one who is seated here to be a judge. There-fore show me by what lawful authority I am brought here, and I will answer it.'

Immediately there was a great shout raised by the multitude in the body of the Hall, praying God to save him. The which so enraged Bradshawe that he shed his pomposity and screeched aloud like a departing pig:

'Whether you have not betrayed your trust will appear when you have given answer to the charge. Instead of answering, you inter-rogate this high tribunal, not stirring your hat to them, which does not become you in your condition.'

169

H.M. altogether ignored such insolence, but pointing with his headless cane to Colonel Cobbett who sat among the judges, saith:

'There is a gentleman can witness I came from the Isle of Wight by force. I do not come here as submitting to an usurped power. I will stand for the privilege of Parliament, rightly understood, as any man here whatsoever. But I see no House of Lords present; I see not a quarter of the Commons; and the King – call you this bringing him to his Parliament? Therefore let me see a legal authority, warranted either by Scripture or by the known laws and Constitution of this realm, and I will answer it.'

Bradshawe descending to base threats, as that if H.M. would not acknowledge the authority of the court they would proceed to what he misnamed justice, the King disdained to take any notice of him, but raised his voice as it were for the benefit of his poor subjects who were cut off from him by the soldiery, saying:

'I desire that you will give me satisfaction in this, for let me tell you it is not mere power that will settle the business of the kingdom. If you proceed by an usurped authority, it will not stand long, and there is a God in heaven will call you to account for it. I do avow it is as great a sin to submit to a tyrannical or any other way unlawful authority, as to withstand a legal one. Wherefore, satisfy God and me and all the world in that, and you shall receive my answer.'

Upon which there was another lusty shout raised for him by the common sort, though threatened by the redcoats to be turned out of the Hall if they would not keep silent. Because of this uproar, I missed somewhat that was said, but I believe Bradshawe spoke to the effect that their purpose was to adjourn until Monday, and that the court affirmed its own authority. H.M.'s reply I heard, which was this-wise:

'I wish for nothing but the bringing of the ship of State to shore when you have cast me overboard; though it is very strange that mariners can find no other way to appease the storm they themselves have raised than by drowning their pilot. But merely to say you have lawful authority will satisfy no reasonable man.'

Bradshawe calling on tinker Fox and his pikemen to withdraw the prisoner, H.M. immediately corrected him with 'The King!'.

170

And as he went away in the midst of his guard, he pointed to the Sword lying on the table, saying with a noble contempt:

'I do not fear that!'

A solemn fast ordered for tomorrow, wherein these self-canonized saints are to seek the Lord, as they blasphemously phrase it, concerning what they name 'God and the kingdom's business'. By which they mean they are for fortifying their spite by hearing the most fiery of their rabbis interpret the Scriptures according to their own giddy minds.

H.M. escorted back to St James's, the people still crying for him, but so strong a guard about his chair that I was not able to exchange word or look with my beloved master.

9

The Moderate Intelligencer (licensed)

Week beginning January 21st.

Three sermons preached this Sabbath in the Chapel Royal at Whitehall (now cleansed of all superstitious ornament), each of an hour's duration, before the Commissioners of the High Court of Justice. Master Hugh Peters mounted the pulpit last, taking as his text, 'To bind their kings in chains', and waxing somewhat wrathful for that he had prepared this sermon to preach to the King at James's, but could not come at him. Says Mr Peters:

'There is a very remarkable passage in Amos. Amos went to preach to Amazia, and Amazia would not let him, yet Amos would preach. I went to preach to the poor wretch, Charles Stuart, and the poor wretch would not hear me, yet lo, here am I preaching in his own chapel.'

Monday, 22nd, the Commissioners met in the Painted Chamber, being sixty-two, who sent down to the Commons' House to command in more. But answer returned that they had not in the chamber the forty required to form a quorum, and so an order given to remove some of the benches in Westminster Hall. After roll-call there, the crier made proclamation for silence on pain of imprisonment, because of the great noise of the people thronging in. Notwithstanding this, at the King's coming a huge shout raised, so that the crier must repeat his proclamation.

The King looked sick, he not having been abed these three nights past, by reason of his dislike of soldiers in his chamber.

Mr Solicitor Cook opened shortly, saying his humble motion to this High Court, in behalf of the people of England, was that the prisoner at the bar be directed to give his positive answer to the charge, either by way of confession or negation. Which, if he should refuse to do, that the matter of charge be taken *pro confesso* and the court proceed to justice. Take what followeth verbatim:

Bradshawe: Sir, you may remember at the last sitting of this court, you were pleased to make some scruples as that you knew not by what authority you were brought here. The court has since that time taken into their serious consideration what you then said, and they are fully satisfied with their authority, and they hold it fit that you should be satisfied therewith too. Their authority they avow to the whole world, and the whole kingdom is to rest satisfied with it. Sir, the court expects that you apply yourself to the charge not to lose any more time, but to give a positive answer thereto.

The King: Sir, if it were only my own particular case, I would have contented myself with the protestation I made the first time I was here, against the legality of the court. But it is not my case alone, it is the freedom of the people of England which is at stake. For if power without law may make law, may alter the fundamental laws of the kingdom, I do not know what subject he is in England can be assured of his life or anything he may call his own. And therefore when I came here today, I did expect particular reasons to know by what authority you do proceed against me. Yet since I cannot persuade you to it, I shall tell you my own reasons, as short as I can, why in conscience I cannot answer till I be satisfied with the legality of this court. All proceedings against any man whatsoever——

(Here the prisoner was interrupted by the Lord President, according to directions given beforehand in the Painted Chamber.)

Bradshawe: Sir, you are about the entering into disputes concerning the authority of this court before whom you are charged as a high delinquent. You may not do it. It is not agreeable to the proceedings of any court of justice, as those who are acquainted with the law are well aware.

The King: Sir, by your favour, I do not know the forms of law, being no lawyer professed, yet I know as much of the fundamental laws of this kingdom as any gentleman within it. And being the guardian of those laws, I cannot see them overturned without demur. If I should impose on any man a belief, without reasons given for it, it were unreasonable; and it is not my opinion, nor yours neither, that ought to decide on the legality of this court, but the known laws of the land. Thus I must tell you why I cannot yield unto——

Bradshawe: I must again interrupt you. It is fit there should be law and reason, and there are both in these proceedings. The vote of the Commons of England in Parliament assembled——

(Here one of the infatuated multitude cried saucily that Colonel Pride had cut down the Commons to a bare rump. Who was taken in charge by the soldiers, according to the crier's proclamation. Much tumult, so that what the King said next was hard to be heard, but it was concerning the right of any man to put in a demurrer.)

Bradshawe: Sir, you have offered something to the court, as that to demur against any proceedings is legal. Sir, I must let you know the mind of the court. They overrule your demurrer. You dispute their authority; but let me tell you, we sit here by the authority of the Commons of England, who have called your ancestors, even the greatest of them, to account.

The King: Show me one precedent.

Bradshawe: Sir, you ought not to interrupt when the court is speaking to you.

The King: I say, sir, by your favour, that the Commons of England were never a court of judicature. I would know how they came to be so.

Bradshawe: You are not to be permitted to go on in these discourses. Clerk, demand an answer.

(Which the clerk did, according to directions given in the Painted Chamber, if the King fell upon that way of debate. But all the King would reply was that he would answer as soon as he was satisfied by what authority the court sat. Whereupon the Lord

President commanded those who had brought him hither to conduct him away again.)

The King: I do require that I give in my reasons why I cannot answer, and give me time for that.

Bradshawe: It is not for prisoners to require.

The King: Sir, I am not an ordinary prisoner.

Bradshawe: Sir, your reasons are not to be heard against the highest jurisdiction in the kingdom who have convened this court. Sergeant-at-Arms, take away the prisoner.

The King: Show me that highest jurisdiction where reason is not to be heard.

Bradshawe: Sir, we show it you here, the Commons of England.

(Which answer caused several Malignants who sat in the galleries to presume to laugh.)

Bradshawe: Sir, you are not to have freedom to use such language as today you have done. How great a friend you have been to the laws and liberties of the people, let all England and the world judge. The next time you are brought here, you will hear more of the pleasure of the court, and it may be their final determination. Sergeant-at-Arms, take away the prisoner.

The King: Well, sir, remember that the King is not at liberty to give in his reasons for the laws and liberties of his subjects.

(At which the ignorant multitude made another *huzza* for him.)

Bradshawe: Clerk, read the default and the contempt. The prisoner is remanded, and this court does adjourn itself till to-morrow at twelve of the clock in the Painted Chamber. Sergeant-at-Arms, will you take away the prisoner!

At his going away, Colonel Hewson sprang from the bench wheron he sat, crying, 'Justice! Justice on the traitor!', and withal spat in his face. Whereat the King drew out his handkerchief, and wiped the spittle from his cheek, and said:

'Well, sir, God has justice in store, both for you and me.'

10

Diary of Colonel Jack Ashburnham

January 23rd. This week's number of *The Moderate Intelligencer* suppressed, because mention made in it of Hewson's spitting, and Mr Dillingham, the author, summoned to the bar of the Commons' House to be sharply admonished.

I coming to Bodurdo's gallery today, the custodian thereof would not admit me, though I offered him double, for there was keen scrutiny made, said he, of those who sat there, and he feared for his place. Was fain, therefore, to get in among the common folk behind the barrier, where, being so far off, I was not able to hear all that passed, save when H.M. spoke, for then the multitude kept quiet to listen. For the rest, great long speeches by Cook and Bradshawe, they exerting all their powers to impress the people.

I suppose the fiends pin their hopes on wearing H.M. down by sheer fatigue, he not sleeping, yet despite his haggard looks, he maintains the most admirable coolness. Nay, more, he continues to turn the table on these parricides, causing Bradshawe to entangle himself with every word he speaks, and driving him into a corner where he can do nought but bluster and thump the arms of his chair. And at length fairly gibbering with rage, he shrieked at H.M. that notwithstanding he disputed the court's authority, he would find they had power to punish him. To which H.M. answered that he found himself indeed before a power, pointing to the soldiery.

When the court adjourned, a new proclamation made by the crier, 'God bless the kingdom of England', which it is thought was intended to prevent the multitude shouting as formerly, 'God bless the King'.

January 24th. Contrary to notice given, no proceedings in the Hall today, there being but forty-seven rogues when they assembled in the Painted Chamber. What they were at there, I know not, and am like to run stark mad for lack of news.

January 25th. My acquaintance, Dr Hackluyt, though a marked man, ventured into an out-room of the Painted Chamber to try if he might not pick up some gleanings for his *Mercurius Pragmaticus.* When the rats emerged from their hole, one of them, John Downes, whispered Dr Hackluyt that in return for money he would let him know what had passed. This Downes is an obscure person, who had some minor post about the Court before the war, but being elected to a seat in the House, attached himself to the cloak-tail of Cromwell, whose jackal he became, and was rewarded with a colonelcy. Now he, it seems, being roped in to swell the Court of Injustice, has grown fearful for his skin, for albeit the people are kept from stirring by the redcoats, their temper is plain, and moreover there is our lusty young Prince of Wales with a rod in pickle overseas.

When it grew dark, Downes came by appointment to a tavern in Southwark, where Dr Hackluyt had engaged a private room, I being present in my guise of a French visitor. After many demands for our discretion, and well oiling of his palm (though I had readier cut the ratlet's gullet), Downes told us thus:

That first there fell out a quarrel between Cromwell and Ireton, the former insisting that there be no further delays, but they proceed to sentence on the pretext that H.M. had refused to answer and therefore was in contempt of court. But Ireton, that cunning lawyer, liked this not. The law, says he, required a solemn calling of witnesses, and if their evidence were published it might impress the people, who were grown dangerously disaffected. Yet because H.M. might shrewdly cross-examine, it were better to hear them in private.

'What witnesses are these?' said I.

'There are nine and twenty of them,' Downes told me, 'the most renegados from the King's armies, others captured and hoping to regain their liberty and get reward. Their testimony was made the more tedious because the Lord President pressed them to say in what month and place they saw the King fight upon his own side. Which put them at a stand, they being for the most part simple swains, who could say no more than that it was at the tedding of the hay or at some time after Plough Monday. One said he had seen the King in bright armour; another, with his sword drawn; a third that 'twas he himself who painted the pole of the Royal Standard when it was first set up at Nottingham. Yet all took care to add, being coached before-hand, that on every occasion of battle there were many slain upon the side of the Parliament.'

But while I made merry with this, Downes fell a-blubbering and spoke these fatal words:

'The court is resolved to proceed to sentence upon Saturday, and to condemn the King as a tyrant, traitor and murderer. And this condemnation is to extend to death.'

I I

True and Humble Representation of John Downes

If I were so hardened a sinner as not to acknowledge my fault, or so ill a subject as my actions would accuse me in the part I played during that most sacrilegious plot against the life of His Majesty, I should lack confidence to petition for mercy. But for my acting in those days, I erred through the defect of my intellect and my terror of Cromwell, not from malice or for rewards.

I was put on the Commission to try His Majesty very much against my will, as were divers others; but Cromwell told us that if we did not execute justice upon the Chief Delinquent, when God had brought him into our hands, the Lord would require of us all the blood and desolation which would ensue by our suffering him to escape. Yet I must needs confess that what went more home with me, he said on another occasion that we had gone too far to retreat, and that if we did not have the King's life, he would have ours.

Having sought every way to excuse myself from taking further part in these illegal proceedings, I was compelled again into the Painted Chamber upon Friday, January 26th, where there was de-bated what we were to do in the Hall next day. Bradshawe was peevish by reason of the scolding of his wife who, so he told us, had been upon her knees to him that morning, beseeching him not to sentence this earthly king, for fear of the dreadful vengeance of the King of Heaven. Even while he was speaking, we were disturbed by the clamour of some citizens' wives in the ante-room, come to plead for the King, who were put out with some roughness by Lieutenant-Colonel Axtell.

We sitting private, all men's tongues were loosed, and Colonel Hewson urged that the King be dressed in his robes and crown to receive sentence, the more to humiliate His Majesty. Which was denied by the rest; yet it was ordered that when the King was brought in, the soldiers add the word 'execution' to their former shouts of 'justice'. Likewise that fresh summonses be issued to the hundred and thirty-five Commissioners named, on pain of the displeasure of the High Court of Parliament. Yet next day, but sixty-seven present in the Hall.

Lord President Bradshawe had a new crimson satin gown for this last day of the trial, to impress the people, to whom, and not to the King, he made his opening speech, he being a gentleman much enamoured of his own eloquence and confident to win their hearts thereby. Yet he had scarce begun his address, with the remark that the prisoner at the bar had been brought several times to answer a charge of high treason exhibited against him in the name of the people of England, when there rang forth from the gallery the voice of that same lady who had made interruption on the first day, she now saying:

'It is false. Where are the people and their consents?'

Whereupon another lady who sat by her, called out that Oliver Cromwell was a rogue and a traitor. There being dangerous applause from the multitude, Mr Axtell leapt up on to the stage below the gallery, flourishing his pistol and commanding his men to fire at the drabs (as he had the impudence to term the Lady Fairfax and her friend Mrs Nelson) if they uttered one word more. But they retired into Bodurdo's house, and order given to the clerks to omit any mention of their protest in the printed records.

Then did Bradshawe resume his speech, but I noted how oft his hand went to his bullet-proof hat as if to assure himself that he still wore that protection. This address of his he caused to be printed in a pamphlet, so I omit it, and hasten on to what fell out next, wherein was my own part. I call God to witness that what I write is true, though not to be found in any records of these proceedings, and I humbly pray that what I write will move the heart of His Gracious Majesty that now is to accord me pardon.

The King having leave to speak (out of the court's great mercy, Bradshawe told him) before sentence was pronounced, he began by saying that this many a day all things had been taken from him save that which was dearer to him than life, his conscience and honour. If, said he, he had had a respect for his life more than for these, certainly he would have made a particular defence. But he having weighty reasons why he could not acknowledge our jurisdiction, requested to declare those reasons before the Lords and Commons in the Painted Chamber. If, said he, he could not get this liberty, then he did protest that all our fair shows were rather specious than real, and that we condemned our King unheard.

Now I, who had my seat at the backside of the court, was so moved by his words that I began to whisper to those who sat on right and left of me that we ought to accede to the King's request. Though they said it would ruin me, I could no longer contain myself, but wept aloud, protesting that if I die for it, yet must I do it. Then, standing up, I cried:

'Have we hearts of stone? Are we men?'

Whereat Cromwell flung round on me, saying in a snarl:

'Are you mad? What do you mean to do? Cannot you be quiet?'

'No, sir,' said I, 'I cannot be quiet. I am not satisfied to give my consent to this sentence.'

Cromwell, with a muttered oath, whispered the Lord President, who said aloud that we were to adjourn into the Court of Wards to consider the King's request. But when we were come there, Cromwell slammed shut the door and advanced upon me for all the world as though he were leading a charge of his Ironsides. I have heard it said that his geny lay in dissimulation, in watching and adroitly seizing opportunities, rather than creating them, and that thus he swam with the tide of human affairs and was assisted by it. But from my personal knowledge of him I can vouch that upon

179

occasion he resembled the tiger rather than the subtle serpent, displaying a force and fury that none could withstand. He demanded of me in high wrath why I had put this trouble and disturbance upon the court. Yet I, though a poor, weak ordinary man, was carried along by my emotion, and answered (and so near as I possibly can, I will set down my very syllabic expressions):

'Sir, God knows I thirst not after the King's blood. All that I desire is the settlement of the kingdom in peace. Should you give sentence of death upon him before you have acquainted the Parliament with his offers to speak with them, in my humble opinion you will do the greatest action upon the greatest disadvantage, and I do not know how ever you will be able to answer for it.'

Cromwell turned in scornful wrath to the Lord President, who was engaged in writing down some invented debate among us to be inserted in the printed accounts and thus conceal from the public the real cause of our adjournment. So near as I remember, Cromwell spoke these words:

'My Lord President, you see what weighty reasons this gentleman has produced that should move him to put this trouble upon you. I wish his conscience does not tell him, whatever he pretends of dissatisfaction, that he only would save his old master. However, it is not the single opinion of one peevish, obstinate man that must sway the court, nor deter them from their duty in so great an affair.'

'But, sir, I am not alone in this,' said I. 'Sir John Bourchier, Mr Dixwell, Mr Love, Mr Waite, did you not confide to me that you were much dissatisfied?'

Not one soul would second me or speak a word for fear, but on the contrary, took me by the sleeve, whispering that I was crazed in my wits to have done this, which would but open the door of a jail for me; and another said that it was not in the power of man to save the King, for the whole Army was resolved that if there were any check in giving judgment, they would immediately fall upon him and hew him in pieces. Colonel Hewson, glowering at me with his single eye, saith he suspected me to be a secret Cavalier, but Cromwell said rather he deemed my aim to be to start a mutiny, withal bidding me remember how it had fared with the mutineers at Cockbush Field.

Yet I, though very fearful, told them, 'twas evident the Parliament expected some such offer from the King, or else why did they make that order that upon any emergency the court should immediately acquaint them with it? (And there was such an order to be seen in the books, if he, Cromwell, had not torn it out, as I have heard since he has done with what else in the proceedings liked him not.) But all I could say would not do. Says Cromwell:

'Waste no more time, but return to your duty, lest you be accursed for putting your hand to the plough and looking back.'

I would in no wise return to the Hall, and in truth I was not able to speak for tears, but made my way into the Speaker's house. Yet ere I left I heard Cromwell say, he would have my signature to the dead-warrant.

I 2

Mercurius Pragmaticus (unlicensed)

January 27th.

There being several passages in this day's proceedings ordered to be struck from the records, note the following.

When the court came back after an adjournment, it was marked that Colonel Downes was not among them, yet Bradshawe says they had unanimously resolved that, since they acted by the supreme authority of the Commons of England in Parliament assembled, they must deny the King's request and proceed to sentence.

Whereafter the Lord President embarked on an oration which lasted full two hours. And notwithstanding I believe he must have taken care to eat liquorice and gingerbread this morning for the strengthening of his voice, he was but in mid-stream when he grew so hoarse 'twas like a frog croaking. Which speech the curious may read at their pleasure, but for my part will say I never heard from the lips of any man such a hodge-podge, what with misquotations intermixed with monk-Latin, with snippets from Cicero and from medieval lawyers torn clean from their context, and irrelevant informations dragged in to impress the people with the speaker's erudition. Nay, I noted Mr Solicitor Cook writhe upon his seat when Bradshawe went so far as to fabricate an axiom from the ancient legal luminary, Henry de Bracton.

Upon my soul, I verily believe that if the Lord President had retained his voice, he would be speaking still, for not content with winding his slow way through history, both English and foreign, to find examples of the punishment of kings, needs must he turn to the Old Testament, where he was like to lose himself as in a labyrinth. When, to the infinite relief of his hearers (I swear even of those on the benches), His Majesty interrupted by desiring to be heard concerning those heavy imputations laid to his charge.

I suppose the Lord President had been working up to his climax, and so was much piqued by the intervention. At any rate he upon a sudden shed the mask of learned judge, and blurted forth the true cause of his enmity against the King thus:

'Sir, you have not owned us as a court, but look upon us as a sort of people met together!'

I never heard so much wounded vanity as was in his tone. But then, swallowing his spleen, he turns preacher, conjuring His Majesty to remember David, whose repentance in the matter of Uriah God was pleased to accept, and heartily desiring His Majesty to a like sad and serious penitence. And having thus mounted the pulpit, spoke of the bloody designs of Malignants against this highest and sublimest court in the kingdom, from which designs God would surely deliver them. And yet, says he, very solemn, 'we do declare with those children in the fiery furnace that would not worship the golden image set up by Nebuchadnezzar, if our God will not deliver us, we are content to perish'.

Which comparison was very strange, seeing what force of soldiers this court had arrayed for its protection both within and without the Hall. More the Lord President would have said, but his voice quite failing, he called for an Oyez and bade the clerk read the sentence which, after a tedious preamble, was as follows:

'For all which treasons and crimes this court doth adjudge the said Charles Stuart, as a tyrant, traitor, murderer and public enemy

182

to the good people of England, shall be put to death by the severing of his head from his body.'

Whereupon the court stood up to signify their consent, and in doing so perforce disclosed to the spectators how few they were in number. The King remained seated, very courteously asking if he might speak a word. I observed Bradshawe flush as if with pleasure that he might show who had the whip-hand, and with saucy insolence he replied that the prisoner was not to be heard after sentence. Then for the first time during all these proceedings did the King betray discomposure, letting fall some sentences of horror. But again recovering himself, said thus:

'I am not suffered to speak. Expect what justice other men shall have.'

During the time when the King was urging to be heard, Axtell scoffed aloud, while some of his soldiers, by his leave, and I suspect by his incitement, did fire powder in their palms, by which they not only offended His Majesty's smell but enforced him to turn away the smoke with his hand. And after this, he fixed his eyes direct on Cromwell, and said he:

'There are some sitting here who well know that if I would have betrayed the liberties and rights of my people, I need not have come hither.' (Which some interpret as meaning that there had been secret offers made to him by Cromwell in return for his life.)

At which Axtell bawled out 'Justice! Execution!', and the soldiers hustled His Majesty out from the Hall, some spitting upon him, and other puffing their tobacco-pipes in his face, a thing he abhorred. Said he, 'Poor soldiers, for a piece of money they would do the same to their commanders.' And one of the guard, being moved, I suppose, by the King's carriage, cried out, 'God bless you, Sir', for which word he was most grievously belaboured by Axtell with his cane. His Majesty observed that it was a hard punishment for a small offence.

His Majesty was hurried away in a sedan-chair carried by two porters, which chair I followed to the midst of King Street, and saw the porters, in reverence, go bare-headed, till Axtell beat them and forced them to put on their caps. And I heard a cry from the multitude who were kept back strait by the soldiery:

'What! do you carry the King in a common sedan, as they carry such as have the plague? God deliver Your Majesty out of such hands.'

In which street I was forced to leave sight of His Majesty, for I was seen to be writing on my tablets, and they threatened to lay me by the heels.

Assault

I

Secret Memoirs of Thomas Herbert

Upon the last day of the pretended trial, I was bidden stay for my master in his own royal palace of Whitehall, a sorry place now, for they had taken away and sold all those carvings and pictures in which he had delighted, and they used it part for quartering of troops and part as a lodging for the Army Grandees. I was stricken with horror to behold His Majesty carried through the gate in a sedan with soldiers belching forth most abominable taunts at him, and he with his dress disordered and his face befouled with spittle. In truth, I believe nobody's sufferings have been so like our Saviour's as were His Majesty's.

Mr Firebrace, and other of his old servants, sought to enter after him, and being thrust back by the guard, broke into loud weeping. Whereat His Majesty remarked:

'You may forbid their attendance, but not their tears.'

When we were private, I showed His Majesty how I had brought his dogs from St James's to please him, but he bade me send them to the Queen, all but an ancient spaniel called Rogue, which he feared would not survive the journey. For he said that nothing now must distract him from his preparations for death. And for the same reason he denied to receive those whom the regicides permitted to come to him, as the Duke of Richmond, the Earl of Southampton, and other noblemen, instructing me to tell them he hoped they did not take it ill, but his time was precious and the best office they could do now was to pray for him.

Only the Lord Bishop of London, Dr Juxon, he received, who had leave to come if he consented to lie under the same arrest. Directly Dr Juxon entered the chamber, he fell a-weeping, upon which His Majesty saith to him in a brisk way:

'Leave off this, my lord, we have no time for it. Let us think of that great work I now have to do. As for these rogues into whose hands I am fallen, let us not speak of them. They thirst after my blood, and they shall have it, and God's will be done.'

The Bishop seeming perplexed by his saying he had a great work to do, His Majesty explained how he believed that, like Samson, he would destroy more Philistines on the day of his death than ever he had done in his life. By which I understood him to mean that in the last tragical act he would justify what he had so oft expressed by word, that rather than yield to the lawless tyranny of the sword, he was content to die.

Being a most devout Christian, he must needs set himself to forgive his murderers from his heart, as our Saviour bade us, and in order to which he requested the Bishop to read with him the example of Christ as contained in the Gospels. But every few minutes, these pious exercises were interrupted by the soldiers, who opened the door without knocking to make sure their royal captive was still in their midst. It was late at night when Dr Juxon returned to Fulham, and as soon as he had taken his leave, my master drew from his finger an emerald ring, bidding me carry it to a certain house in Channel Row at the backside of King Street.

I trembled at the thought of such a mission, but His Majesty told me he was sure that Colonel Thomlinson would give me the password which would enable me to go through the many guards. And said he, you must hand this ring to the mistress of the house, saying nothing. Being come to the house, I discovered the lady to be none other than Mrs Jane Whorwood, who desired me to stay in the parlour till she returned, which she did in no long time, and gave me a little cabinet, sealed with three seals, saying only:

'Pray deliver this into the same hand that sent the ring.'

I wondered was there some instrument, as a file, secreted there, for I knew Mrs Whorwood by reputation as a bold and meddlesome dame, who oft had conspired to snatch His Majesty out of the hands of his captors, when in my opinion she ought to have been attending to her wifely duties in Oxfordshire. The word securing my return to Whitehall, I found the soldiers intruded upon my master at night already in his chamber, so he whispered me that I should see the cabinet opened on the morrow.

Morning being come, the Bishop was early with His Majesty,

who after prayers, broke the three seals upon the cabinet and invited me to look therein. I was much surprised to see but a few trifling jewels, most part broken Georges and Garters.

'I have two young children who are prisoners like myself,' says the King. 'See here all the wealth I have left to give them.'

Some of the presbyterian ministers, who had published a protest against the illegal High Court of Justice, came to offer to pray with His Majesty, who thanked them, but said he had made choice of Bishop Juxon and would have no other. The King and Dr Juxon being closeted together, Colonel Thomlinson required my attendance. My heart was like to break, imagining that I, the last of the King's poor servants, was to receive my dismissal, but it fell out quite otherwise. Says Colonel Thomlinson:

'I have applied to his Excellency, the Lord General, that the King may be removed back to St James's. For I must disclose to you, Mr Herbert, that the deed you wot of is to be done upon him in the street outside Whitehall, and that between the hours of ten in the morning and five in the afternoon on Tuesday. That is to say, if they are able to get sufficient hands to the dead-warrant, for many have refused to sign, of whom I am one.'

I being too much stricken to reply, he went on to say that if His Majesty remained here, he would be disturbed by the setting-up of the scaffold, and it was for this charitable reason he had applied himself to General Fairfax. But he had found his Excellency in effect a prisoner in his own house, with guards about it, and so timid that the most Colonel Thomlinson could wring from him was, His Majesty might be moved on Monday very privately after dark, in case of demonstrations by the people.

During the forenoon of Monday, His Majesty was much occupied in sorting and burning some privy papers and his cipher keys, and likewise instructing me anent his legacies. Alas, he had little save his books to leave. I observed he seemed more dejected than during the preceding days, and when I carried in his dinner, he scarce touched the food. I supposing him afflicted with the natural terrors of a violent death, he seemed to guess my thoughts, and confided to me that what troubled him was an ordeal through which he must pass this very day. With a cruel kindness, his murderers had given leave that his younger children, the Princess Elizabeth and the Duke of Gloucester, come to take farewell of him. And he feared that the Lady Elizabeth, a maid of fourteen who had ever been delicate, might never recover from the shock of this parting.

Two circumstances fell out on Monday which I must not forget to mention. The first was a letter to the Parliament from the Prince of Wales, who enclosed a blank sheet of paper signed with his name, begging them to set down thereon any terms they chose in return for his father's life. But they laid it aside with contumely. To the King himself there came a messenger from the Army Grandees, who for the last time offered him his life if he would consent to their proposals. But as soon as His Majesty had read some few of these demands, he tore up the paper, saying that he would rather become a sacrifice for his people than betray their laws, liberties, lives and estates to so intolerable a bondage of armed faction.

2

A True Relation of what the King said to me the last time I had the happiness to see him. By the Princess Elizabeth

My Lord Northumberland, in whose charge I was kept at Syon House, brought me with my brother Gloucester in a closed carriage to Whitehall on the afternoon of January 29th. And being come into His Majesty's presence, I could not control my tears. But the King, taking me into his embrace, besought me not to weep, for he had particular things to say unto me which he durst not write, lest his enemies take the paper from me.

'But, sweet heart,' said he, 'you will forget what I say.'

I told him I would never forget it while I lived, and promised that I would set down every word on paper ere I went to my bed that night. He wished me, he said, not to torment myself for him, for it was a glorious death that he would die, being for the Church, the laws of the realm, and the liberty of the subject. He told me what books to read against popery, and said that I should have his copy of Bishop Andrewes' sermons, which would be my shield if I were permitted to go to the Queen my mother in France. (I would not disclose to His Majesty a whisper I had heard, that instead, my brother and I were to be sent to Carisbrooke Castle in the Isle of Wight, for so long his own prison.)

Then His Majesty gave into my hands all his remaining jewels, except the George he wore, which was cut in an onyx with great curiosity and set about with twenty-one fair diamonds. It had a secret spring which, on being released, disclosed a picture of the Queen my mother. His Majesty said that he had forgiven all his enemies, and commanded me, with my brothers and sisters, to forgive them likewise, but never to trust them, for that indeed they had been very false to him, and he feared to their own souls likewise. And spoke further thus:

'Tell James it is my last command that he should no longer look upon Charles as his elder brother only, but be obedient to him as his Sovereign. And tell your mother that my thoughts have never strayed from her, and that my love will be the same to the last.'

Gloucester standing silent all this while, clinging to my skirts, the King took him up upon his knee, caressing him, and bidding him not to fear, for he should hear nothing but what was for his good.

'Sweet heart,' the King said, 'I have heard that these people of the Army intend to make you King, but that is not for you to take upon you if you regard the welfare of your country and your own soul.'

Upon which the child looked very steadfastly at him.

'Mark, Harry, what I say,' the King continued, his voice being strained as though he must force the words out. 'They will cut off your father's head, and perhaps make you a king. But heed carefully, child, you must not be made a king while your brothers Charles and James do live, and this I strictly charge you.'

Whereat the child fetched a deep sigh, and said:

'I will be torn in pieces first.'

Which answer, falling unexpectedly from one of such tender years, it made the King rejoice.

Then did His Majesty bestow on me as a parting gift his pocket Bible, telling me that it had been his constant companion and greatest comfort through all his sorrows, and he hoped it would be mine. Withal he blessed and embraced us many times, until as we clung to him, he called to my Lord Bishop Juxon to take us away. The King leaned his head against the window, endeavouring to stifle his bitter grief, but catching a view of us as we passed through the doorway, he ran to snatch us once more to his bosom.

This is all I can remember at present of what the King said to me.

3

True and Humble Representation of John Downes

I, holding to my resolution to have no more to do with the proceedings against the King, took my seat in the Commons' House at nine in the morning of January 29th, where I found the benches mighty bare, for many had gone out of town. We had but just begun our deliberations, when in rushed Cromwell, shouting:

'Those who sat in the High Court of Justice shall set their names to the dead-warrant. I will have their hands now.'

Then I and several more protested that it was against our conscience, yet this would not serve. The looks of Cromwell were so wild that I trembled, remembering the stories (which I think had bottom) that in his youth he was pate-crazed. He seemed so now in truth, at horseplay one moment and the next shedding abundance of tears. And while he breathed fire against me in the Commons' House, as I went with him towards the Painted Chamber he hugged me close, telling me that we were come to the very threshold of the promises and prophecies. For, said he, God was about to bring His people into the Land of Promise, and that His chariots are twenty thousand of angels. Alack, I knew well that this was indeed the strength of the New Model Army, in which I held a commission, and that as my commanding officer, Cromwell could have me shot to death as a mutineer if I durst disobey his orders.

When we assembled in the Painted Chamber we numbered but fifty-nine, though sixty-seven had risen to their feet to confirm the sentence in Westminster Hall. Spread out upon a table was the dead-warrant, dated January 26th, the day before sentence was pronounced, and bearing upon it fifteen signatures. There was a hot quarrel toward between Mr Solicitor Cook and Commissary Ireton, for says Cook, if we go by the law, a fresh warrant must be drawn, signed and dated today. No, says Ireton; some of these fifteen who have already signed cannot be relied on to do it again. There is no time, says he, for such niceties; we must retain the original warrant but alter the date.

While they thus argued it, Cromwell seemed as it were drunk, at one minute praising the Lord for His favour to poor, weak, despised Saints (as he termed the Army), and the next daubing with ink the face of Mr Henry Marten, who straightway returned the compliment. I cannot well describe how it was with him, only by saying he was like a Tom o' Bedlam got loose from his chains. As witness how he used his cousin, Mr Richard Ingoldsby. For Mr Ingoldsby coming among us to speak with an acquaintance, Cromwell seized him by the shoulders, crying out that all this while he had escaped, but he should no longer tempt God with carnal cowardice. Says Mr Ingoldsby, I have denied from the beginning to have aught to do with the trial of the King, and have not sat once in Westminster Hall. Yea, says Cromwell, you have been backward in the work of the Lord, and now must be forced to your duty. And with that he called on Mr Marten, they two together hustling Mr Ingoldsby to the table, where they put a pen into his hand and guided it to sign his name. And though I will not sin against the truth and say, there was the like force used with me, I do avow that I was threatened with my very life if I did not write my signature.

All this while the Lord President Bradshawe was urging that beside each name there should be a seal with a coat-of-arms impressed on it, for the sake of pomp and dignity. But because most of those who signed had no right to coat-armour, needs must he send out to borrow signet-rings from his acquaintance. Which hugely delighted Colonel Pride, who could not read nor write, but making a scrawl upon the paper, clapped his hands like a child to see the brave coat-of-arms beside it.

In the end, it was but an ill-looking document, several erasing their signatures and others written over them. One, I think it was Mr Edmund Harvey, who crossed out his name, said he feared that otherwise this dead-warrant would prove his own.

Having thus confessed how I came to be guilty of this most heinous crime, I can but cast my life and all at the feet of His Gracious Majesty that now is, whose great clemency is well known, and for whom this humble petitioner shall ever pray. . . .

4
Unfinished Autobiography of Cornet George Joyce

It grieved me sore that I was given no seat in the High Court of Justice, there being none under the rank of major nominated. Yet Cromwell whispered me in my ear that he thought there would be work for my zealous arm anon, more glorious even than that I performed at Holmby House, but not pleasing to particularize. Meanwhile I must stay content to feast my eyes upon the preparations for a sacrifice so savoury in the nostrils of the Lord.

On the Sabbath before, I was much edified by the sermon preached by Master Peters in the purged chapel at Whitehall, wherein he did apply to Charles Stuart the frightful curse pronounced against the King of Babylon. And skipping nimbly through Scripture, Master Peters promised the Lord other peace-offerings, for says he, in Psalm 149 it is written that the Elect will bind nobles in fetters of iron and execute judgment upon the heathen. By which it is evident, says he, that no Malignant, small or great, shall escape the Lord's vengeance.

Upon Monday, the pious work of erecting the altar of sacrifice was begun, by placing of rails along that line of posts which has ever stood from east to west before the Banqueting House to Holbein's Gate. I rejoiced to think that needs must Charles Stuart hear this hammering ere he was carried in a chair to James's when it grew dark. As for me, I could not seek my couch nor go indoors to the fire (though it was as sharp a night as ever I remember), but kept my vigil where the great work was to be done, ruminating upon the end of the ungodly, which would be as the fate of Gog and Magog, their flesh feeding the fowls of the air, and the beasts of the field lapping their blood.

With holy joy I watched one Lockier, a master mason, knock out one in the long line of windows in the Banqueting House, through which aperture the Man of Sin was to step to his doom. And to the carpenter and his journeyman who were erecting the scaffold level with the bottom of this window, I said that they were building that which would be more pleasing to the Lord than Solomon's temple, albeit this was but of deal planks and not of cedarwood overlaid with pure gold. But they being carnal men, had no relish for their blessed toil, pausing often to slap their arms about their bodies for warmth and blow upon their fingers. They cared not what they were building, said they, being concerned only that they should have double wages for so dangerous a work.

When they went home, I lingered still, taking a sentry's turn about the altar, which was surrounded by a waist-high rail hung with black baize. Viewing the cheap deal coffin which was to receive the carcase of Charles Stuart, I chanted aloud with Jeremiah, 'Declare ye among the nations and publish and conceal not, Babylon is fallen, Bel is confounded, Merodach is broken in pieces.' There joined me anon a humble brother in the Lord, who carried a lanthorn in his hand and a sack upon his shoulder. He told me his name was Tench, a joiner by trade at the sign of the Drum in Houndsditch. His father being hanged as a spy by the Malignants in 1644, he had nursed in his heart a just desire for vengeance and (how marvellous are the ways of the Lord!) behold, such was given into his hands.

For, said he, coming to view the place of sacrifice, he had met with godly Master Peters, who observed to him that Charles Stuart, knowing his own guilt and fearful of hell-fire, would perchance make some resistance when he came to the block. And therefore, says Master Peters, do you provide hooks and pulleys to drag him down if need be, these being as the fleshhooks which Moses was commanded to place before the altar which he built in the wilderness. These same Tench had hastened to come by, together with four iron staples which he bought out of his own purse. And with his hammer and other tools he drove in the staples, working right manfully into the small hours of the morning, I encouraging him all the while by chanting of psalms.

He said to me that he looked to sell these staples for a goodly sum when the sacrifice had been offered. It grieved me to find his thoughts occupied with filthy lucre, for hitherto I had deemed him one of the Elect.

5

Secret Memoirs of Thomas Herbert

By the good offices of Colonel Thomlinson, Hacker was induced to withdraw his guards from the bedchamber when we came to St James's, where my dear master was to spend his last night upon earth. Yet even so I marvelled to hear His Majesty's even breathing through the long dark hours, which told me he slept sweetly, whereas I, when not stark awake, tossed and turned in nightmare. From such an incubus I was awakened by the King's voice asking what ailed me. Whereupon I recounted at length how I had fancied that the late Archbishop, Dr Laud, had come into the chamber in his pontifical habit, being very pensive and sighing much, and kissing His Majesty's hand, fell prostrate. With many other details which I now forget.

The King heard me out with his wonted patience, and said my dream was remarkable; then asked me what o'clock it was. I told him but two, yet he would rise, for, said he, he had a great work to do that day, for the which he would be well prepared. When I had lit the candles, I marvelled anew at the care wherewith he chose the raiment he would wear, but said he:

'Herbert, this is my second marriage day; I would be as trim as may be, for before night I hope to be espoused to my blessed Jesus. And since the weather is sharp, pray lay out an extra shirt, lest I chance to shiver, and thus have the imputation of fear laid upon me. I would have no such imputation. I fear not death; it is not terrible to me. I thank my God I am prepared.'

Even as the King thus arrayed himself, there sounded from without the throb of drums and the loud trample of horse upon the frozen ground of the Park. At this I trembled so much that I could scarce hold the brush with which I was tending his hair. He rallied me gently, saying:

'Pray, though it has not long to stand upon my shoulders, take the same pains with my head as you were used to do.'

My Lord Bishop Juxon arrived betimes and was closeted with His Majesty for an hour in private. I did violence to my presbyterian convictions by attending His Majesty at the service of Matins afterwards, and rejoiced that I had done so, for there was somewhat remarkable which I had been sorry to miss. Matins being ended, the King inquired of Dr Juxon with a hint of rebuke in his tone, whether he had chosen of himself to read St Matthew's account of the crucifying of our Saviour as the second Lesson. But his lordship showed him how it was the proper Lesson for the day according to the calendar of the Church of England. Which coincidence made me very pensive and consoled the King exceedingly.

At ten of the clock, there came a timid knock upon the door, and I opening, found there Hacker, who appeared quite altered in his mien, being by nature brutish but now subdued. He faltered that it was time to go to Whitehall. Upon my reporting this to the King, he, as one in command of the situation, bade me say he had not yet completed his thanksgiving for the Sacrament. After a while there came another knock, and at this His Majesty says to me:

'Pray open the door. Hacker has given us a second warning.'

Both Dr Juxon and I being like to swoon, His Majesty helped us to our feet, bidding us take courage, and pausing to give me as a memento the silver watch which hung at his bedside, stepped nimbly forth. As we went through the gardens, he espied Colonel Thomlinson standing apart with a sad countenance, to whom His

Majesty beckoned, and I observed him slip into the Colonel's hand his gold toothpick case.

'If it please God to restore my son,' says he, 'this small memorial may save your life. I give it you in token of my gratitude for all your courtesy while I have been in your charge.'

Come through the gate into the Park, we beheld two ranks of foot soldiers drawn up so as to form a lane right across to White-hall, who, at the King's appearing, made a loud roll upon their drums. This, I suppose, was to drown any cries of sympathy from such of the common folk who were present. Yet I must remark that the redcoats themselves, who had offered His Majesty such barbarous insults at his trial, seemed now as tamed as Hacker. And when the King called out to them, 'March apace, good fellows!', they obeyed him as readily as if they had been his own Cavaliers.

His Majesty walked between Dr Juxon and Colonel Thomlin-son, and I behind them, with a company of halberdiers close about us. I heard His Majesty say that he was glad to have this exercise, for in regard it was a bitter cold morning, without a little motion he would be indisposed to what he intended to speak upon the scaffold. But though the soldiers behaved themselves with decency, the King was not to escape abuse on this his last promenade, a sorry fellow, whose name, I learnt afterwards, was Tench, walking abreast of him and belching forth dark hints of mutilation. Until at length Dr Juxon, though the mildest of men, quite lost his temper, and complained wrathfully to Hacker, who bade the wretch be gone.

(Yet I must note here, being most painful to record each trifle which fell out that day, that the poor old spaniel, Rogue, supposed shut up ere we left St James's, had contrived to steal out after his master, which Tench, stooping between the legs of the soldiers, seized upon, and afterwards tied in his cellar, charging a fee to those who came to view the dog.)

We entered Whitehall by the Park Gate, and so across the Horse Guard Yard and The Street, passing through the Stone Gallery to His Majesty's own apartments. Here the King at once resumed his devotions, which were interrupted by some fanatic ministers who would intrude themselves upon him, and had the impudence to inquire of His Majesty if his peace was made with God. Who sent out to them Dr Juxon with this answer:

'I hope you do not deem me so ill a Christian as to have been so long in prison and have that to do now. And I tell you plainly that you who have so often prayed against me, shall never pray with me in this hour. You may, if you please, pray for me, and I will thank you for it.'

After some space, His Majesty rose from his knees with a cheerful and serene countenance, exclaiming:

'Now let the rogues come! I have forgiven them, and am prepared for all I have to undergo.'

Alas, what he must undergo before the pangs of death was a long and unaccountable delay, for the bells tolled noon, and still there was no sign of his murderers. I presumed to entreat His Majesty to partake of some dinner, but he, having received the Sacrament, saith he was resolved to eat no more earthly food. Then did Dr Juxon add his entreaties to mine, reminding His Majesty that he might swoon in such extreme cold and after so long fasting; whereat he consented to eat half a manchet of bread and drink a glass of claret.

From all I have written it may be thought that His Majesty had no fear to conquer, but I can testify it was far otherwise. He was exceeding sensitive, and from certain remarks he let fall, I perceived that the memory of his grandmother, the Queen of Scots, who was bestially hacked to death by an unskilled executioner, haunted his mind. And there had been those sinister threats uttered by the wretch Tench, as though some butchery were intended.

And yet, I know not whether to impute it to a very extraordinary measure of supernatural assistance, or something within himself, he passed through this last act of his tragedy with so much true greatness, without disorder or any sort of affectation, that even the most fierce among his enemies were fain to confess that though they had vanquished him, it was not in their power to subdue him.

6

Unfinished Autobiography of Cornet George Joyce

At length I come to that feat for which the Lord chose me while I was yet in my mother's womb.

Upon the morning of the great sacrifice, Cromwell sent for me, and said that he would have me keep company with him and attend upon him whithersoever he went that day. But gave no reason for this order. We entered the chamber of Commissary Ireton, who lay in bed at Whitehall, honest Major Harrison having crept in beside him for warmth. At the fire stood other of the Saints, as Colonel Hercules Huncks, Colonel Phayre, and Lieutenant-Colonel Axtell. To whom Cromwell saith:

'Those named to have charge of the great business must sign the warrant to the executioner.'

Then all at once began to make excuse, saying that albeit they had searched their hearts with prayers and tears to that God to whom all nations were less than a drop in a bucket of water, and had received assurance that the Lord was with His Elect in what they were about today, for one carnal reason or another they were not able to sign. As Mr Axtell said, he had no schooling, so could not write his name, and Mr Harrison had the belly-ache so sore he was not able to rise. At which there fell out some cross passages, Cromwell upbraiding them as peevish froward fellows. Says he:

'I have sought the Lord day and night that He would rather slay me than put me upon the doing of this work, but His answer is ever the same, that He hath stirred up the armies of the Lion of Judah to be His instrument in the destruction of this idol.'

Yet in the end of it, he was constrained to write the signatures of two of them, and to send for Colonel Hacker to make a third.

After which he carried me into the Painted Chamber where the Lord President Bradshawe and some of the Commissioners were sitting, and there was brought in the common hangman, one Brandon, who had been fetched by a troop of horse from his dwelling in Rosemary Lane. Him they offered £30 to perform his office; but he being of a low spirit said that at the pronouncing of sentence against Charles Stuart he had taken a vow and protestation, wishing God to perish his body and soul if ever he appeared on the scaffold to do that act. And saith further that his assistant, one Ralph Jones, a cleaner of the dunghills, had fled on purpose to avoid it.

The Lord President was sharp with him, but neither threats nor the raising of his fee could move this craven beast, and so he was close shut up till after the sacrifice had been offered.

Then was the *Sergeants' Call* ordered to be beat upon the drums throughout the regiments of Hewson, Pride and Hacker, and thirty-eight sergeants being assembled, Hewson offered one hundred gold pieces and quick promotion to whosoever would undertake the godly work. Word coming to Cromwell that none would volunteer, he turned out from the chamber where he was all save his secretary, Mr Robert Spavin, and myself, and embracing me, he spoke these pregnant words:

'Brother Joyce, I have long suspected that thou art another Gideon, and justly to be called the most valiant of men.'

As he thus spoke, he drew off the cover from some object which leaned against a chair, and I beheld the bright execution axe which had been fetched from the Tower that morning. Satan tempting me, I said with Gideon that I was the least in my father's house, to which Cromwell made answer that nonetheless I should cut off the Midianites as one man.

'Up then and about it,' says he, 'since thou art he whom the Lord hath chosen. For now must be fulfilled the prophecy wherein the Beast hath one of its heads wounded to death. The grapes of Babylon are fully ripe, and wilt thou deny to thrust in the sickle?'

I presumed to descend to profane speech, saying that there would doubtless be Malignants lurking near the scaffold, who would dog my footsteps until they had revenge upon me. And likewise the common rout had shown clearly that they liked not this deed, and I would be from henceforth a marked man. Cromwell condescended to my weakness, drawing me apart into a window, and telling me that I should be so well concealed by a vizard and false beard that none should know me. And whispered:

'Directly you have done your work, you shall be speeded into Ireland, where a regiment awaits you, Colonel Joyce.'

Upon this I bade Satan and his wiles be gone, and I would no longer with Judah fear the chariots armed with scythes of the Canaanites. Cromwell told me I must have an assistant, whereat I picked upon a stalwart trooper of mine named Wrathwood who, for a just fee, agreed, yet only on the condition that he held up the head in silence, lest his voice betray who he was when he spoke the customary words, 'Behold the head of a traitor.'

At which the divine impulse to mirth seized upon Cromwell, who says between his laughter:

'Since these words are ever answered by "So perish all the King's enemies", in truth it is better that you stand mum.'

[*Editorial Note*. Here the manuscript breaks off abruptly, and is not resumed. But a later, unknown hand has added the following:

The next Sabbath but one after Charles I was beheaded, Robert Spavin, secretary to Lieutenant-General Cromwell at that time, invited himself to dine with me and brought several others along with him to dinner. Their principal discourse at meat was only who it was that beheaded the King. One said it was the common hangman; another, Hugh Peters; others also nominated, but none concluded. Robert Spavin, as soon as dinner was done, took me by the hand and carried me to the south window. Saith he:

'These are all mistaken, they have not named the man who did the act. It was Lieutenant-Colonel Joyce. I was in the room when he fitted himself for the work, stood behind him when he did it, when done went in again with him. There is no man knows this but Cromwell, Commissary Ireton and myself.'

This Joyce died in Ireland an. 1651 of a putrid fever. He was very much disturbed in his sickness and lay raging and swearing and still pointing at one thing or another, which he conceived was visible before him.]

7

Letter from Bishop Juxon to King Charles II

Little Compton in Gloucestershire. February 1st, 1649.

May it please Your Majesty. The horrid wickedness which hath been acted was so far beyond the apprehensions of all men, that it is no wonder if we are struck with that amazement as not yet to have recovered our wits. For though we had too great cause to look every day to hear of the murder of the King, yet that it should be performed in the light of the sun, I think no man could imagine. Had not your royal father, of blessed memory, laid upon me the most strict command, even with his dying breath, to give you an exact account of that most execrable parricide committed upon him, I would not have added to Your Majesty's affliction, nor mine own, in thus enlarging upon it. Yet such was that blessed martyr's wish, he foreseeing that the printed accounts would be very defective by reason of the strict censorship here, and likewise because, he being separated from all else who had any kindness for him, none save myself can testify truly to his last acts and words.

I beseech Your Majesty to pardon so unworthy an account as I shall give, my spirits being quite disordered and my old body much fatigued with the haste of fleeing hither to my country seat, Fulham Palace being taken from me by the regicides, and my person threatened with arrest.

There was one circumstance fell out which the modesty of the performers in it may conceal from Your Majesty. My Lords of Hertford, Lindsey and Southampton, so soon as that wicked judgment was given in Westminster Hall, sent a joint petition to Parliament in this-wise: 'That since His Majesty was presumed by the law to do no wrong himself, but did it all by them, his Councillors, as they had the honour to act under him, so they prayed they might have the honour to suffer instead of him upon the scaffold.' So happy was His Majesty in the love even unto death of the best and ablest of his subjects.

Yet he said to me upon several occasions that his greatest comfort was that God had given him that charity which was the noblest triumph over his destroyers, and he would have the pleasure of dying without any taint of desired revenge. And ere he rose from his knees at St James's on that fatal morning, he spoke aloud these memorable words:

'Oh God, though they think my kingdoms on earth too little to entertain at once both them and me, yet let the capacious kingdom of Thy infinite mercy at last receive both me and my enemies.'

It was near half past one o'clock when Colonel Hacker came with a file of soldiers to fetch His Majesty to the scaffold. Mr Herbert was in so swooning a condition that the King excused him from further attendance; but when I likewise begged to remain behind in the chamber, His Majesty would not consent, reminding me that it was my sacred duty to minister to the dying.

We passed through the Stone Gallery, which was lined with pikemen, behind whom knelt some humble servitors of the King, who lamented grievously for him. The soldiers, marvellous to relate, made no effort to restrain them, but stood with bowed heads, afflicted rather than insulting. This was the more remarkable because among them I recognized some of the very men who sat up always in his bedchamber at St James's, and would not suffer him to go into any other room to say his prayers or to relieve the ordinary necessities of nature.

At the instant His Majesty stepped through the window on to the scaffold, the sun which till this time had been mantled in thick cloud, burst forth to shine full upon him. He, as at his pretended trial, took close and composed view of the scene, regarding with unchanged countenance the block (which was made a-purpose so low that he must lie flat to reach it, an instance of their barbarous malice), and the two headsmen, habited in long woollen frocks such as butchers wear, with grizzled periwigs and false beards.

Then did he step to the breast-high rail and beheld the neighbourhood quite filled with soldiers, both horse and foot, full-armed and with their standards displayed. Nonetheless the common folk were present likewise, crowding the roof tops and standing a-tiptoe to see between the ranks of the military. They made no sound when they perceived the King, for I think their spirits were as benumbed as were their bodies in that freezing cold.

Since I have such strict injunctions laid upon me to conceal nothing from Your Majesty anent this awful scene, I must confide to Your Majesty that there was one fear haunted your blessed father, and that was lest the axe be blunted, either by accident or by brutish intent. For besides the staples and pulleys which seemed to threaten some hideous massacre, there were upon the scaffold some fifteen persons, who moved restlessly, so that the swinging of their cloaks often brushed against the dread instrument. And this apprehension His Majesty voiced several times during his speech, bidding his murderers have a care of the axe.

There had been until this moment the same continuous drumming as had been used when His Majesty came through the Park; but now it ceased and there fell a tense silence. Yet there being no possibility of his words penetrating to his poor subjects, the King addressed his speech to those upon the scaffold, which words Colonel Thomlinson took down in shorthand, kneeling upon one knee and supporting his tablets on the other (for which reverence he is like to suffer severe reprimands). Sir, he has sworn most solemnly to me that he will contrive to get His Majesty's speech printed at large in Holland. But lest he fails, I will here repeat unto Your Majesty those more pregnant passages while they are fresh in my mind; and I must not forget to note how the King's voice was quite freed from that hesitation which had afflicted him since childhood.

He saith first that he held it his duty, as a king, a good Christian, and an honest man, to clear himself of the odious charges brought against him. He called God to witness, to whom he must shortly give account, that he never did begin a war against the two Houses of Parliament; they began it by demanding control of the militia, which they confessed was his, yet would have it from him. And to be short, says he, if anybody will look at the date of the commissions, his and the Parliament's, calling men to arms, they would find proof who it was commenced these unhappy troubles. Then pointing to me, he said:

'I hope there is a good man there will bear me witness I am a

205

good Christian, that I have forgiven all, even those in particular who have been the chief cause of my death. Who they are, God knows; I do not desire to know. I pray with St Stephen that this may not be laid to their charge.'

Thereafter His Majesty spoke somewhat which was against my counsel. Many times during our private discourses, he had returned to a sin which, said he, lay heavy on his conscience, to wit, his consent to the execution of the Earl of Strafford, saying that it was not through ignorance, but by following the persuasions of worldly wisdom, that he had suffered innocent blood to be shed by a false pretended way of justice. I took leave to advise him, he was over-scrupulous. And yet his now public confession of this sin was a most extraordinary instance of his true Christian humility.

'Yet for all my innocence,' said he, 'God forbid that I should call in question His judgments upon me. Many times He does pay justice by an unjust sentence. I will say only this, that the unjust sentence I suffered to take effect upon my Lord of Strafford is punished now by a like injustice upon me.'

Then did he as it were set forth his last will and testament to his subjects, for, said he, his regal duty was to endeavour their welfare even to his latest breath. And spoke thus:

'Believe it, sirs, you will never do right until you give God His due, the King (that is, my successor) his due, and the people their due. For the first, the affairs of the Church must be regulated by a national synod, freely called, freely debating among themselves. For the King, the laws of the land will clearly instruct you in that. For the people, I must tell you that their liberty consists in having those laws by which their life and goods may be most their own. It is not having a share in government, that is not pertaining to them. A subject and a sovereign are clean different things. The people's privilege is freely to elect members who will represent them in parliament without molestation.'

At which words there was an angry hum from the officers on the scaffold, for they knew he hit at them who had lopped off the majority in the House of Commons by the hand of Colonel Pride. His Majesty, to drive home his point, concluded loudly thus:

'Sirs, it was for this that now I come here. If I would have surrendered to an arbitrary way, to have all laws changed according to the power of the sword, I needed not to have come. And therefore I tell you, and I pray God it be not laid to your charge, that I am the martyr of the people.'

His Majesty now turned him to make preparations for death, but I whispering in his ear that he should bear witness to the religion of the Church of England, he thanked me heartily, saying he had almost forgot that; and though his conscience in religion was known to all the world, he did declare here publicly that he died in the Anglican faith as he found it left him by his father. Then with that sweet courtesy which never deserted him, turning to his murderers, he saith:

'Sirs, excuse me for this long discourse. I have a good cause and I have a gracious God. I will say no more.'

As I assisted him to don a silken nightcap, I marvelled to observe how steady were his hands, no flurry of spirits, no disorder of speech, his eyes as lively and quick as ever. It was far otherwise with me, who could but falter out some dry, formal words, reminding His Majesty that there was but one short stage more which, though turbulent and troublesome, yet he might consider that it would carry him a great way, even from earth to heaven. To which His Majesty returned this noble answer:

'I go from a corruptible to an incorruptible crown, where no disturbance can be, no disturbance in the world.'

Then sighing a little, as a man weary for his rest, he took off his cloak and doublet, but by reason of the extreme cold, resumed his cloak again. And here I must record how the last earthly care of your blessed father was for Your Majesty. He had most strictly charged me beforehand that I convey the George he wore into your hands, together with a small paper containing the heads of his speech. Both of which he now gave me, speaking the one word, 'Remember'. And then, with a pleasant countenance, as it might have been at his royal *couchée*, he felt in his pockets and found therein two small seals, which he bade me send to the Lady Elizabeth, your sister.

Sir, my courage failed me at that moment, so that I turned

aside that I might not witness the striking of that sacrilegious blow which deprived Your Majesty of a father and his realm of the protector of its laws and liberties. I would fain have stopped my ears likewise; for what told me that all was over was not the customary cry of the heads man (who stood mum), but such a dismal universal groan from the thousands of common folk, as it were with one consent, as I never heard before and desire never to hear again.

Immediately thereafter came shouting of orders as upon a field of battle, and both horse and foot soldiers scattered the people, driving them every way and smiting them with the flat of their swords. And this by command given beforehand. Nor did my grey hairs spare me from their violence, for straightway they seized upon me, jumbling me about until they had filched from my pocket the paper and the two seals and the George. Which last, containing a picture of Your Majesty's royal mother, I hear they intend to sell.

8

Mercurius Elencticus (unlicensed)

January 31st, 1649.

Yesterday's *Pragmaticus* being suppressed, he appeareth here under a new name, and gives you short what *Pragmaticus* would have told you.

They were inhumanly barbarous to the King's dead corpse. His head thrown down by him that held it up, which bruised the face. His hair and clothing sold by parcels. The block cut into chips, as likewise the sand sprinkled with his sacred gore, were exposed for sale as goods in a market, which were greedily bought, but for different ends, by some as trophies of their slain enemy, and by others as precious reliques of their beloved prince. Others again bought pieces of the scaffold dyed with his blood, for which the soldiers took a shilling or a half-crown, more or less, according to the quality of the customers. But none without ready money.

And after his body was coffined, as many as desired to see it were permitted at a certain rate, by which means the soldiers got store of monies, in so much as I heard one say:

'I would we had two or three more Majesties to behead, if we could but make such use of them in lieu of our arrears.'

9
Secret Memoirs af Thomas Herbert

When I heard from the multitude that groan or sigh or wail (I know not which to term it) which has since haunted my dreams, I knew that all was over and began to faint. My Lord of Southampton who, for a great sum, had got leave to attend upon our master's corpse, succoured me, with brisk words rather than with physic, and conjured me to assist him in his pious vigil, for Dr Juxon was put under restraint.

Into the Banqueting House came a file of soldiers, bearing a coffin fitter for a pauper than a prince, and in truth I heard it cost but six shillings. Axtell marched before and used base language, refusing my lord's demand that the corpse be embalmed, but says he in a scoffing manner:

'If you think there is any sanctity or holiness in it, you may pay it your respects.'

My lord and I received the coffin, reverently laying it across two stools, and throughout that night we sat huddled in our cloaks beside it. Whitehall was liker a camp than a palace, with tramp of guards being changed, both within and without, so that it was borne home upon me how in very truth this kingdom was under the rule of the sword.

As the new clock on Whitehall Gate struck two, I felt the hair upon my nape to rise with terror, for there came slow and heavy footsteps approaching down the stair. By and by the door opened and two persons entered, so muffled up that I could not see their faces. Verily I deemed them phantoms. They paid us no attention but came to the coffin, the lid of which one of them tried to lift, yet could not, so drew his sword and with the pommel knocked up the lid. And folding his arms he gazed for a long space in silence upon that which lay therein. Says his companion:

'What government shall there be?'

'The same as is now,' says the first. And speaking so, he touched his sword.

Though I could not distinguish anything of this man's features, by his voice I knew him to be Oliver Cromwell, who, I suppose, must satisfy himself as if he still doubted the effecting of his hellish cruelty.

My lord and I going to close the coffin lid again, a shaft of moonlight touched the dead King's face, which smiled as perfectly as it had been alive, with a kind of quiet triumph.